HEAT EXCHANGE

SHANNON STACEY

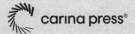

Dear Reader,

I love New England and have enjoyed sharing that love with my readers. New Hampshire and Maine, which are both states I've called home, have also been home to my characters. And now it's time to head to my original home state of Massachusetts.

Family relationships have always been at the heart of my stories, and in *Heat Exchange* you'll meet the Kincaid family. But for the Kincaids, family means more than parents and siblings. You'll meet the firefighters and the community whose roots are as strong and deep as any family tree's.

I hope you enjoy this new series and, if you do, I hope you'll let me know! All of the ways to contact me are listed on my website, shannonstacey.com, and I love to hear from readers.

Best wishes,

Shannon

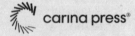

carina press®

ISBN-13: 978-0-373-00278-8

Heat Exchange

Copyright © 2015 by Shannon Stacey

Edited by: Angela James

Recycling programs for this product may not exist in your area.

www.CarinaPress.com

Printed in U.S.A.

HEAT EXCHANGE

For Angela James and everybody who's been a part of the Carina Press team. We've had quite an adventure over the past five years, and I'm thrilled to be continuing this journey with you.

ONE

LYDIA KINCAID COULD pull a pint of Guinness so perfect her Irish ancestors would weep tears of appreciation, but fine dining? Forget about it.

"The customer is disappointed in the sear on these scallops," she told the sous-chef, setting the plate down.

"In what way?"

"Hell if I know. They look like all the other scallops." Lydia had a hairpin sticking into her scalp, and it took every bit of her willpower not to poke at it. Her dark hair was too long, thick and wavy to be confined into a chic little bun, but it was part of the dress code. And going home with a headache every night was just part of the job. "Ten bucks says if I wait three minutes, then pop that same plate in the microwave for fifteen seconds and take it out to her, she'll gush over how the sear is so perfect now."

"If I see you microwaving scallops, I'll make sure the only food you ever get to touch in this city again is fast food."

Lydia rolled her eyes, having heard that threat

many times before, and accepted a fresh plate of scallops from the line cook. The sous-chef just sniffed loudly and dumped the unacceptable batch in the garbage, plate and all. She was pretty sure the guy spent all his off time watching reality television chefs throw tantrums.

Three hours later, Lydia was in her car and letting her hair down. She dropped the bobby pins and elastic bands into her cup holder to fish out before her next shift and then used both hands to shake her hair out and massage her scalp.

She hated her job. Maybe some of it stemmed from the disparity between the cold formality of this restaurant and the warm and loud world she'd come from, but she also flat-out wasn't very good at it. The foods perplexed her and, according to the kitchen manager, her tableside manner lacked polish. Two years hadn't yet managed to put a shine on her. The tips were usually good, though, and living in Concord, New Hampshire, cost less than living in Boston, but it still wasn't cheap.

She'd just put her car in gear when she heard the siren in the distance. With her foot still on the brake, she watched as the fire engine came into view— red lights flashing through the dark night—and sped past.

With a sigh, she shifted her foot to the gas pedal. She didn't need to hold her breath anymore. Didn't need to find the closest scanner. Nobody she loved was on that truck so, while she said a quick prayer for their safety, they were faceless strangers and life wasn't temporarily suspended.

And that was why she'd keep trying to please people who wouldn't know a good scallop sear if it bit them on the ass and taking shit from the sous-chef. That job financed her new life here in New Hampshire, including a decent apartment she shared with a roommate, and it was a nice enough life that she wasn't tempted to go home.

Her life wasn't perfect. It had certainly been lacking in sex and friendship lately, but she wasn't going backward just because the road was longer or harder than she'd thought. She wanted something different and she was going to keep working toward it.

Thanks to the miracle of an apartment building with an off-street parking lot, Lydia had a dedicated parking spot waiting for her. It was another reason she put up with customers who nitpicked their entrées just because they were paying so much for them.

Her roommate worked at a sports bar and wouldn't be home for another couple of hours, so Lydia took a quick shower and put on her sweats. She'd just curled up on the sofa with the remote and a couple of the cookies her blessed-with-a-great-metabolism roommate had freshly baked when her cell phone rang.

She knew before looking at the caller ID it would be her sister. Not many people called her, and none late at night. "Hey, Ashley. What's up?"

"My marriage is over."

Lydia couldn't wrap her mind around the words

at first. Had something happened to Danny? But she hadn't said that. She said it was over. "What do you mean it's over?"

"I told him I wasn't sure I wanted to be married to him anymore and that I needed some space. He didn't even say anything. He just packed up a couple of bags and left."

"Oh my God, Ashley." Lydia sank onto the edge of her bed, stunned. "Where did this even come from?"

"I've been unhappy for a while. I just didn't tell anybody." Her sister sighed, the sound hollow and discouraged over the phone. "Like a moron, I thought I could talk to him about it. Instead, he left."

"Why have you been unhappy? Dammit, Ashley, what is going on? Did he cheat? I swear to God if he stepped out—"

"No. He didn't cheat. And it's too much for me talk about now."

"If you had been talking to me all along, it wouldn't be too much now. You can't call me and tell me your marriage is over and then tell me you don't want to talk about it."

"I know, but it's…it's too much. I called to talk to you about the bar."

Uh-oh. Alarm bells went off in Lydia's mind, but there was no way she could extricate herself from the conversation without being a shitty sister.

"I need you to come back and help Dad," Ashley said, and Lydia dropped her head back against the sofa cushion, stifling a groan. "I need some time off."

"I have a job, Ashley. And an apartment."

"You've told me a bunch of times that you hate your job."

She couldn't deny that since a conversation rarely passed between them without mention of that fact.

"And it's waiting tables," Ashley continued. "It's not like I'm asking you to take a hiatus from some fancy career path."

That was bitchy, even for Ashley, but Lydia decided to give her a pass. She didn't know what had gone wrong in their marriage, but she did know Ashley loved Danny Walsh with every fiber of her being, so she had to be a wreck.

"I can't leave Shelly high and dry," Lydia said in a calm, reasonable tone. "This is a great apartment and I'm lucky to have it. It has off-street parking and my space has my apartment number in it. It's literally *only* mine."

"I can't be at the bar, Lydia. You know how it is there. Everybody's got a comment or some advice to give, and I have to hear every five minutes what a great guy Danny is and why can't I just give him another chance?"

Danny really *was* a great guy, but she could understand her sister not wanting to be reminded of it constantly while they were in the process of separating. But going back to Boston and working at Kincaid's was a step in the wrong direction for Lydia.

"I don't know, Ash."

"Please. You don't know—" To Lydia's dismay, her

sister's voice was choked off by a sob. "I can't do it, Lydia. I really, really need you."

Shit. "I'll be home tomorrow."

"WE GOT SMOKE showing on three and at least one possible on the floor," Rick Gullotti said. "Meet you at the top, boys."

Aidan Hunt threw a mock salute in the direction of the ladder company's lieutenant and tossed the ax to Grant Cutter before grabbing the Halligan tool for himself. With a fork at one end and a hook and adze head on the other end, it was essentially a long crowbar on steroids and they never went anywhere without it. After confirmation Scotty Kincaid had the line, and a thumbs-up from Danny Walsh at the truck, he and the other guys from Engine 59 headed for the front door of the three-decker.

Some bunch of geniuses, generations before, had decided the best way to house a shitload of people in a small amount of space was to build three-story houses—each floor a separate unit—and cram them close together. It was great if you needed a place to live and didn't mind living in a goldfish bowl. It was less great if it was your job to make sure an out-of-control kitchen fire didn't burn down the entire block.

They made their way up the stairs, not finding trouble until they reached the top floor. The door to the apartment stood open, with smoke pouring out. Aidan listened to the crackle of the radio over the sound of his own breathing in the mask. The guys from Ladder 37 had gained access by way of the window and had a woman descending, but her kid was still inside.

"Shit." Aidan confirmed Walsh knew they were going into the apartment and was standing by to charge the line if they needed water, and then looked for nods from Kincaid and Cutter.

He went in, making his way through the smoke. It was bad enough so the child would be coughing—hopefully—but there was chaos in the front of the apartment as another company that had shown up tried to knock down the flames from the front.

Making his way to the kid's bedroom, he signaled for Cutter to look under the bed while he went to the closet. If the kid was scared and hiding from them, odds were he or she was in one of those two spots.

"Bingo," he heard Cutter say into his ear.

The updates were growing more urgent and he heard Kincaid call for water, which meant the fire was heading their way. "No time to be nice. Grab the kid and let's go."

It was a little girl and she screamed as Cutter pulled her out from under the bed. She was fighting him and, because his hold was awkward, once she was free of the bed, Cutter almost lost her. Aidan swore under his breath. If she bolted, they could all be in trouble.

He leaned the Halligan against the wall and picked up the little girl. By holding her slightly slanted, he was able to hold her arms and legs still without running the risk of smacking her head on the way down.

"Grab the Halligan and let's go."

"More guys are coming up," Walsh radioed in. "Get out of there now."

The smoke was dense now and the little girl was doing more coughing and gasping than crying. "My dog!"

Aidan went past Kincaid, slapping him on the shoulder. Once Cutter went by, Kincaid could retreat—they all stayed together—and let another company deal with the flames.

"I see her dog," Aidan heard Cutter say, and he turned just in time to see the guy disappear back into the bedroom.

"Jesus Christ," Scotty yelled. "Cutter, get your ass down those stairs. Hunt, just go."

He didn't want to leave them, and he wouldn't have except the fight was going out of the child in his arms. Holding her tight, he started back down the stairs they'd come up. At the second floor he met another company coming up, but he kept going.

Once he cleared the building, he headed for the ambulance and passed the girl over to the waiting medics. It was less than two minutes before Cutter and Kincaid emerged from the building, but it felt like forever.

They yanked their masks off as Cutter walked over to the little girl and—after getting a nod from EMS—put an obviously terrified little dog on the girl's lap. They all smiled as the girl wrapped her arms around her pet and then her mom put her arms around both. Aidan put his hand on Cutter's shoulder and the news cameras got their tired, happy smiles for the evening news.

Once they were back on the other side of the engine and out of view of the cameras, Kincaid grabbed the front of Cutter's coat and shoved him against the truck. "You want to save puppies, that's great. If there's time. Once you're told to get the fuck out, you don't go back for pets. And if you ever risk my life again, or any other guy's, for a goddamn dog, I'll make sure you can't even get a job emptying the garbage at Waste Reduction."

Once Cutter nodded, Kincaid released him and they looked to Danny for a status update. They had it pretty well knocked down and, though the third floor was a loss and the lower floors wouldn't be pretty, the people who lived in the neighboring houses weren't going to have a bad day.

Two hours later, Aidan sat on the bench in the shower room and tied his shoes. Danny was stowing his shower stuff, a towel wrapped around his waist. He'd been quiet since they got back, other than having a talk with Cutter, since he was the officer of the bunch. But he was always quiet, so it was hard to tell what was going on with him.

"Got any plans tonight?" Aidan finally asked, just to break the silence.

"Nope. Probably see if there's a game on."

Aidan wasn't sure what to say to that. He didn't have a lot of experience with a good friend going through a divorce. Breakups, sure, but not a marriage ending. "If you want to talk, just let me know. We can grab a beer or something."

"Talk about what?"

"Don't bullshit me, Walsh. We know what's going on and it's a tough situation. So if you want to talk, just let me know."

"She doesn't want to be married to me anymore, so we're getting a divorce." Danny closed his locker, not needing to slam it to get his point across. "There's nothing to talk about."

"Okay." Aidan tossed his towel in the laundry bin and went out the door.

A lot of guys had trouble expressing their emotions, but Danny took it to a whole new level. Aidan thought talking about it over a few beers might help, but he shouldn't have been surprised the offer was refused.

He'd really like to know what had gone wrong in the Walsh marriage, though. He liked Danny and Ashley and he'd always thought they were a great couple. If they couldn't make it work, Aidan wasn't sure he had a chance. And lately he'd been thinking a lot about how nice it would be to have somebody to share his life with.

A mental snapshot of the little girl cradling her dog filled his mind. He wouldn't mind having a dog. But his hours would be too hard on a dog, and he wasn't a fan of cats. They were a little creepy and not good for playing ball in the park. He could probably keep a fish alive, but they weren't exactly a warm hug at the end of the long tour.

With a sigh he went into the kitchen to rummage for a snack. If he couldn't keep a dog happy, he probably didn't have much chance of keeping a wife happy. And that was assuming he even met a woman he wanted to get to know well enough to consider a ring. So far, not so good.

"Cutter ate the last brownie," Scotty told him as soon as he walked into the kitchen area.

Aidan shook his head, glaring at the young guy sitting at the table with a very guilty flush on his face. "You really do want to get your ass kicked today, don't you?"

"MAYBE I SHOULDN'T have called you. I feel bad now."

Lydia dropped her bag inside the door and put her hand on her hip. "I just quit my job and burned a chunk of my savings to pay Shelly for two months' rent in advance so she won't give my room away. You're stuck with me now."

Tears filled Ashley's eyes and spilled over onto her cheeks as she stood up on her toes to throw her arms around Lydia's neck. "I'm so glad you're here."

Lydia squeezed her older sister, and she had to admit that coming back was about the last thing she'd wanted to do, but she was glad to be there, too. When push came to shove, her sister needed her and when family really needed you, nothing else mattered.

When Ashley released her, Lydia followed her into the living room and they dropped onto the couch. About six months after they got married, Danny and Ashley had scored the single-family home in a fore-closure auction. It had gone beyond *handyman's special* straight into the rehab hell of *handyman's wet dream*, but room by room they'd done the remodeling themselves. Now they had a lovely home they never could have afforded on their salaries.

But right now, it wasn't a happy home. Lydia sighed and kicked off her flip-flops to tuck her feet under her. "What's going on?"

Ashley shrugged one shoulder, her mouth set in a line of misery. "You know how it is."

Maybe, in a general sense, Lydia knew how it was. She'd been married to a firefighter, too, and then she'd divorced one. But the one she'd been married to had struggled with the job, tried to cope with alcohol and taken advantage of Lydia's unquestioning acceptance of the demanding hours to screw around with every female who twitched her goods in his direction.

That wasn't Danny, so other than knowing how intense being a firefighter's wife could be, Lydia didn't see what Ashley was saying.

"He's just so closed off," her sister added. "I feel like he doesn't care about anything and I don't want to spend the rest of my life like that."

Lydia was sure there was more to it—probably a

lot more—but Ashley didn't seem inclined to offer up anything else. And after the packing and driving, Lydia didn't mind putting off the heavy emotional stuff for a while.

"I should go see Dad," she said.

"He's working the bar tonight. And before you say anything, I know he's not supposed to be on his feet that much anymore. But you know he's sitting around talking to his buddies as much as being on his feet, and Rick Gullotti's girlfriend's supposed to be helping him out."

Rick was with Ladder 37 and Lydia had known him for years, but she struggled to remember his girlfriend's name. "Becky?"

Ashley snorted. "Becky was like eight girlfriends ago. Karen. We like her and it's been like four months now, which might be a record for Rick."

Lydia looked down at the sundress she'd thrown on that morning because it was comfortable and the pale pink not only looked great with her dark coloring, but also cheered her up. It was a little wrinkled from travel, but not too bad. It wasn't as if Kincaid's was known for being a fashion hot spot. "And Karen couldn't keep on helping him out?"

"She's an ER nurse. Works crazy hours, I guess, so she helps out, but can't commit to a set schedule. And you know how Dad is about family."

"It's Kincaid's Pub so, by God, there should be a Kincaid in it," Lydia said in a low, gruff voice that made Ashley laugh.

Even as she smiled at her sister's amusement, Lydia had to tamp down on the old resentment. There had been no inspirational *you can be the President of the United States if you want to* speeches for Tommy's daughters. His two daughters working the bar at Kincaid's Pub while being wonderfully supportive firefighters' wives was a dream come true for their old man.

Lydia had been the first to disappoint him. Her unwillingness to give the alcoholic serial cheater *just one more chance* had been the first blow, and then her leaving Kincaid's and moving to New Hampshire had really pissed him off.

Sometimes she wondered how their lives would have turned out if their mom hadn't died of breast cancer when Lydia and Ashley were just thirteen and fourteen. Scotty had been only nine, but he was his father's pride and joy. Joyce Kincaid hadn't taken any shit from her gruff, old-school husband, and Lydia thought maybe she would have pushed hard for her daughters to dream big. And then she would have helped them fight to make those dreams come true.

Or maybe their lives wouldn't have turned out any different and it was just Lydia spinning what-ifs into pretty fairy tales.

After carrying her bag upstairs to the guest room, Lydia brushed her hair and exchanged her flip-flops for cute little tennis shoes that matched her dress and would be better for walking.

"Are you sure you want to walk?" Ashley asked. "It's a bit of a hike."

"It's not that far, and I won't have to find a place to park."

"I'd go with you, but…"

But her not wanting to be at Kincaid's was the entire reason Lydia had uprooted herself and come home. "I get it. And I won't be long. I'll be spending enough time there as it is, so I'm just going to pop in, say hi and get the hell out."

Ashley snorted. "Good luck with that."

It was a fifteen-minute walk from the Walsh house to Kincaid's Pub, but Lydia stretched it out a bit. The sights. The sounds. The smells. No matter how reluctant she was to come back here or how many years she was away, this would always be home.

A few people called to her, but she just waved and kept walking. Every once in a while she'd step up the pace to make it look like she was in a hurry. But the street was fairly quiet and in no time, she was standing in front of Kincaid's Pub.

It was housed in the lower floor of an unassuming brick building. Okay, ugly. It was ugly, with a glass door and two high, long windows. A small sign with the name in a plain type was screwed to the brick over the door, making it easy to overlook. It was open to anybody, of course, but the locals were their bread and butter, and they liked it just the way it was.

Her dad had invested in the place—becoming a partner to help out the guy who owned it—almost ten years before his heart attack hastened his retirement from fighting fires, and he'd bought the original owner out when he was back on his feet. Once it was solely Tommy's, he'd changed the name to Kincaid's Pub, and Ashley and Lydia had assumed their places behind the bar.

After taking a deep breath, she pulled open the heavy door and walked inside. All the old brick and wood seemed to absorb the light from the many antique-looking fixtures, and it took a moment for her eyes to adjust.

It looked just the same, with sports and firefighting memorabilia and photographs covering the brick walls. The bar was a massive U-shape with a hand-polished surface, and a dozen tables, each seating four, were scattered around the room. In an alcove to one side was a pool table, along with a few more seating groups.

Because there wasn't a game on, the two televisions—one over the bar and one hung to be seen from most of the tables—were on Mute, with closed-captioning running across the bottom. The music was turned down low because Kincaid's was loud enough without people shouting to be heard over the radio.

Lydia loved this place. And she hated it a little, too. But in some ways it seemed as though Kincaid's Pub was woven into the fabric of her being, and she wasn't sorry to be there again.

"Lydia!" Her father's voice boomed across the bar, and she made a beeline to him.

Tommy Kincaid was a big man starting to go soft around the middle, but he still had arms like tree trunks. They wrapped around her and she squealed a little when he lifted her off her feet. "I've missed you, girl."

She got a little choked up as he set her down and gave her a good looking over. Their relationship could be problematic at times—like most of the time—but Lydia never doubted for a second he loved her with all his heart. Once upon a time, he'd had the same thick, dark hair she shared with her siblings, but the gray had almost totally taken over.

He looked pretty good, though, and she smiled. "I'm glad you missed me, because it sounds like you'll be seeing a lot of me for a while."

A scowl drew his thick eyebrows and the corners of his mouth downward. "That sister of yours. I don't know what's going through her mind."

She gave him a bright smile. "Plenty of time for that later. Right now I just want to see everybody and have a beer."

A blonde woman who was probably a few years older than her smiled from behind the bar. "I'm Karen. Karen Shea."

Lydia reached across and shook her hand. "We really appreciate you being able to help out."

"Not a problem."

Lydia went to the very end of the back side of the bar and planted a kiss on the cheek of Fitz Fitzgibbon—her father's best friend and a retired member of Ladder 37—who was the only person who ever sat on that stool. She supposed once upon a time she might have known his real first name, but nobody ever called him anything but Fitz or, in her father's case, Fitzy.

There were a few other regulars she said hello to before getting a Sam Adams and standing at the bar. Unlike most, the big bar at Kincaid's didn't have stools all the way around. It had once upon a time, but now there were only stools on the back side and the end. Her dad had noticed a lot of guys didn't bother with the stools and just leaned against the polished oak. To make things easier, he'd just ripped them out.

About a half hour later, her brother, Scotty, walked in. Like the rest of the Kincaids, he had thick dark hair and dark eyes. He needed a shave, as usual, but he looked good. They'd talked and sent text messages quite a bit over the past two years, but neither of them was much for video chatting, so she hadn't actually seen him.

And right on Scotty's heels was Aidan Hunt. His brown hair was lighter than her brother's and it needed a trim. And she didn't need to see his eyes to remember they were blue, like a lake on a bright summer day. He looked slightly older, but no less deliciously handsome than ever. She wasn't surprised to see him. Wherever Scotty was, Aidan was usually close by.

What did surprise her was that the second his gaze met hers, her first thought was that she'd like to throw everybody out of the bar, lock the door and then shove him onto a chair. Since she was wearing the sundress, all she had to do was undo his fly, straddle his lap and hold on.

When the corner of his mouth quirked up, as if he somehow knew she'd just gone eight seconds with him in her mind, she gave him a nod of greeting and looked away.

For crap's sake, that was Aidan Hunt. Her annoying younger brother's equally annoying best friend.

He'd been seventeen when they met, to Lydia's twenty-one. He'd given her a grin that showed off perfect, Daddy's-got-money teeth and those sparkling blue eyes and said, "Hey, gorgeous. Want to buy me a drink?"

She'd rolled her eyes and told him to enjoy his playdate with Scotty. From that day on, he had seemed determined to annoy the hell out of her at every possible opportunity.

When her brother reached her, she shoved Aidan out of her mind and embraced Scotty. "How the hell are ya?"

"Missed having you around," he said. "Sucks you had to come back for a shitty reason, but it's still good to see you. I just found out about an hour ago Ashley had called you."

"She just called me last night, so it was spur-of-the-moment, I guess."

"It's good to have you back."

"Don't get too used to it. It's temporary."

She'd always thought if she and Scotty were closer in age than four years apart, they could have been twins, with the same shaped faces and their coloring. Ashley looked a lot like both of them, but her face was leaner, her eyes a lighter shade of brown, and her hair wasn't quite as thick.

Scotty was more like Lydia in temperament, too. Ashley was steadier and liked to try logic first. Scott and Lydia were a little more volatile and tended to run on emotion. Her temper had a longer fuse than her brother's, but they both tended to pop off a little easy.

They caught up for a few minutes, mainly talking about his fellow firefighters, most of whom she knew well. And he gave her a quick update on their dad's doctor not being thrilled with his blood pressure. It didn't sound too bad, but it was probably good Ashley had called her rather than let him try to take up her slack.

Then Scotty shifted from one foot to the other and grimaced. "Sorry, but I've had to take a leak for like an hour."

She laughed and waved him off. "Go. I'll be here."

He left and Lydia looked up at the television, sipping her beer. She only ever had one, so she'd make it last, but part of her wanted to chug it and ask for a refill. It was a little overwhelming, being back.

"Hey, gorgeous. Want to buy me a drink?" What were the chances? She turned to face Aidan, smiling at the fact she'd been thinking about that day just a few minutes before. "What's so funny?"

She shook her head, not wanting to tell him she'd been thinking about the day they met, since that would be an admission she'd been thinking about him at all. "Nothing. How have you been?"

"Good. Same shit, different day. You come back for a visit?"

"I'll be here awhile. Maybe a couple of weeks, or a month." She shrugged. "Ashley wanted to take some time off, so I'm going to cover for her. You know how Dad is about having one of us here all the damn time."

His eyes squinted and he tilted his head a little. "You sound different."

"I worked on toning down the accent a little, to fit in more at work, I guess. Even though it's only the next state over, people were always asking me where I was from."

"You trying to forget who you are?" It came out *fuh-get who you ah.* "Forget where you came from?"

"Not possible," she muttered.

He gave her that grin again, with the perfect teeth and sparkling eyes. They crinkled at the corners now, the laugh lines just making him more attractive. "So what you're saying is that we're unforgettable."

She laughed, shaking her head. "You're something, all right."

Aidan looked as if he was going to say something else, but somebody shouted his name and was beckoning him over. He nodded and then turned back to Lydia. "I'll see you around. And welcome home."

She watched him walk away, trying to keep her

eyes above his waist in case anybody was watching her watch him. Her annoying brother's annoying best friend had very nice shoulders stretching out that dark blue T-shirt.

Her gaze dipped, just for a second. And a very nice ass filling out those faded blue jeans.

TWO

AIDAN WAS JUST having a beer. Shooting the shit with the guys. Figuring out when they could get in some ice time at the rink. What he *wasn't* doing was checking out his best friend's sister.

That was Lydia over there, for chrissake. Scotty's sister. Tommy's daughter. She was bossy and sarcastic and pretty much the last woman on Earth he could mess around with. Except Ashley, who was all of those things *and* married to Danny, which put her one rung higher on the off-limits ladder. But he'd never been attracted to her the way he was to her sister.

Last he knew Lydia didn't even like him very much.

So why had she given him a look that said she might have mentally stripped him naked and was licking her way down his body?

He took a slug of his beer, trying to work it out in his head. She'd definitely been looking at him. The only other person in range had been Scotty, and she sure as hell hadn't been looking at *him* like that. And he hadn't imagined the heat, either. That woman had been thinking some seriously dirty thoughts. About him.

Yanking his T-shirt out of his jeans in the hope it would be long enough to cover the erection he was currently rocking seemed a little conspicuous, so he turned his body to the bar and rested his forearms on it. He seriously needed to get a grip.

He couldn't disrespect Tommy Kincaid by lusting after his daughter. The man was not only a mentor of sorts and a second father to him, being his best friend's dad, but he was the reason Aidan was a firefighter.

He'd been eleven years old when his family's minivan got caught up in a shit show involving a jackknifed 18-wheeler, two other cars and a box truck full of building supplies. His memories of the accident itself were hazy. Screeching tires. Shattering glass. His mother screaming his father's name.

But the aftermath imprinted on his memory so clearly it was like a movie he could hit Play on at will. A police officer had gotten them all out of the vehicle and Aidan had held his little brother's hand on one side and kept his other hand on his little sister's baby carrier.

A firefighter was working on his dad, whose head had a lot of blood on it. Aidan's mom was dazed and sat leaning against the guardrail, holding her arm. When his little brother called out to her, she didn't even look at him.

Then a woman started screaming and there were a

lot of shouts. The firefighter who was holding some bandaging to his dad's head looked over his shoulder and then back to his dad. Aidan could tell he wanted to go help the woman who was screaming, so he stepped forward.

"I can hold that," he told the firefighter. "Just show me how hard to press."

The firefighter hadn't wanted to. But the screaming and the voices grew more urgent and he had Aidan kneel down next to him. After making sure Bryan put his hand on Sarah's carrier and wouldn't move, Aidan took over putting pressure on his dad's head wound.

"You're okay, Dad," he said, looking into his father's unfocused gaze. "Just keep looking at me and we'll wait for an ambulance together."

He'd been the one to give the paramedics their information and tell them his father took a medication for his blood pressure. Then he'd given them a description of his mom's demeanor since the accident. After asking them to retrieve Sarah's diaper bag from the van, he'd cared for his siblings until his aunt arrived.

The firefighter had shown up at the hospital and given him a Boston Fire T-shirt. "You did good, kid."

Aidan hadn't really known what praise and pride felt like until he looked into the man's warm eyes. "Thank you, sir."

"Some people are born to take charge in emergencies. It's a special thing and not everybody's got it.

When you grow up, if you decide you want to save lives, son, you look me up. Tommy Kincaid. Engine Company 59."

Aidan rubbed the Engine 59 emblem on his T-shirt and smiled. He'd been only sixteen the first time he showed up at the old brick building that housed Engine 59 and Ladder 37, looking for Tommy. He met Scotty that day and together they'd never looked back. Friendship. A little bit of trouble here and there. Training. Testing. They'd been inseparable. Aidan didn't know if it was a favor to Tommy or if Fate played a hand, but when the station assignments went out, they'd even been assigned to the same engine company.

His extremely white-collar parents hadn't been able to reconcile their hopes for their oldest son with his drive to serve the public, and things were still rough between them. And maybe his old man was embarrassed to only have one of his sons working with Hunt & Sons Investments—Sarah being destined for more feminine pursuits, like marriage and motherhood, according to their father—but Aidan wouldn't be swayed.

Tommy had become his father figure. Scotty and Danny and the rest of the guys were his brothers. This was his family, and he knew they had his back, anytime and anyplace.

Messing around with Lydia Kincaid was a bad idea. Like a *sticking a fork in a toaster while sitting in a bathtub cocked off your ass* kind of a bad idea.

"Earth to Hunt," Scotty said, and Aidan felt an ugly jolt of guilt for even considering messing around with Lydia while standing right next to her brother, for chrissake. "What the hell's wrong with you?"

"Nothing. Wicked tired is all."

"What's her name?"

Aidan snorted. "I wish."

"Piper's got a friend I could hook you up with. Her name's Bunny, and she's not bad."

"I'm too old for chicks named Bunny."

Scott shrugged. "I don't think that's her real name. At least I hope it's not. But whatever, man. Your loss."

Aidan didn't exactly wallow in regret. He was tired of it. He was tired of women who saw his face and didn't look any further. He was sick of women who got off on banging firefighters and the women who saw him outside the rink with his bag and wanted to spend a little time with a hockey player.

He didn't mind at all if a woman wanted to use him for hot, dirty sex. But he also wanted her to laugh with him and enjoy a quiet evening on the couch. And he needed her to stroke his hair when the day was shitty and to hold him when the nightmares came.

Lydia's laughter rose above the noise of the bar, but Aidan didn't turn to look. He just knocked back the rest of his beer and kept his eyes on the television.

THE OVERLY CHIPPER chime sound that indicated an incoming text made Lydia very reluctantly open her eyes the next morning. Ashley's guest room mattress had seen better days and it had taken her forever to fall asleep.

With a groan, she reached over to the nightstand and felt around until she found her phone. She had just enough charger cord to read the message without picking her head up off the pillow.

What the hell, girl?

She had no idea what the hell, since she wasn't even awake yet. But then she realized it was a group text, the group being her two best friends, Becca Shepard and Courtney Richmond. With Ashley as their fourth, they'd been inseparable growing up, and there was a group text going on more often than not.

This time it was Becca, and Lydia wondered which of them the message was aimed at. Probably her.

Before she could respond, another text from Becca came through.

Heard you were at KP last night. Ninja visit?

Lydia didn't have time to compose a reply before a response from her sister popped up.

I'm taking some time off. L's home to cover for me.

How long?

Don't know.

Since Ashley was not only awake, but able to type coherently, Lydia dropped the phone onto the blanket and closed her eyes again. Kincaid's didn't open until eleven, so she didn't have to jump out of bed.

But when the phone chimed again she realized that, even if she didn't join in the conversation, the alerts would drive her crazy. After a big stretch, she picked up the phone again.

GNO!

That was Courtney, and Lydia rolled her eyes. While a girls' night out was appealing, she barely had her feet under her. She hadn't even worked a shift at the bar yet, so trying to get time off would be tough.

Soon. Stop at KP & say hi if you can.

That might hold them off for a while. Long enough to get coffee into her system, at least.

That turned out to be the end of the messages, but Lydia knew she'd tipped past the mostly awake point and wouldn't be able to go back to sleep now. After unplugging her phone, she made a quick stop in the bathroom and then headed downstairs.

Once she reached the top of the stairs, she could smell the coffee and followed the aroma to the kitchen. Ashley was sitting at the table, her phone in hand, and she looked up when Lydia walked in.

"Hey, how did you sleep?"

"Like a baby." It was a lie, but Ashley already felt bad about asking her to come home. No sense in piling on guilt about it. And even a crappy mattress was better than staying at her dad's.

Once she'd made her coffee, she sat down across from her sister and sipped it. If it wasn't so hot, she'd guzzle the stuff. Lydia was a better cook than Ashley, but her sister was definitely better at making coffee.

After a few minutes, Ashley put down her phone and looked at her. "It's been ten days."

"Ten days?" A week and half had gone by before her sister bothered telling her that her marriage was over?

"I thought he'd come back, you know? Like maybe he'd blow off some steam and then we'd talk about it. But he didn't come back. And when I called him, he just closed up and it was like talking to a machine." Ashley stared at her coffee, shaking her head. "More than usual, even. So the more I hope we can work it out, the more he does the thing I can't live with anymore."

Lydia took the time to consider her next words carefully. She had her sister's back, 100 percent, but sometimes having a person's back wasn't as cut-and-dried as blindly agreeing with everything they said. "He's always been quiet. I don't know how many times I've heard the other guys call him the ice man. It's not just with you."

"He can be however he wants with other people, especially the other guys. I'm his *wife*. If I'm upset and worried or pissed off, I need to feel like he at least cares."

"Have you thought about counseling?"

Ashley shrugged. "I mentioned it once and he changed the subject. I'm not sure what the point would be in talking to somebody when he doesn't talk."

"That *is* the point. A professional can help you guys communicate, including helping him break through whatever block he's got up and talk to you."

"I left a message on his voice mail, asking him if we could set up a time to meet somewhere for coffee. If he shows up, I'll mention it."

"Just don't make it about him—that *he* needs help because he can't communicate. Make it about you feeling like it would be good for your marriage."

She nodded. "Assuming he even calls me back. He keeps texting me, but I want him to stop taking the easy way out and actually talk to me. I want to hear his voice."

"Where's he staying? With his parents?" Ashley's mouth tightened and Lydia leaned back in her chair. "No. Don't even tell me."

"He's staying with Scotty."

"Of course he is." Lydia's hand tightened around the coffee mug and it took supreme will not to chuck it at the wall. "Is Scott working today?"

Ashley looked at her, and then slowly shook her head. "Don't, Lydia. You'll only make it worse."

"It's not right. You're his sister."

"It's better than not knowing where Danny is or having him shack up with God knows who."

"There are plenty of other guys who could offer him a couch," Lydia argued. "He could crash with Aidan or Rick. Jeff. Chris. Any of them. It didn't have to be *your* brother. In our father's house."

When Ashley just gave a small shrug, Lydia wanted to shake her. As far as she was concerned, Scott had crossed a line and she wanted her sister to be pissed off about it. To demand the respect and loyalty the Kincaid men should be showing *her*, and not Danny.

But she knew Ashley wasn't wired the same way she was and it took a lot to make her angry. Just like their mother, once she'd had enough, she could give Lydia and Scott a run for their money, and that's what Lydia wanted to see.

"Did I really jam you up by asking you to come back?" Ashley asked. "I'm sorry about what I said about your job, by the way. I was so desperate to get out of being at the bar, but that was dirty."

"I forgive you because God knows I've vented at you often enough. That's what sisters are for. And you didn't jam me up at all. You were right about me hating that job and, when I go back, I'll find one I like more."

"You should go back to bartending. You're a natural."

Lydia shrugged. Bartending was something she was good at and she honestly enjoyed it, but she'd taken the waitressing job because she wanted something different. Tending a bar that wasn't Kincaid's Pub had seemed at the time like it might be too painful for her.

"I thought about going to school," she said. "But I spent weeks looking at brochures and stuff online and nothing jumped out at me. If I'm going to invest that time and money, I want it to be for something I *really* want to be, you know?"

"If I had the chance to go to college, I'd go for

office or business stuff. I don't even know what it's called, but I think it would be awesome to work in a medical clinic, like for women's health."

"Have you thought about going to the community college?" They'd both been thrown into work young and college had never been a big deal in their family, but if Ashley wanted to go, she should.

"Danny and I talked about it a while back. He was supportive, but Dad made a big deal out of needing me at Kincaid's and you were getting a divorce. Plus working around Danny's hours would be a pain. It was easier to forget about it."

Lydia shoved back at the guilt that threatened to overwhelm her and make her say something stupid, like offering to stay in Boston so Ashley could go to college. Her dad had accused her of being selfish when she'd taken off, and maybe she was, but she couldn't be responsible for everybody's lives. She was still working on her own.

"I'm going to take a shower," Lydia said when it became clear Ashley had nothing else to say at the moment. "We should go out for breakfast."

"I already made pancake batter. I was just waiting for you to get up."

Her sister wasn't the best cook in the world, but she made amazing pancakes. "I hope you made a lot. I'm starving."

Ashley's face lit up with a real smile. "I know you and my pancakes. I practically had to mix it in a bucket."

AIDAN HELD UP a metal rod and looked over at Scotty. "What is this? Does this go somewhere?"

They both looked at the piece of playground equipment they'd spent the past hour assembling, and then Scotty shrugged. "It doesn't look like it goes anywhere."

"I don't think they said, 'Hey, let's throw a random metal rod in there just to mess with the idiots who have to put it together,' do you?"

"I don't know. If you set something on fire, I know what to do with it. Building things? Not my job."

Chris Eriksson joined them, scratching at a slowly graying beard. "I don't think you're supposed to have extra pieces. A bolt maybe. A few nuts. That looks important."

"Where did the instructions go?" Aidan asked, scanning the playground to see if they'd blown away.

"There were instructions?"

"Funny, Kincaid." Eriksson shook his head. "My kid's going to climb on this thing. If we can't figure it out, we're breaking it down and starting over."

Aidan stifled the curse words he wanted to mutter as he started circling the playground structure. They were surrounded by an increasingly bored pack of elementary students and a photographer waiting to snap a few pictures of the kids playing on the equipment the firehouse had donated and built. When Eriksson had come to them, looking for some help for his son's school, they'd been all-in.

And they still were. This was their community

and they all did what they could. But it would have been nice if somebody had been in charge of the directions. After a few minutes, one of the teachers— a pretty brunette with a warm smile—moved closer and beckoned him over.

"We built one of these where I did my student teaching, and I think it's a support bar for under the slide," she whispered. "If you look up at it from underneath, you should see the braces where it bolts on."

"Thank you."

"No, thank you. We really appreciate you volunteering your time."

He gave her his best public relations smile, secure in doing so because of the ring on her finger and lack of *I'm hitting on a firefighter* vibe. "Just doing our part for the children, ma'am."

She nodded and went back to her students, leaving him relieved he'd judged the situation correctly. Having a teacher flirt with him in front of her students would be a level of awkward he didn't care to experience. He'd learned fairly quickly that, for whatever reason, there were women out there who really liked men in uniform, with police and fire uniforms ranking right up there. Fake kitchen fires were rare, but not unheard of, and it seemed like every firehouse had a story about busting through a front door to find the lady of the house wearing little to nothing.

For a few years, he'd been like a kid in a candy store, so to speak, but it had gotten old after a while.

He'd grown to hate not being sure if a woman was attracted to him or his job, so one time he'd actually told a woman he was interested in that he was a plumber. It was a lie he kept going for several weeks, until she suffered a plumbing emergency and he was forced to admit he had no idea why disgusting water was backing up into her bathtub.

That had been his longest relationship, surviving his confession and lasting about a year and a half. He'd even been thinking about an engagement ring, but she struggled with his job and in the end, she opted out. Or rather, she opted for a guy who worked in a bank and was home by five and never worked weekends.

There had been a few almost-serious relationships since then, but they always fizzled out under the strain of his job. Flipping back and forth between day tours and night tours was something that came naturally to him at this point, but it was a lot harder on the people in his life.

He tried to stay hopeful, but sometimes it was hard to be optimistic about finding a woman he'd spend the rest of his life with. Even Scotty's sisters—who'd grown up with Tommy Kincaid and surrounded by firefighters—hadn't been able to make their marriages to firefighters work. Sure, there were a lot of strong marriages if he looked around enough, but it got discouraging at times.

"Hey, Hunt, you gonna stand around yank—" Scotty bit off the words, no doubt remembering just in time they had a young audience. "Doing nothing, or are you gonna help?"

Once they'd gotten the metal rod bolted into the proper position, Chris Eriksson turned testing it out into a comedy skit that made the children laugh and then, finally, it was time for some press photos. The kids gave them a handmade thank-you card that the firefighters promised to hang on their bulletin board, and then it was time to get back to the station. Several guys had agreed to cover for them, but only for a few morning hours.

Once they were on their way back, in Eriksson's truck, Chris looked over at Scott. "Hey, I heard Lydia's back."

Aidan was glad he'd been too slow to call shotgun and was wedged into the truck's inadequate backseat because he felt the quick flash of heat across the back of his neck. He was going to end up in trouble if he didn't figure out how to stifle his reaction to hearing Lydia's name.

But the way she'd looked at him at Kincaid's last night...

"Yeah," Scotty said. "She's going to help out at the bar so Ashley can take a little time off while she and Danny figure out what the hell they're doing."

"I heard Walsh was staying with you. That's cozy."

Aidan wondered if Lydia knew that part yet, because he couldn't imagine she'd take it well. He'd known the Kincaid family almost a decade and a half, and he knew that Ashley was the older sister, but Lydia was the junkyard dog. If you messed with the family, Ashley would try to talk it out with you, but Lydia would take your head off your shoulders.

"Lydia can worry about the beer and burgers and stay out of the rest of it," Scotty said.

Aidan laughed out loud. "I wouldn't recommend you tell *her* that."

"Hell, no. I'm not stupid."

As they got close, Eriksson sighed. "Fun time's over. Chief says we've gotta clean the engine bays today. And everything else that needs cleaning."

"That's bullshit," Scotty said. "I swear to God, the guys on night tour last week were all raised in barns. We should go drag their asses out of bed and make *them* clean up."

Aidan didn't mind the thought of filling the time around any runs with cleaning. It was mindless work that would keep him from having to look his best friend in the eye until he'd gotten a handle on thinking dirty thoughts about the guy's sister.

He didn't think the *she started it* excuse would cut it with Scott Kincaid.

THREE

Lydia almost made it to Kincaid's Pub without getting sidetracked. She might have made it all the way if she hadn't heard sirens in the distance, which made her think of her brother. And thinking about her brother brought her back to the fact that—in her eyes—he'd chosen a fellow firefighter over his own sister.

She detoured down an alley and then over two blocks until she was standing in front of three stories of old, red brick. The bay doors were open so she could see the gleaming fronts of both trucks—Engine 59 written over the door on the left and Ladder 37 written over the right in big gold letters that gleamed against the chalky brick.

When she was a little girl, she'd thought it was a castle. She'd even drawn it into a picture for art class, the bricks towering behind a dark-haired princess in a long pink gown. The assignment had been fairy-tale illustrations, so the teacher had drawn a sad face on her picture. Lydia had been crushed. She'd also been the one who hid the unsealed bag of pastrami in the depths of the art teacher's desk supply cabinet, but nobody knew that but her.

Over the years, the tall and narrow brick building became less of a princess castle and more of a place that competed for her father's attention. More often than not, it had won. But there was no denying this place was woven into the fabric of her life.

There were a couple of webbed folding chairs in front of L-37, so she knew the guys had been sitting on the sidewalk, but there was nobody out there now. She stepped inside the open bay door, running her hand down E-59's glossy, red side as her eyes adjusted to the light.

She'd shown up in high temper, but the sights, sounds and smells of the house wrapped around her like a blanket that brought her familiar comfort, even if it chafed a little bit.

"Can I help you?"

Lydia looked at the guy standing in front of her, who looked as if he was about twelve years old. "I'm looking for Scott Kincaid."

He frowned, and then his expression morphed into a wide grin. "You must be his sister. You look just like him. I'm Grant Cutter. I was assigned here right after you moved away, I guess."

"Lydia," she said, shaking his hand. "Is Scotty around, do you know?"

"He was back in the cage with the air tanks. Let me—" There was a clang of metal and Grant broke off, peering around the end of the truck. "Here he comes. Hey, Scotty, your sister's here."

When her brother stepped around the back of the truck, a clipboard in his hand, Lydia nodded. "Hey, Scotty."

"Hey." He handed the clipboard to Grant. "Can you take this to Cobb?"

"Sure thing."

"Don't just put it on his desk or he'll claim he never saw it. Hand it to him directly." When Cutter nodded and headed for the stairs, Scotty turned his attention to Lydia. "Aren't you supposed to be at the bar?"

"I was on my way and took a little detour. I've got enough time and Don's cooking." Don had been with the bar since before the ownership and name change, and her dad trusted him with a key and the safe combination. If she ran late, he'd cover out front until she got there.

"So just a little detour for grins, or were you looking for me?"

She knew him well enough to hear the slight edge in his voice, which meant he was already feeling defensive. And that meant he knew he was doing something wrong. "I stopped by to talk about Danny, actually."

"Oh yeah?" Her brother put his hands on his hips, tilting his chin up slightly. "What about him?"

He knew very well what about him. "You don't think maybe it would have been more appropriate if he stayed with one of the other guys?"

"I have a spare bedroom and the other guys don't. Doesn't make sense for him to crash on a couch or burden a family when I have an extra bed. And when a guy's having a hard time, you try to be there for him. It's called loyalty, you know."

"How about your loyalty to our sister? Where's *that* loyalty?

"Lower your damn voice. And I *am* being loyal to our sister. If Danny goes out and rents an apartment, and then starts making do for himself, it's just that much harder for them to get back together, and that's what we all want, right?"

"It doesn't matter what *we* all want. Do you want them back together because it's better for Ashley or because it's better for Danny?"

"I think it's better for both of them. If I didn't, I wouldn't *want* them back together. I love Ashley—and you're a liar if you claim you think otherwise—but I love Danny, too. He's like a brother to me."

"I get the whole brotherhood thing, trust me. I know all about it. But you're taking it too far in this case, Scott. You need to remember whose brother you *actually* are."

"You haven't even been around for two years. Who the hell are you talking to about remembering who you are? You left. You walked away."

"I left because of the same stupid bullshit Ashley is going through now, but at least when I left Todd, you had my back. It sucks that you don't have hers."

"You're out of line, Lydia."

"No, *you're* out of line."

The younger firefighter—Grant, she thought—walked back into the bay as she shouted at her brother and froze. After looking back and forth between the two of them, he turned and retraced his steps to make a hasty exit.

"Great. Nothing like a family spectacle to brighten everybody's day," Scotty said, his voice dripping with sarcasm.

"Ashley should be able to visit her own father without running into Danny," Lydia said, trying to dial back the temper. Not because she cared about being a spectacle, but because she wouldn't get anywhere butting heads with him. "You have to see that."

He shrugged. "Ashley goes in the front door. Danny always uses the back stairs. She probably wouldn't even know he was there."

"Trust me, she'd know."

"It's not like she's in the habit of stopping by for regular visits, anyway."

"That's not the point. She should be able to if she wants to. The family home should be a safe place for her."

He rolled his eyes so hard she wondered if it hurt. "That's a little dramatic, even for you. They're just going through a rough patch."

"I'm going to show you dramatic in about thirty seconds if you don't get your head out of your ass. It doesn't matter if it's just a rough patch or if they end up divorced. Right now, they're separated and Danny shouldn't be living under Dad's roof."

"Look, Lydia, I'm working here, okay? And I'm not tossing Danny out. So why don't you go to work and leave Ashley and Danny's marriage to them." He turned and started walking away.

"I'm not done talking to you," she said, and he flipped her the bird without looking back.

Lydia inhaled deeply through her nose, trying to resist the urge to run after him and bring him to the ground in a full body tackle. That would be a family spectacle they wouldn't get over anytime soon.

When Scotty walked away, leaving Lydia alone in the bay, Aidan knew he needed to leave it well enough alone. Not only because he should mind his own damn business, but because Lydia in a temper could be a lot to handle.

But when her shoulders sagged and she looked up, as if looking for some kind of divine guidance, he walked around the back of the truck. "Hey, Lydia. You okay?"

She jumped, and he wondered if the heat in her face was from being startled or if she was thinking about whatever it was she'd been thinking last night. "Oh, hey. I didn't know you were there."

When she tucked her hands in the back pockets of her jeans, it took every ounce of control Aidan had to keep his eyes on her face. But his peripheral vision happened to be excellent, so he couldn't miss the way the Kincaid's Pub T-shirt she was wearing stretched over her breasts when she put her arms behind her.

"Sorry. I wasn't trying to eavesdrop, but you guys aren't great at keeping things quiet."

She shrugged. "I don't care who knows. So I'm pissed my brother's letting Danny stay with him. It's not a secret."

Aidan didn't have a lot of experience with family dynamics outside of his own, and his own family was nothing like the Kincaids, but he suspected there was more to this than Danny crashing in Scott's spare room.

If things were heated and sides were being taken, he could see it. If Danny had gotten caught stepping out on Ashley or he'd put his hands on her or something, then Scotty would have to close the door in his face. But as far as he knew, Danny and Ashley were just going through a rough patch and needed a little space.

He held up his hands in a conciliatory gesture. "I'm Switzerland."

"Yeah, right." She shook her head, looking around the bay. "There's no Switzerland when firefighters are involved. Brotherhood first. Everybody else gets what's left."

And there was that *more to it* that he'd suspected might be an underlying problem. "That's not entirely true, you know."

She arched an eyebrow at him. "And you know what it's like to be on *this* side of it how exactly? Doesn't your family count money for a living?"

"It's a little more complicated than that, but I see what you're saying. But to us firefighters, that whole brotherhood thing kind of *includes* our families."

"In theory, maybe."

"Look, I love Tommy. You know that. He's been more of a father figure to me than my own father has been, but he's a hard-ass. Any…shortcomings he might have in the nurturing category might be his personality and not the job."

She stared at him for a few seconds, that dark gaze locked with his, and then she smiled. "Good effort, kid."

Kid? What the hell was that? She might have four years on him, but what was with the patronizing pat on the head? "It's my take on it. Whatever."

"This is exactly why I'm stuck back here again. Ashley can't even show her face at the damn corner market—never mind the bar—without somebody trying to convince her Danny's such a great guy and if she could just be more understanding and more supportive and give him another chance." She took her hands out of her pockets to point at him. "Not a single one of you—not even her own father or brother—has told her that maybe she did the right thing for *her* and that Danny needs to make an effort to resolve their problems, or that *he* needs to be more understanding and supportive."

Goddamn, but she was hot as hell when she got fired up. He tried to shove that awareness to the back of his mind, but it wasn't exactly a switch that could be flipped. "I admit that sucks."

"Yeah, it does." She stopped pointing at him, but he could still see the temper on her face and in the set of her shoulders. God help Scotty should he walk back in at that moment. "But I'm here now. And since you say you know my family so well, you know I'm not going to let anybody shit on Ashley. If Danny gets his head out of his ass, then good. If not, screw him."

She turned and walked away before he could say anything, not that he had any idea what to say to that. He actually was fairly neutral on the matter of the Walsh marriage, whether Lydia wanted to believe him or not. He liked them both a lot and he hoped they worked things out. And if they couldn't, he hoped the split was amicable and they both found happiness. That was about it for him.

Even though she left without giving him a chance to respond, he had to admit he liked watching her leave. She was a little taller than average, and nice and curvy. The long, angry strides did nice things for her ass, and Aidan was once again left with a Lydia-inspired hard-on.

And there wasn't a damn thing he could do about it.

The last thing he needed was to get caught jerking off in the bathroom. That had happened to a new kid once and they'd called him Palmer for so long they would have forgotten his real name if it wasn't written or sewn on his gear.

"Is my sister gone?"

Scotty's voice killed the hard-on as effectively as a cold shower. "Yeah. You're not exactly her favorite person at the moment."

"No shit." Scott walked to the bank of metal lockers and yanked his open. "No wonder Todd drank so much and went looking for less bitchy company."

Anger rose in Aidan's chest and he turned away before it spilled out. Siblings fought and he was aware nobody knew your soft spots like family, but that was a cheap shot. It wasn't Lydia's fault her ex had turned out to be an asshole. And blaming her made Aidan want to plant his fist in his best friend's face.

"That guy was a dickhead," was all he said.

"Yeah, he was." Scott sighed and slammed his locker. "I didn't mean that. She just… God, she drives me crazy, you know?"

Aidan was starting to know a little something about being driven crazy by Lydia, yes. Just, in his case, for an entirely different reason.

Danny Walsh watched Lydia leave from the third-story window. He could tell by the way she was walking that she was pissed off and he knew she must have stopped by to see Scott. Those two pushed each other's buttons without even trying.

Leaving the window, Danny turned off the television he'd had on for background noise while he cleaned up the living room area and then went into the kitchen. After giving the beef stew he'd made a quick stir, he turned the slow cooker to low. They used the slow cooker a lot because it meant not having to throw a meal away and start over if they had to go on a run before they got a chance to eat it.

He pulled out his phone and sent a group text announcing lunch was ready and then pulled out a stack of paper bowls and a loaf of bread. There wasn't a lot of butter left in the tub in the fridge, so he jotted that down on the list they kept on the door. Hopefully it would be enough for today.

The guys started showing up, serving themselves from the slow cooker before taking seats around the huge and ancient kitchen table. Danny was pretty sure the chairs were all older than him, with yellow vinyl seats spackled here and there with duct tape, but they were sturdy and nobody had ever complained enough to merit stretching the budget for new ones.

"That's all the butter there is," he warned them. "So have a little more bread and a little less butter with your bread and butter."

"Guys on night tour probably ate the shit with a spoon," Scotty mumbled as he scraped half the butter off his bread and wiped it on Rick's slice.

Danny ignored the jab, but he made a mental note to talk to Cobb and Gullotti later about the possibility of growing discontent in the house. The crew that manned Ladder 37 on the opposite shifts as Gullotti's wasn't pulling their weight when it came to domestic matters and that needed to be nipped in the bud. If these guys had to scrub the toilet, they all had to scrub the toilet.

"Did I hear a woman yelling in the bay earlier?" Jeff Porter asked, stretching across the table to spin the lazy Susan until it stopped on the seasoned salt, which he put on everything he ate.

"Lydia stopped by," Scotty said. "Looking for me."

"Ah. I thought maybe somebody had a new ex who wasn't happy about the ex part."

Danny sprinkled pepper on his stew, but on the inside he cringed at the word *ex*. Not in a million years had he ever thought it could happen, but now it looked as though he was on the road to having an ex-wife and it hurt. Ashley was his wife and he wanted her to stay that way.

"Must be almost time for Karen to go," Jeff said. "Right, Rick? This is the longest you've dated anybody that I can remember."

"I like Karen," Rick said around a mouthful of stew.

"I do, too," Grant said. "She's pretty and funny. And wicked smart, too."

They all looked at Grant, and red crept up his neck. He'd taken a big bite of potatoes and carrots as soon as he finished talking, so he chewed awkwardly as they stared, and then swallowed hard.

"I didn't mean anything by that," he said. "I meant that Rick should keep dating her because she's pretty and funny and stuff. Even if they broke up, I wouldn't make a move. Plus she's kinda old. I mean for me."

That made a few of them wince, and Jeff laughed. "Stop talking and eat your stew."

"Damn right you wouldn't make a move," Scotty said. "You don't date the other guys' ex-girlfriends. Or ex-wives or sisters or…hell, mothers or daughters. You don't fish in the station's pond."

Danny happened to be looking at Aidan when Scotty spoke, so he saw the way his mouth tightened and the tops of his ears turned red. But it was only a few seconds and Danny wondered if maybe he'd imagined it.

Grant gave Scotty a skeptical look. "At the rate Gullotti racks up ex-girlfriends, we'll either have to break that rule or go looking for women out in the boonies somewhere."

Danny shook his head. "That's one rule you don't want to break because that's drama nobody here wants. Relationships get messy and that kind of personal friction can tear a house apart."

"How did you end up married to Scotty's sister, then?" Grant asked. "She's Tommy Kincaid's daughter, even. Isn't that like a double rule-breaking?"

The last thing Danny wanted to do was talk about his marriage, even if it was currently a good example of the kind of drama he was talking about. So far things were still good between him and Scotty, but if things went any further south between Danny and Ashley, Scotty might feel a need to choose sides.

"I was actually up in Lynn at the time and met Ashley at a wedding for some mutual friends. I met Tommy and the rest of the family after about a month, I guess, but I didn't transfer here until after Ashley and I were engaged."

Silence filled the kitchen after he spoke and Danny knew why. Each of them was remembering that he and Ashley were separated and that there was a possibility of friction between him and Scotty if there was a divorce and it turned messy.

But that wasn't going to happen because he wouldn't let it. If Ashley wanted a divorce, he'd sign the papers. She could have the house. She could have whatever she wanted, and he wouldn't fight it. He loved her too much to drag them both down into hostility and court battles.

The ache in his chest he'd suffered off and on since the day Ashley told him she needed space flared up, and Danny took a breath to steady himself. Being emotional never helped any situation. And it certainly wasn't going to help this awkward silence that was threatening to ruin everybody's appetites.

"So everybody's current on the house fund for the month," he said, changing the subject. "Everybody take a look at the list before the end of tour and add anything you can think of so we can put together a grocery run."

As Danny expected, the guys all started talking about things they were almost out of, and he was free to eat his stew in peace. It was good stew, but now it tasted like sawdust and stuck in his throat.

If only his own house was as easy to manage as his firehouse.

FOUR

ONCE AGAIN BEING behind the bar in jeans and a dark green Kincaid's Pub T-shirt didn't just stir up mixed emotions for Lydia. It put all of her feelings in a blender and spun them around on the highest speed setting.

On the one hand, there was probably no place else in the world she was as comfortable. The bar was practically her second home. On the other hand, she'd expected to grow up and leave it behind someday, and almost had. Being there was a confusing mash-up of warm nostalgia and cold panic that she was taking a giant step backward.

She'd almost gotten away once before, when she was married to Todd. They met at a benefit hockey game—he was a probie at a nearby firehouse at the time—and he'd said all the right words. They got married in a small civil ceremony six months later. When he rented them an apartment she thought was too far from both his firehouse and Kincaid's, he'd told her it was a nice neighborhood with great schools for the children they'd have. And as he steered her toward leaving more and more of the responsibility for the bar in Ashley's hands, she believed him when he said it was important to him that she make a beautiful home for their family.

It had taken her almost three years to recognize that he was systematically isolating her from the community that considered her family and him still a newcomer. Since she was trying to make a home for children Todd wasn't around to make—a fact she was thankful for now—she wasn't behind the bar at Kincaid's, listening to stories about the guy who froze up on the ladder or who was using his job to get laid.

Of course, nobody wanted to be gossiping about Tommy Kincaid's son-in-law so, though her dad and siblings hadn't really liked Todd, they'd never heard anything concrete enough to merit interfering with her marriage. But they'd supported her when she moved home and divorced him. He'd moved to Worcester and she'd gone back to the pub.

But every day she'd left her dad's house and walked to Kincaid's for her shift, she'd felt as if she was spinning her wheels. There was nothing left for her there. She had zero interest in ever being involved with another firefighter. And, whether or not it was justified, she'd divorced one of them. In a climate of sticking together and seeing things through, the fact she hadn't done that in her marriage made some people look at her a little sideways. She'd finally gotten fed up and, in a desperate attempt to change her life, moved to New Hampshire.

And now she was back. And even though she could tell herself it was only temporary, it didn't feel that way. It felt more like stepping back into her life after a two-year vacation.

"Hey, doll, can I get another Bud Light?" Lydia turned to the customer sitting at the bar and cocked her head, giving him a look. "Uh, sorry. Can I get another Bud Light, please? Ma'am?"

She laughed and got him his beer. She wasn't answering to doll for anybody, but being too much of a bitch cut into the tips. Over the years she'd learned how to get her point across without driving customers away.

The sound of a glass smashing on the floor caught not only Lydia's attention, but that of everybody in the bar. There was no heckling, though. Just silence as the nonlocal customer who'd knocked his glass off the table looked at her like a deer caught in headlights.

"You gotta kiss Bobby," she called to him.

The guy's eyebrows drew together. "What? Who's Bobby?"

She pointed at the framed and signed photograph of Bobby Orr that hung on the wall. It had its own track lighting and was bolted to the wall so well it would take somebody hours and power tools to steal it. It was the heart of Kincaid's.

"You want me to kiss a picture?"

"You don't have to kiss the glass. Just kiss your fingertips and tap them on his cheek." She showed him, stopping just short of touching the glass because kissing Bobby for no reason might be bad luck.

The story, no doubt embellished by years and alcohol, told of two young men hired before the bar's grand opening, back in the day. They'd been setting up the beer mugs the day before they'd opened and each dropped a couple of glasses. One of them, rumored to be a fine young hockey fan, had laughed and kissed the picture of Bobby Orr the owner had just finished bolting to the wall.

"Help me, Bobby, or I'll have all my wages docked before I've earned any."

After work, one of them had landed in the hospital with a burst appendix. The hockey fan, however, had won enough off a scratch ticket that night to buy a used Camaro. Lydia wasn't sure how much of the story was true but, since the first morning the bar had been in business, very few had taken the chance.

"You must be kidding." The guy shook his head. "I don't really get into the whole jinx thing. Sorry."

Chad, the young dishwasher, who was already sweeping the broken glass into a dustpan, looked at the customer with big eyes. "You must not be from around here."

"Hey, it's up to you," Lydia called. "But in 2011, a customer broke a plate and she chose not to kiss Bobby."

"And she died a horrible, gruesome death, right?" the customer asked, his mouth curved up in a smirk.

Lydia shrugged one shoulder. "Not that I know

of. But she did trip on the sidewalk outside and need eleven stitches in her knee. And she had to beg a ride to the hospital because it turned out she parked illegally and her car was towed while she was having lunch."

"Is she serious?" he asked Chad.

The kid nodded. "I didn't work here yet, but I heard about it. You should just do it, sir. Better safe than sorry, you know?"

With skepticism written all over his face, the customer slowly stood and walked across the bar with everybody watching. Then he kissed his fingertips and pressed them to Bobby Orr's glass-covered cheek.

A cheer went up and then everybody went back to what they were doing before the glass broke. Lydia winked at the customer. "Refill's on the house."

A few minutes later, her phone chimed and she leaned by the cash register to read the message. Strictly speaking, employees weren't supposed to be screwing around with their phones, but she figured if her old man didn't like it, he could tend his own bar.

It was from Ashley.

Everything going okay?

Guy called me doll and Bobby got kissed. Just another day at KP.

There was a long pause while her sister typed a response.

Let me know if anything comes up. I can't tell you how much I appreciate this. Really.

Having stood behind the Kincaid's bar while going

through a marriage ending, Lydia did have an idea of how much her sister appreciated it. And it was so much worse for Ashley.

Danny Walsh was one of them. Not just a member of the firefighting community—the brotherhood—but he was family. He'd become tight with Scott and Aidan, and Tommy thought the world of him. He was loved and respected, and people were no doubt having some trouble wrapping their minds around why Ashley wouldn't want to be married to him anymore.

Not that it was really their business but, in Lydia's experience, that wouldn't stop them from having opinions. Opinions they'd be all too happy to share with Ashley while she was trying to work. Lydia could handle this, she thought. For Ashley's sake. And once her sister felt strong enough to step back behind the bar, she'd be free to go.

Based on how her pulse kicked up every time the door opened, that day couldn't come fast enough. She didn't want to admit it—even to herself—but she was looking for Aidan, and that little dip of disappointment she felt every time it wasn't him alarmed her.

What kind of idiot would stand there and think about how hard it was for both her and her sister to be married to firefighters while lusting after a firefighter?

Lust being the key word, she decided. As long as she kept it to a very private sexual attraction that nobody else knew about, there was no harm, no foul. She was simply a woman who hadn't dated in a while having a purely physical reaction to a handsome guy with a hot body and a naughty grin.

Of course, she wouldn't blame him if he avoided the place for a few days. She'd been pissed off at Scotty and, since he'd walked away, poor Aidan had gotten the overflow. She'd been bitchy with him and he didn't deserve it. On the other hand, maybe it had been a good thing. If it kept Aidan out of her sight, she wouldn't have to figure out why seeing him was having this kind of affect on her all of a sudden.

It was no big deal, she told herself, setting Kincaid's coasters in front of a couple who sat at one of the tables. All she had to do was tend the bar, bide her time, keep her pants on and then get the hell out of Boston.

"Maybe I'm not too old to date a woman named Bunny," Aidan said, setting the weights back on the rack.

Grant Cutter, who'd been spotting him, tossed him a towel. "Too late."

Sitting up so he straddled the bench, Aidan wiped the sweat from his head and bare torso. "What do you mean too late?"

"Scotty wanted to go to some club and his girlfriend would only go if Bunny went, but she didn't want to be a third wheel. You didn't answer your phone, so he called me and made me go."

"Aren't you a little young?"

"So was Bunny." Grant frowned. "But not *too* young. Not that young, I mean."

"Relax." He hadn't been serious about wanting to date her, anyway. He was more just giving voice to the fact he really wanted to get laid. "I knew what you meant."

"And I think Bunny's out of the picture anyway, since Scotty's not seeing Piper anymore."

Aidan frowned. "Since when?"

"I guess when he left her place this morning, she told him not to bother coming back."

"Huh." He'd only seen Scotty for a few minutes that morning. They had a full crew, so Cobb had sent Scotty to another house to cover for a guy who called in sick.

"She was asking him about his benefits and then she asked him if the insurance would cover her getting a nose job if they got married. He said he wasn't getting married anytime soon and then she said if she got knocked up, he'd have to."

"So he was running like his ass was on fire when he left there this morning," Aidan said, shaking his head. Sometimes Scott made some noise about trying to find the right woman and settling down, but they'd all known Piper wasn't her. Especially if, as Grant implied, she was as young as her friend Bunny.

The younger guy looked at the clock for what seemed like the thousandth time, and Aidan gave him a questioning look. "You going somewhere?"

"I have a date tonight. Like a real date, not a wingman thing. Her name's Nicole and she's pretty awesome."

"Does she know you went out with Bunny last night?"

Grant looked down at his shoes and shook his head. "She knows I went out with Scotty and some friends. She didn't ask. I wouldn't have lied to her if she'd asked. And it wasn't really a date with Bunny. I was just extra, you know."

"Relax, kid. I'm just messing with you."

Grant kept on talking, telling him where he met Nicole—at his nephew's ball game—and pretty much her entire life story, but Aidan half tuned him out. Calling the other guy kid had yanked him back to the moment Lydia had looked him in the eye and called him that.

"Good effort, kid."

He didn't believe it had just popped out of her mouth. She'd been considering what he'd said and had plenty of time to think about her response while looking at him. And even when he'd been seventeen and she'd seemed so much older at twenty-one, she'd never called him that.

No, Aidan was pretty sure it had been deliberate, but he couldn't wrap his mind around why.

The alarm sounded and both of them were on their feet immediately. They met the other guys on their way through the kitchen, but there was no talking as they listened to the call. A motor vehicle accident involving an SUV, a pickup and a cyclist, with injuries. Witness unable to confirm if it was steam or smoke on-scene.

Once they'd each weighed themselves down with fifty-plus pounds of gear and hit the sirens, they rolled out, E-59 first with L-37 right behind. They always rolled together—the pumper truck with various water hoses and wrenches, and the ladder truck with the variety of ladders, tools and rakes. As soon as they cleared the bays, the doors closed and they were off.

They arrived on-scene to find some very pissed-off people yelling at each other. There was no steam and no smoke, and the injury appeared to be a scuff down the side of the cyclist's leg. It didn't stop him from swinging his helmet at one of the other pissed-off, yelling people, trying to hit the guy in the head.

"Whoa!" Jeff Porter yelled, wading into the fray. One of the senior firefighters with Ladder 37, he was a big man with a big voice that mixed equal parts authority and menace.

Everybody stopped talking, until the guy in the button-down shirt and tie waved his hand at the crumpled nose of his SUV. "Who's going to pay for this?"

"I ain't your insurance company, son," Porter barked. "Are you hurt?"

"No, but I want this fixed."

"I ain't a body shop, either." Porter looked at the others. "Anybody hurt?"

The cyclist shook his head while the woman who'd

presumably been driving the pickup glared. Porter repeated the question and she shook her head.

"Look at my vehicle," SUV guy said, gesturing again at his front end. "Look at it!"

"Maybe if you'd been looking at the front of it instead of your phone, you would have braked," the woman said.

Aidan exchanged looks with Cutter, Walsh and Cobb as he leaned against the truck to watch. There was nothing to do here but leave them to the cops and tow trucks, once Porter was done playing peacemaker.

"How'd you get involved in this?" the big guy asked the cyclist.

"I was behind this dumbass when he rear-ended that dumbass and I didn't want to cool down, so I went out around. This dumbass flings his door open and down I go."

"What kind of moron goes around a car on the left?" SUV guy demanded.

"What kind of moron runs into a big-ass bright red pickup?" the cyclist shot back.

Porter looked at the police officers and shook his head. "Good luck, guys."

"That was a waste of time," Cutter said when they were back in the truck.

"You never know," Aidan replied. "Besides, the time it wasted is less time until you can get ready for your hot date with Nicole."

That perked the kid up. "True. You got any plans for tonight?"

"Nope." Just going home to his empty apartment, where he'd try to convince himself that being able to walk around in his boxer briefs, belch without apology and scratch whatever might itch was a payoff for being alone.

ASHLEY CHECKED THE RINGER volume on her phone and then rolled her eyes at her own stupidity. It was turned up all the way, just as it had been when she'd checked it an hour before.

Danny wasn't going to call tonight.

Even though it was her own damn fault, she put her hand over her queasy stomach and fought back another wave of tears. She was going to dehydrate if she kept it up.

She'd pushed him too far. Even as she pushed at him, hoping for a reaction, she'd known on some level she was going too far, but she hadn't stopped. While she was afraid of the possible consequences, she was even more afraid of living the rest of her life in what had come to feel like an emotional vacuum.

When she said the worst of it—that she wasn't happy and wasn't sure she wanted to be married to him anymore—she'd been hoping she'd finally break through his wall of reserve. She was starving for an emotional response from him, even if it was anger.

Instead he'd accepted what she'd said with nothing more than a clenched jaw and left.

When her cell phone rang, Ashley almost knocked it off the couch in her rush to grab it. Her heart was pounding, but it was her father's number on the screen. Her thumb hovered over the button that would reject his call, but some subliminal part of her brain refused to forget the fear she'd felt the night Fitzy Fitzgibbon had called to tell her Tommy had had a heart attack and was in an ambulance. She'd answered every call from her dad since then.

"Hello?"

"What are you doing?"

As usual, the question sounded demanding and a little judgmental rather than conversational, and she bristled. "I'm folding laundry."

That wasn't entirely true. She'd dumped the basket of clean clothes on the couch, but she hadn't so much as matched a sock yet. Mostly she was staring at a repeat of some crime drama on the television while thinking about her husband.

"You and your sister need to come over in the morning," he told her.

"Why?" She tried not to wonder whether Danny would be upstairs in her brother's apartment tomorrow morning, but she couldn't help it. Unless he'd changed his shift schedule, he wasn't on day tour tomorrow and there was a possibility she'd run into him. While she wanted to see Danny, she didn't want to see him with her entire family present.

"What do you mean why? My daughters can't

come visit me? I barely got to talk to Lydia at the bar, and there's something I want to talk to her about."

Ashley could hear the underlying annoyance in his voice, and she wondered how her sister had managed to piss their old man off already. "I'll tell Lydia when she gets home."

No, she wouldn't, but she'd leave her a note. Between lying awake dwelling on her screwed-up marriage and not working nights at the bar, her sleep patterns were scrambled and she was waking up with the sun. To keep from turning into a zombie, she was going to bed earlier than she had since middle school.

"How are you doing?" her dad asked, and his voice was as close to tender as it could get.

"I'm doing okay."

"Are things any better? Between you and Danny, I mean."

"We're working on it." Another lie, this one slightly bigger than the last. "It's going to take time."

"You take too much time and you'll get used to being apart, and I know that's not what you want."

It wasn't what she wanted, but what her marriage had become wasn't what she wanted, either. As tempting as it was to call Danny and tell him she was sorry—that she'd temporarily lost her freaking mind—and that she wanted him to come home, that wasn't going to solve the problem. When the relief faded, she'd still want something from Danny he seemed incapable of giving her.

"I'm not going to rush this, Dad. If we're meant to be together, it'll work out."

She heard his snort loud and clear over the phone. "You make it sound like kind of destiny crap. It won't just work out. You have to *work* at working it out."

Ashley bit down on the sarcasm burning to be let loose. Mr. Marriage Counselor, he wasn't. "I know."

"He's a good man, Ashley."

Tears blurred the television screen. "I know that, too."

"Good. I'll see you in the morning, then."

As usual, he hung up without giving her a chance to say goodbye, and Ashley tossed the phone onto the coffee table. Then she flopped over onto the pile of clothes and squeezed her eyes shut. She didn't want to cry again, dammit.

But her father's voice wouldn't get out of her head. "*He's a good man, Ashley.*" And the pile of laundry had nothing of his. Her shirts. Her underwear. Her socks. None of his, which for some reason made her feel incredibly alone. And this time there was no stopping the tears.

FIVE

LYDIA WALKED UP the cement front steps of the Kincaid family's three-decker the next morning and paused in the shade of the deep porch. Not surprisingly, Ashley had declined to accompany her on this trip, which was the answer to a summons from their father.

She'd seen him at Kincaid's, but they hadn't really had the chance to catch up. It wasn't an easy place to have personal conversations without withdrawing to the windowless, claustrophobic office Lydia avoided whenever possible.

Not that they'd be having a heart-to-heart. Tommy Kincaid wasn't much for those, and he probably wouldn't ask much about her life in New Hampshire. Quite frankly, she wasn't sure why he'd asked her to stop by at all.

She knocked and then walked in without waiting for an answer. Her dad would be in the battered leather recliner that was so perfectly molded to his body, nobody else could comfortably sit in it.

Their first-floor unit was definitely stuck in the '80s. Her mom had started making some noise about updating it, but then they'd gotten the diagnosis that changed their lives. And, because her parents weren't the kind of people who *did* doctors, they'd gotten it too late. Lydia wasn't sure if it was some kind of shrine to her mom or if her dad was just lazy, but nothing had been changed since then that hadn't worn out beyond use or been broken.

She went into the living room, wishing she'd stopped for a coffee along the way. At this hour, there would probably be a couple of inches left in her dad's coffeepot, but it would be cold. And unless she'd seriously misjudged his ability to adapt to an ever-changing world, he didn't have a Keurig yet.

"Hey, Dad."

"There's my girl." He lifted his face so she could kiss his cheek, setting the remote control on the arm of the recliner so he could squeeze her hand. "It's nice having you back behind the bar. You always did have a way with the customers."

"At least somebody thinks so," she said, thinking of her job in Concord. Beer and burgers just came more naturally to her, she guessed, sitting on the couch.

"I heard you showed up at the house yesterday to cause a scene," he said, and she realized that was the motive behind the summons. She was here for a lecture.

"I did *not* show up there to cause a scene. I went there to talk to my brother. There's a difference." She didn't expect him to see it, though. In his mind, personal business didn't belong on the job.

"It's none of your business, Lydia."

She'd made a decision before leaving Ashley's that she wasn't going to let her dad get her back up, but she could already see it wasn't going to be an easy resolution to keep. "Since I had to quit my job and dip into my savings to pay ahead on my rent, I think Ashley's marriage is very much my business. And that's above and beyond the fact you're all my family. That's supposed to matter, too."

"Mind your mouth," he said, which was code for *don't tread too closely to calling me out for things I do wrong.*

"You don't think it's a little rude to have Danny staying here?"

He considered it for a few seconds, and then shook his head. "He's not staying with me. And, even if he was, he's been part of this family for a long time. You want me to see him out on the streets?"

"Oh, please. There are a lot of options between staying under your roof and being out on the streets."

"He's staying with Scotty, not me."

Lydia rolled her eyes. "Again, under your roof."

"Your brother pays rent. He's allowed to have a guest."

Losing her temper with her father never got her anywhere but in a shouting match she couldn't win, so she tried to swallow some of her anger. "I know he rents the second-floor apartment, but you're still his

father and you still own the house. I think you guys
could have taken into consideration how awkward
it might be for Ashley, having Danny living here."

"He's not living here. He's just…what do they call
it? Couch-surfing. He's just crashing until Ashley
comes to her senses." As if he could sense the storm
of words she was about to unleash on him for that bit
of bullshit, her dad just kept right on talking. "And
speaking of renting, we've been renovating the third-
floor apartment. It's almost done."

"Yeah? You going to rent that to Danny, maybe?"

"No, I was thinking you could rent it."

Oh, hell no. "Why would I do that?"

"You can't stay with your sister forever."

The word *forever* pinballed around in her mind and
she suffered a rare moment of being struck speech-
less. He couldn't possibly believe she'd come back
to Boston to stay. She knew Ashley had told him she
just needed a little time and Lydia was going to cover
for her. At no time did either of them imply she was
moving back for good.

"And you might get in the way of her and Danny
getting back together," he continued, just making it
worse.

Lydia had gone toe-to-toe with her father many
times over the years. Ashley might be older, but she
was always willing to step back and let her sister do
the talking for her and their younger brother. Lydia
knew her father would never lay a hand on any of

them in anger, so she'd never had any fear of getting in a shouting match.

There was still a line, though—only so far she could push before it became serious disrespect—and Lydia wasn't sure she could get into this without crossing that line.

"It's important for a couple going through a tough time to have plenty of alone time," he continued.

"Yeah, you're the person we all go to for marriage counseling," she muttered.

He gave her such a hard look, she actually dropped her gaze to her hands. They weren't supposed to bring up the fact that children weren't deaf and they all knew Mom was on the verge of throwing Dad out when she got sick. Even when they tried to be quiet, her dad had a voice that carried through the walls and they'd all known. Then the cancer came and nobody ever mentioned those times again.

"I'm here for Ashley," she said quietly. "And if Ashley wants alone time with Danny, she'll let me know. If they try to reconcile, I'll do whatever I can to help make that happen."

He seemed satisfied, and he picked up the remote control again. Once the channel surfing started, the conversation was usually over. "You should go upstairs and smooth things over with your brother. I don't like when you kids fight."

Both of the Kincaid men in one morning? She was tempted to claim she had to get to work, but that probably wouldn't work on the guy who owned the business. "I'll talk to him later. He might not even be up yet."

"He's up. No reason to put off the conversation."

With a sigh that let him know just how she felt about his demands, Lydia pushed off the couch and walked through the house to the back. Stepping out onto the back deck, she leaned against the railing for a few minutes, just breathing in the fresh air.

She wasn't sure if it was their zodiac signs or the stars being misaligned when she was born or some kind of magnetic opposition built into their DNA, but she and her father had never been able to communicate. They loved each other. That was never in doubt. But they drove each other batshit crazy like nobody's business.

Once she'd calmed down enough so she could probably have a reasonable conversation with the other family member who had a knack for driving her batshit crazy, Lydia went up the wooden steps to the second-floor deck and knocked on the glass slider that led into Scott's living room.

She was looking at a very dead plant in a ceramic black bear by her right foot when the door slid open. "What kind of loser can't keep pansies alive?"

"I don't know much about pansies," a deep voice said, and Lydia jerked her head up to look into the pretty blue eyes of Aidan Hunt.

Aidan enjoyed the way Lydia's eyes widened when she saw him standing in the doorway instead of her brother. She blushed, which made her cheeks pink, and her lips parted slightly.

He liked looking at her mouth.

"Oh. I thought you were my brother."

"I figured as much." He stepped aside. "Come on in. He's in the shower right now, but he shouldn't be too much longer."

Unlike the first-floor apartment, the second floor had been freshened up since the last time she'd seen it. Mostly cosmetic, with laminate floors instead of the old carpet, and new paint. And Scotty didn't own much, but what he did was good quality. Like the leather sofa and love seat in front of a huge flat-screen television.

"I'm here on the old man's orders," she told him, moving to the fridge.

Aidan managed to be in the perfect spot to check out her ass when she bent over to see what Scotty had on hand. "Sometimes it's easier to go along than to argue with him."

"So Scott and Ashley tell me." She grabbed an orange juice and closed the door. "I haven't gotten the knack of that yet."

"It's good for him." Aidan leaned against the kitchen island and crossed his arms. "To be challenged, I mean. Not many people talk back to him."

She took a swig of the juice and screwed the cap back on the bottle. "Is Danny here?"

He noticed the tightness around her mouth—since he was still looking at it—and knew she still wasn't okay with Danny staying at the Kincaid house, no matter which unit he was in.

"Yeah, he's in his room. Uh, the guest room. We have some free time, so we're going to do…some stuff."

She smiled, then, and that curve of her lips made him acutely glad the island was between them so she couldn't see him from the waist down. "Stuff, huh? Sounds very mysterious and guy-like."

"Men of mystery. That's us."

"Maybe a little trip to the strip club? Hit the gun range or the batting cages? Maybe stop at the salon and get pedicures?"

"Pedicures?" He laughed. "Hey, you never know. Those boots are hard on our feet."

"I'd pay good money to get my hands on a black-mail photo of Scotty getting a pedi—"

She broke off when Danny walked into the room, and Aiden felt the tension ratchet up a notch.

When Danny saw Lydia, he stopped in his tracks and his expression seemed to close off, as if he was feeling no emotions whatsoever. "Hi, Lydia."

Aidan watched her, hoping she wouldn't lose her temper or simply walk out the door. That wouldn't do anybody any good, and he knew for a fact Scotty being at odds with his sister upset him. If he heard her yelling and rushed out to defend Danny, it would get ugly and Scotty would be almost impossible to work with until it was resolved.

But Lydia's expression softened and she crossed

the kitchen to wrap her arms around his neck. "Hi, Danny."

They embraced for a moment and then, when they broke apart, Danny gave her a half smile. "I wasn't sure if you were going to hug me or kick me in the balls."

"Neither was I," she said, and they all laughed. "I'm kidding. It's good to see you."

"I hear it makes you unhappy that I'm staying here. Because of Ashley." He gave a little shrug of his shoulders. "I can find a couch to crash on at somebody else's place if you think this is too hard for her."

Since Aidan had overheard Lydia's feelings on the matter when she expressed them in no uncertain terms to Scotty the day before, he was surprised when she shook her head. "I might have overreacted. A little."

Danny's mouth quirked into a smile. "A little?"

"I was so focused on Ashley and being a good sister and making sure somebody stood up for her that, until I saw your face, I forgot we like *you*, too."

"A little?"

She grinned. "A little."

"Are you sure? Because I don't want to cause problems between you and your brother, or your old man."

"I'm sure. And I know Ashley wouldn't want you couch-surfing, either."

"How's she doing?"

Aidan watched Lydia struggle with an answer,

even taking a sip of her orange juice before answering. "She's okay, I guess. Maybe you should call her."

"Yeah, maybe." He slapped his hand on the counter and forced a smile. "I'm running to the corner market for a few things before we head out. You guys need anything?"

Scotty walked in at that moment, a towel wrapped around his waist while he scrubbed at his hair with another. "What's going on?"

"I'm heading to the market. You need something?"

They were all good, and as soon as Danny was gone, Scotty gave his sister a look. "I didn't hear any yelling."

"It's all good," she said. "And I'm supposed to apologize for causing a scene yesterday."

"I guess I'm supposed to accept it, then."

Aidan shook his head at the strangeness of the Kincaid family dynamics and went into the living room space. The apartment was too open concept to give them any real privacy to make their half-assed apologies, but he didn't need to stand at the island and watch. He knew it wouldn't take long. Scott and Lydia both had tempers with a low flash point, but they also burned out almost as quickly.

Sure enough, in less than two minutes, the siblings were laughing and Aidan exhaled a deep sigh of relief. The storm had passed. This one, anyway.

"Why do you have a ceramic bear on your back deck with dead flowers in it?" Lydia was asking.

Aidan could see Scott shrug from where he sat

on the couch. "It was a gift from a woman I dated a while back."

"Interesting gift."

"Black bear. Yellow flowers in it. It was supposed to be a Bruins thing."

"That's sweet," she said. "How come you broke up?"

"She just wasn't the one."

Aidan laughed. "She wasn't the one whose name he said in his sleep is what he means."

"Screw you," Scotty shot back. "I'm going to get dressed. Try not to spill all my secrets, Hunt."

"I'm heading out," Lydia told him. "But I'll talk to you later."

Scotty waved goodbye before disappearing into his room, and Aidan stood as Lydia walked toward him. "Feel better now?"

"Yeah, I do. I don't like fighting with my brother, believe it or not. And I love Ashley, but I can't kick Danny while he's down." She shrugged. "I guess I should mind the bar and my own business."

It was close enough to what Scott had said so he had to fight not to grin. "I don't think minding your family's business is a bad thing. I wouldn't mind mine interfering now and again."

"It's their loss," she said in a quiet voice rich with sincerity.

The affection she clearly had for him shone in her eyes and it kicked his heart rate up, even though he knew it only came from having known each other for so long. "Thanks."

"I should head out and let you guys get ready for your pedicures."

Aidan chuckled. "Not quite that glamorous. We're helping Rick Gullotti build a wheelchair ramp for his landlords."

"Hot day for it."

"Yeah, but we've all got the time off. Maybe I'll stop by the bar later for a beer. And to say hi."

He said it casually because, as far as he knew, they were friends and it seemed like something a friend could say without deeper meaning, but she cocked an eyebrow at him. "Maybe I'll see you around, then, kid."

"Definitely," he said as she opened the glass slider and stepped out onto the deck.

And the first chance he got, he was going to get to the bottom of this *kid* thing.

SIX

An hour before closing time, Lydia gave up on seeing Aidan walk through the door. It was late enough so if he hadn't stopped in by now, he probably wasn't going to.

She figured he wasn't doing the night shift at the station or he wouldn't come in and have a beer beforehand. And if he had to be in at eight tomorrow morning, ten o'clock at night was a little late to head out for a drink.

It had probably just been a throwaway line anyway. *Hey, maybe I'll stop in and say hi.* She'd heard it many times before. Sometimes people popped in to say hello and sometimes they found better things to do.

Hoarse laughter caught her attention and she looked to the back corner of the bar where her dad and his buddy Fitz were perched on stools, one on each side of the polished wood. Besides that pair, there were a couple of firefighters she didn't really know sitting at the bar, and three guys she pegged as not from around there sitting at one of the tables.

"Hey, Dad," she called. "Are you going to be here awhile longer?"

"Yeah, I got another half an hour or so in me."

He shouldn't, she thought. He should be home in bed already. "I'm going to go check the other room, then."

When her dad waved her away, Lydia grabbed an empty bus pan from under the bar, along with a rag and the spray bottle of cleaner. The more she did now, the closer she was to being able to go home once she'd locked the door. The kitchen closed at nine, so all she had to do was cash out the register, clean up the last few mugs and wash the floor.

The room wasn't too bad, most of their patrons knowing enough to bring their empties to the bar when they were done, but she found a couple of bottles on the floor next to the leg of the pool table. And there was a half-full bottle balanced precariously on top of the rack of pool cues. Shaking her head, she dropped it into the bus pan.

Movement at the door caught her eye, and she turned to watch Aidan walk through the door. Heat suffused her body and she moved away from the opening before he saw her. While she could see the door from the alcove, she couldn't see the bar. She imagined him going over and shaking her dad's hand, though. Maybe accepting a beer.

"Kinda late," she heard her father say. The place was quiet enough so his loud voice seemed to echo through the bar. "We'll be closing up soon."

"I was going by and figured I'd say hi for a few minutes. See if anybody was around."

"Lydia's in the pool table room. If they made a mess, that bus pan might be heavy. And she's gotta put the chairs up. Go give her a hand, would ya?"

Great. *Thanks a lot, Dad.*

Lydia grabbed the spray bottle and spritzed the nearest table before wiping it down. And when Aidan stepped into the alcove, she gave him a welcoming smile. He was wearing a Boston Fire T-shirt with a pair of faded jeans, and his hair looked freshly washed. She wanted to run her fingers through it and see if it felt as soft as it looked, but she curled them in the cleaning rag instead.

"Hey, kinda late to start the night, isn't it?" she asked.

He held up the open bottle of beer. "Told you I'd stop by. But it took forever to build that damn ramp and then Gullotti's landlady insisted on making supper for us. After that, we went upstairs to his place because he needed a hand moving some furniture. Next thing you know the night's gone and we've all got to work tomorrow."

"But you still came here? Just because you said you might stop by."

"I wasn't going to but I took a shower and I wasn't tired and…" He set the bottle on one of the tables she hadn't wiped yet and alarm bells went off in her mind. "There's something I wanted to talk to you about."

He walked slowly toward her as he said it, his voice

low. She could almost feel the energy crackling between them, and she tried desperately to remember this was Aidan Hunt. He was Scotty's best friend. He was a firefighter. He could be an annoying pain in the ass. That was three strikes and he was out.

"What is it you want to talk about?" she asked, surprised her voice sounded as steady as it did.

"You keep calling me *kid*."

She tried to ignore the way he moved into her personal space, but it wasn't easy. He smelled too good and she was eye level with that hollow at the base of his throat.

"I'm not a kid anymore," he continued when she didn't say anything.

Oh, she knew that. But calling him *kid* was her way of reminding herself he was her younger brother's best friend. Or attempting to, anyway. It didn't seem to be working.

"You're younger than I am," she said, with a new tone in her voice that bordered on husky.

Touching him would be a mistake. She pressed her hands to the wall behind her, the old brick coarse under her palms.

When Aidan braced his hands against the wall, too—one on either side of her head—Lydia's breath caught in her chest. He was close enough so she could smell his shampoo and the slight tang of his aftershave. And he was close enough to kiss her.

She was *not* going to touch him.

"Not by enough years to even count," he said, "unless you're scraping the bottom of the barrel looking for reasons why I shouldn't kiss you."

"There are so many reasons you shouldn't kiss me, I don't need to scrape the bottom of the barrel."

With his hands still braced against the wall, he dipped his head low, so his mouth was close to her ear. "Trust me, I know. But it's all I think about so unless you tell me you don't want it, I'm going to kiss you anyway."

His breath was hot on her neck, making the soft wisps of her hair tickle her skin. Lydia knew she should tell him she didn't want him to kiss her, but she couldn't make herself say the words. "It would be a lie."

Aidan's cheek grazed hers and she sighed at the contact. His lips pressed lightly against the corner of her mouth and then she had a brief moment of staring into his pretty blue eyes before his mouth was on hers.

Her fingers curled against the wall, the brick rasping her nail tips like an emery board. Their breaths mingled and the desire that had been building in her since he walked into the bar her first night back solidified into a needy ache. He kissed her until she made a hungry sound deep in her throat, and then lifted his right hand from the wall to cup the side of her face.

"Why do I want you so much?" he whispered against her lips.

"It doesn't make any sense."

"It doesn't." He brushed his thumb over her cheekbone, looking into her eyes. "I don't care."

His mouth closed over hers again, more demanding this time. Giving up on her determination not to touch him, Lydia ran one hand up his chest and buried the other in his hair. It was as soft as it looked, and she moaned against his lips when he put his hands on her hips and pulled her hard up against him.

The sound of a breaking plate jerked her back to her senses. When he lifted his head, looking in the direction of the noise, she sidestepped so she was no longer between him and the wall. *Saved by the jinx.* "I should be out there. I need to go."

"Or you could stay here and kiss me some more."

She laughed, and it sounded a little more high-pitched than usual. "I'll feel bad if the poor schmuck doesn't kiss Bobby's picture and then gets hit by a car or something."

Aidan nodded and picked up a chair, turning it upside down in his hands. "Go ahead, then. I'll put up the chairs and bring the bus pan back."

"Thanks."

Lydia wasn't surprised to see that her dad had already taken care of making sure their customer fended off the broken glass jinx, and she also wasn't surprised when her dad gave her an odd look. It hadn't occurred to her that she might look like a woman who'd just been kissed and the only guy back there was Aidan Hunt.

"It's hot as hell in that alcove," she said, hoping to fend off any questions.

As expected, he latched on to the easy answer.

"I've been thinking about replacing the ceiling fans with something with bigger paddles."

"Good idea. Aidan's finishing up the last of the chairs and he'll bring the bus pan out."

"Took you a while."

She wasn't sure if he meant anything by that other than general criticism, but she kept her back to him and focused on the cash register. Hitting the button to pop it open, she took out some ones and started counting. "We got talking about Scotty's apartment. It came out nice."

As she'd hoped, Fitz took over the conversation, wanting to know how the third-floor renovation was going. Leaving them to it, she counted and bundled the bills in the register drawer.

When she heard Aidan set the bus pan on the bar, she took a deep breath before turning to face him. It was weak to avoid making eye contact, but she could almost feel her father's presence behind her, so she concentrated on putting the spray bottle back under the bar. "Thanks. I appreciate it."

"Not a problem. You want me to take it out back?"

"I'll get it for her, son." Her dad got off his stool, jingling the key ring clipped to his pocket. "Time to lock up, everybody."

Aidan slapped his hand on the bar, which startled Lydia into making eye contact with him. He smiled. "I'll see you around."

She nodded and grabbed the bus pan, even though

her dad had said he'd take it. It was something to do with her hands. "Thanks again for the help."

Her dad walked him and the other customers to the door, talking and laughing with them in that easy way he had with the patrons, and she watched them go. There was a little tension in Aidan's shoulders, which probably mirrored her own.

Once he'd locked the doors, her dad sighed and gestured to Fitz. "Help out, old man. Let's get this place cleaned up so my girl can get home."

Not that she was in any hurry, Lydia thought. It wasn't as if she'd be getting any sleep. With the memory of that kiss to relive and savor, she had a feeling she'd do more sheet-twisting and pillow-punching than sleeping.

You're an asshole, plain and simple. Aidan curled his fingers over the edge of the porcelain sink bowl the next morning, staring at his reflection in the mirror.

Kissing Lydia Kincaid in the pool room of Kincaid's Pub with Tommy sitting at the bar made him an asshole. Looking Scotty in the face two hours ago when they'd shown up for the day tour without saying a word about what he'd done made him an asshole. And the real kicker was that he wanted to kiss her again.

No matter how he tried to justify it in his mind, he couldn't make those simple facts go away. He wanted Lydia and he shouldn't. Therefore, he was an asshole.

"Hey, Hunt, you dead?" Jeff Porter pounded on

the bathroom door. "I think Eriksson does the best mouth-to-mouth, if you need a little pick-me-up."

"I'm not dead," Aidan shouted back. "Gimme a freakin' minute."

"You've had a lot of minutes. I'm gonna take the Halligan to the door in not too many *more* minutes."

Aidan yanked open the door and glared at the big man as he pushed by. "You ladder guys need to learn some manners. Here, it's all yours."

Porter grinned and slapped him on the shoulder. "I'm good. I was just bustin' your balls."

"Asshole." Aidan went into the kitchen to see if there were any doughnuts left. There were two cinnamon sugar ones, which were everybody's least favorite, but they met the definition of junk food, so he grabbed a mug of coffee and sat down in front of the box.

The last thing Aidan needed was anybody trying to bust his balls. They were on the verge of exploding all on their own, without any help. He'd hoped kissing Lydia would get the need out of his system, but it had backfired on him.

It might have gotten the overwhelming need to kiss her out of his system, but now he'd been left with an even more overwhelming need for more. More Lydia. More kissing and more touching. More of her voice in his ear when it was low and husky with desire. More of her hands on his body.

He broke off a chunk of doughnut and shoved it into his mouth. Maybe a sugar high would help.

After taking a long swallow of coffee to wash it down, he took another bite. Then another. Fifteen minutes later, the doughnuts and coffee were setting up like concrete in his stomach, and he leaned back in his chair and debated on catching a quick nap.

Scotty walked in at that moment and poured a cup of coffee. Then he peeked in the doughnut box and scowled when he saw that it was empty. "You didn't save me one? What the hell kind of friend are you?"

Guilt punched Aidan in the gut, and he felt the blood drain out of his face. If Scotty only knew just how bad a friend he was. He should tell him, he thought. He should tell Scott he'd kissed his sister and let him do what he had to do. Maybe he'd take such a beating from her brother that he'd shy away from ever being within touching distance of Lydia again.

"Jesus, Hunt. I was kidding. What the hell's wrong with you?" Scotty hooked a chair rung with his foot and dragged it away from the table so he could sit down.

"I'm just tired. I thought maybe I could fend off the urge to nap with a sugar rush. But mostly I just feel like I need a longer nap now."

"You're turning into an old man. You need a girl-friend, my friend."

"I don't think getting laid is going to cure my need for a nap."

"Not just getting laid, dumbass. A real girlfriend. You're getting into a rut and you need somebody to have fun with. To go to the movies and shit with, you know?"

Aidan stared into his empty coffee mug so he wouldn't have to look his friend in the face. He didn't want to go to the movies with a girlfriend. He wanted to go some place private with Lydia and maybe re-enact some late-night movies. Which, of course, he should *not* be thinking about right now, with Scott in the room.

"You're one to talk," Aidan said. "Grant told me you and Piper are no more."

Because he looked over when he said it, he saw Scott's expression change. He actually looked regret-ful, if not downright sad, which was different for him. "She was just chasing the bennies, and she was will-ing to get knocked up to get them."

The idea a woman would get pregnant deliberately to get a ring and benefits made Aidan angry on Scot-ty's behalf. "Grant said she was after a nose job?"

"Yeah. That's a helluva story for the grandkids, huh? Well, kids, your grandma wanted plastic sur-gery, so she trapped me with an unplanned pregnancy and that's why I drink so much."

"Heartwarming." Aidan set the empty mug back on the table. "Sorry it didn't work out. Maybe the next one."

"Maybe we're destined to be single. We should move in together and I'll just leave all my shit around and you'll clean up after me, like that old TV show my dad used to watch."

"Yeah, I don't think so."

"Hey, Kincaid," they heard Gullotti call from the other room. "Come give me a hand for a minute."

Scotty knocked back the rest of his coffee and stood up. "No rest for the awesome, my friend."

Aidan watched him rinse his cup and set it upside down on the drying mat before leaving the kitchen. There might be a weird kind of domesticity around the station, but he had no intention of becoming *The Odd Couple* with Scott Kincaid, best friend or not. He was still holding out hope he'd find the perfect woman who loved him and could handle his job and wanted to have some kids and a dog.

His thoughts turned to the woman who didn't make any secret about not loving the firefighting, though. He wasn't sure how she felt about him, kids or dogs, but he already knew that while she *could* handle his job, she didn't want to go through it again.

Pulling out his phone, he cast a guilty glance in the direction Scotty had gone, and then pulled up his texting app. Cursing himself for a weak, stupid son of a bitch, he tapped on Lydia's name.

Hey. You busy?

It probably took only seconds for her to type in her response, but it felt like forever.

A little, but not slammed. What's up?

Just wanted to say hi.

Hi back.

He smiled at his phone, but then felt like an idiot. It was like being back in high school again.

Before he could come up with anything brilliant or charming to say, another text from popped up.

Getting busy but text me your schedule later and I'll take a turn saying hi.

Okay, he typed. *Talk to you soon.*

Just as he hit Send, the alarm sounded. He took the few seconds to rinse his coffee mug and tucked his phone in his pocket. Once in the bay, he stepped into his gear and grabbed his helmet and coat.

"Great," Eriksson said as he jogged by. "Another fucking genius barbecuing on the second-floor deck of a three-decker."

"You're kidding."

Danny climbed into the driver seat of Engine 59 and flipped the siren on. "Let's go save the structure from the morons who live in it."

SEVEN

LYDIA ENJOYED THE COOL breeze washing away the last traces of humidity as the sun started dropping in the sky. She and Ashley were walking to a little Italian place they loved, and since they had plenty of time before they met Becca and Courtney, they took their time.

Karen, Rick Gullotti's girlfriend, had offered to take a shift and give Lydia a night off, and she'd jumped at the chance without even running it by her dad. She hoped spending some time with her friends and Ashley would distract her from the fact she hadn't seen Aidan in several days. There had been a few *just saying hi* texts here and there, but she hadn't seen that face of his since the night he kissed her at Kincaid's.

"Oh my gosh, Lydia Kincaid!"

They stopped to chat for a minute with what seemed like the hundredth person who recognized Lydia and wanted to welcome her home—this time an elderly former elementary school teacher who never let anybody forget she had to teach all three Kincaid kids how to read. Maybe she should have worn a hoodie.

"Danny texted me earlier," Ashley told her when they'd started walking again.

"Really? Is that good or bad?"

"I don't know. I was mad when I got the text. I wanted him to call me instead, so I could hear his voice. I miss his voice, a lot."

"You miss *him*."

"Yeah. But he wanted to set up a time when he could come get some more of his stuff."

Lydia sighed. "Maybe when he does, you should tell him you miss him."

"He wanted to coordinate the time so I wouldn't be there."

Her sister's quietly spoken words broke Lydia's heart and she stopped walking. "Ashley, do you really want this separation?"

"I don't know." They faced each other on the sidewalk and Lydia saw the strain in Ashley's eyes and around her mouth. "I wasn't happy with him. I'm not happy without him. I keep telling myself it's because this part is the hardest and I'll be happy…someday."

"I know I'm starting to sound like a broken record, but you guys really need to talk." The more time she spent back in Boston, the more convinced she became that neither Ashley nor Danny wanted a divorce.

"I think I'm going to tell him to come over when I'm home. He can have his stuff if he takes a few minutes to talk to me."

"I'm not sure ransoming his belongings is a step forward in marital communications."

Ashley shrugged and put her hand on the door of the restaurant. "Maybe not, but it's a start."

She yanked the door open and walked inside before Lydia could say anything else. Becca and Courtney waved to them from a back table, and Lydia felt her mood magically improve just from seeing their faces.

Courtney was rocking some kind of chic, blond, sharply angled haircut and sophisticated makeup, probably inspired by her fancy office job. Becca was going to keep holding on to her big hair and black eyeliner until it came back into style, Lydia thought, hugging them each in turn.

They all talked over each other for a few minutes, catching up. Thanks to texting, email and late-night phone calls, there wasn't a lot of catching up to do, but nothing beat the energy of being all together in the same place.

The wine flowed and they each ate an entire week's worth of carbs. Maybe more, Lydia thought, looking at the mess of empty pasta plates and bread baskets they'd made of the table.

They were all considering dessert when Lydia's phone chimed and she saw that it was from Aidan. Even though nobody would be able to see the screen from their seats, she felt compelled to hold the phone under the edge of the table with her head bowed to read his message.

I want to see you.

They were just words on the phone screen, but in her mind Lydia heard Aidan's deep voice saying them, and a chill went down her spine.

Are you drunk texting me?

No. If I was drunk I would text that I want to... never mind. See? Not drunk.

Screw that. She wanted to know what he wanted to do, in detail.

Maybe you should get drunk later and text me the end of that sentence.

Or I could get drunk and show up at your place to DO the end of that sentence to you.

She laughed and, when Ashley cleared her throat and Lydia looked up, realized they were all staring at her. "Sorry. I really hope you guys weren't talking about something terrible or sad right then."

"Who are you talking to?" Ashley asked.

"Nobody." She looked back down at her phone to type a response.

I'm staying with Ash, so no. And you have to stop.

"Nobody seems funny," Becca said, propping her chin on her hand. "Is he hot?"

"Who says it's a he?"

Stop what?

"You look flustered," Courtney said. "A little hot and bothered, even."

"No, I certainly don't look hot and bothered. Or if I do, it's because it's hot in here, but I'm not both-ered." Maybe just a little.

She turned her attention back to her phone.

Stop saying stuff like that. Remember all the reasons you shouldn't kiss me?

And then we kissed anyway.

Dammit, that was true.

No more kissing.

"It's definitely a he," Ashley said, and Lydia looked up. "Just tell us who this nobody is and be done with it."

"I can't."

Her sister gave her a sharp look, mimicked slightly by the two women who had been her best friends for her entire life. "What do you mean you *can't*? That's very different from *won't*."

Her phone chimed again.

Okay. No more kissing. Gotta go.

Disappointment coursed through her, even though she was the one who'd put it out there first. And had something suddenly come up or had he lost his interest in texting her the second she ended any possibility of further intimacy?

"You can't tell anybody," Lydia said, setting her phone screen-down on the table. "I mean *anybody*. Especially you, Ashley."

"You know we won't. And why especially me?"

"Because it was Aidan."

Ashley's expression didn't change. "Aidan who?"

"Aidan Hunt."

Her expression changed then, with her eyes and

her mouth both making big O shapes. "He's Scotty's best friend."

"Yeah." Lydia took a sip of her wine because her mouth was suddenly dry.

"He's a firefighter."

"Yeah."

"And he's like a second son to Dad."

"I know." Strike. Strike. Strike. Three strikes and he should be out. She'd already done the baseball thing. "It's no big deal. He texted something funny and I laughed. Not really a big deal."

"And anybody but us might believe that," Becca shot back.

"Are you sleeping with Aidan Hunt?" Ashley asked, her face still stuck in the *you can't be serious* position.

"No, I'm not sleeping with him." Lydia paused for a few seconds, and then she shrugged. "But I did kiss him. Or he kissed me. We kissed."

"When?" all three of them asked at the same time.

"A few nights ago, at the bar." She told them what happened that night because, if she could trust anybody in the world, it was these three women.

"And you haven't seen him since?" Courtney asked.

"No. We've both been busy and he did two night tours. He's texted me a few times, but that's about it."

Ashley leaned back in her chair, shaking her head. "I can't believe he had the balls to kiss you with Dad right around the corner."

"He must have *really* wanted to kiss you," Courtney said, and then she sighed dreamily. She'd always been the romantic of the bunch.

Becca shook her head. "He's Scott's best friend, though. Isn't there like some kind of code or something?"

Before Lydia could answer, Ashley jumped in. "Not only would Aidan sleeping with you be against the best friend code or bro code or whatever the hell it's called, but they're firefighters with the same company. Sisters are off-limits."

"I know all about firefighters," she said, her voice a little sharp.

"And that's the other thing," Ashley said. "You swore you'd never get involved with another firefighter ever again."

"I'm not getting involved with him. We kissed one time."

"And now you guys are texting," Becca pointed out. "And he's making you laugh and blush."

"That's more of a relationship than I've had in two years," Courtney said.

Ashley snorted. "Hell, that's more of a relationship than my marriage is right now."

"It's not a relationship. It's not even close to a relationship. Did you guys decide what you're having for dessert?" she asked, abruptly changing the subject.

She'd had her heart broken and her life turned upside down by a firefighter before, and she'd struggled having a father and brother doing the job. She wasn't ever going to open her heart to a firefighter again.

The best way to keep that from happening was to keep her legs closed, but she already knew that was going to be a lot harder than keeping her heart closed.

AIDAN SHOVED INTO Gullotti and hooked his stick past him to send the puck toward the net. Walsh dove for it, easily catching it in his glove, and Gullotti laughed.

"Mrs. Broussard could have gotten that between the pipes," he taunted.

Aidan jabbed the guy with an elbow and then skated away before he could retaliate, either verbally or physically. Being told he wasn't as good as the guy's elderly landlady was bad enough.

His head wasn't in the game. Well, it wasn't *really* a game. It wasn't even a practice for league play. It was more of a pickup game just to keep everybody from getting too rusty and to blow off some steam on the ice.

Scotty skated up to him, also laughing. "You suck today, Hunt, and you never suck on the ice. What are you thinking about that's better than hockey?"

No way in hell was Aidan answering that question. Not honestly, anyway. After days of flirtatious texts, he'd finally gotten the one he was waiting for.

Dad's going to Fitz's to watch the game instead of watching it in the bar. Wednesday nights are slow. You should stop by and say hi.

That wasn't an invitation he needed to hear twice.

She'd have plenty of downtime to lean against the bar and talk to him face-to-face, instead of over the phone, and Tommy wouldn't be there giving him looks that probably didn't mean anything outside of Aidan's paranoia.

"Guess I'm getting old," was all he said.

"Bullshit. If you're getting old, I'm getting old. And that ain't happening anytime soon."

After another forty minutes on the ice, Aidan was starting to wonder, though. They hadn't had a lot of practice time lately, since most of the guys preferred being outside when the weather was good, and he was going to have even more aches and pains tomorrow morning than he had this morning. Four hours knocking down a fire in a warehouse, with several more hours checking for hot spots and killing flare-ups had sucked more than usual because Mother Nature brought the heat and humidity in spades.

When their time ended, they hit the locker room and Aidan let the steaming hot water beat down on him, hoping it would help to keep some of the stiffness at bay. The guys talked and laughed around him, and he took comfort in the familiarity of it, even while guilt gnawed at him.

He was flat out lying to Scotty now. Maybe it was a lie of omission, but that was just as bad, if not worse. Deliberately going behind his friend's back to hide the fact things were getting hot between him and his sister was about as bad as it could get.

Once he forced himself to shut the shower off, he

wrapped a towel around his waist and rubbed the water out of his hair with another as he walked to where he'd left his bag on a bench.

"I could use a beer," Walsh said. "And a burger. What do you think the chances are I can get served at Kincaid's?"

"You're always welcome there," Scotty said. "You know my old man doesn't have a problem with you."

"It's your sister I'm worried about."

"Lydia's cool. And I know Ashley was going to some kind of bridal shower thing with a friend of theirs tonight, so she won't be around."

Aidan watched Danny consider it for a moment, and then he nodded. "I could really use a burger and a beer."

"That sounds like one helluva plan," Gullotti said. "Kincaid?"

When Scotty nodded, Aidan felt a sinking feeling in the pit of his stomach. The lack of customers and Tommy not being around meant nothing if everybody else they knew—including her brother—showed up.

"How about you, Hunt?"

"Yeah," he said. "I could go for that."

He got dressed, tuning out whatever small talk they were making, and trying to mentally shift from *talk Lydia into going out back and making out* to *don't even look at Lydia because he might give away how badly he wanted her.* It sucked, but there really wasn't a valid reason he could offer up as to why none of them should visit one of their favorite haunts. Especially since anything he could come up with—gas leak, health code violations—would be something Scotty would know before him. Or be able to disprove the story with one *what the hell* phone call.

Aidan was just going to have to suck it up and pretend his interest in the gorgeous bartender was the same as it had always been—she was his best friend's sister and therefore a friend. They could chat. They could laugh. But he couldn't kiss her up against the brick wall again.

They'd ridden over to the rink in two vehicles, so they all threw their bags and sticks into the back of Scotty's truck. Then they divided between that and Gullotti's jacked-up Jeep for the ride to Kincaid's, with Aidan automatically getting shotgun in the truck.

"You feeling all right?" Scotty asked when they were almost there. Grant and Gavin, who were each the young guy in their companies, were chatting in the backseat.

"Yeah, why?"

"I don't know. Your game seemed off tonight, and you're pretty quiet. Something going on?"

Aidan swallowed past the lump in his throat and stared out the passenger window. Maybe if they'd been alone and not in a moving vehicle, he would have been honest. But it wasn't the time. "Nope."

"You're not going through some kind of midlife crisis or something, are you? I already told you, we're not old enough for shit like that."

Aidan laughed. "No crisis, though I wouldn't mind the Corvette that supposedly comes with it."

"Maybe a hot blonde in the passenger seat."

Or a hot brunette with a hotter temperament and dark eyes a man could lose himself in. "Maybe a rich, hot blonde whose daddy has Bruins season tickets. What the hell, let's give him season tickets to the Patriots, too."

"Just in case we ever meet her, I'm calling dibs right now."

They were laughing when Scotty pulled the truck down the narrow alley that led to a small parking lot reserved for Kincaid's employees and the upstairs tenants. Cutter parked on the street and they met up outside the door.

The good feeling Aidan had managed to momentarily capture faded with every step he took toward the door. The night was going to be very different from how he'd spent a good part of the day imagining it and, instead of enjoying Lydia's company, he was going to be doing everything possible to avoid it.

The thrill Lydia felt when Aidan walked through the bar's front door was short-lived. The look he gave her was nothing short of apologetic and she knew why when he stepped inside and Scotty, Danny, Grant Cutter, Gavin Boudreau—who was with Ladder 37, though she didn't really know him—and Rick were right on his heels.

They weren't part of the plan. None of them were, but especially her brother.

"Hey, guys," she said when they all stepped up to the bar. "Did you all just randomly happen to arrive at the same time?"

"We were playing some hockey," Grant told her. "And then Danny said he was in the mood for a burger and a beer and then we were *all* in the mood for burgers and beer."

"You came to the right place, then," she said, giving him her work smile. She actually liked the young guy well enough, but it wouldn't be very professional to have her expression mirror what she was actually feeling on the inside.

There were a lot of bars that served burgers in Boston. If Tommy hadn't gone out of his way to turn Kincaid's Pub into a second home for the local firefighters, she could be flirting with Aidan already.

He didn't look any happier about it than she did. He was down near the end of the bar, standing with her brother, and every time she looked at him, his gaze skittered away. The knowledge he was that worried about Scotty's opinion of their relationship—or flirtation or whatever she should call it—was annoying.

She took her order pad out of her apron pocket and slapped it on the bar, then pulled out a pen. "Okay, let's have it."

Grant hadn't been kidding about them all being in the mood for burgers and beer and, once they all had a drink, they disappeared into the pool room. A minute later, she heard the rattle of pool balls being cued up and male laughter. It caught the attention of three women sitting at one of the tables, and she wondered how long it would be before the men had company.

Then she wondered which one of them would try to lay claim to Aidan and felt a surge of jealousy. If any one of them put a hand on him, all three of them would find themselves out on the sidewalk pretty damn quick.

When the woman facing her met her stare and did a double take, as if the look on Lydia's face had startled her, Lydia forced a smile and went to give the cook the burger orders.

She had no claim on Aidan and he was free to do whatever—or whomever—he wanted. So they'd kissed once and exchanged a bunch of text messages. On the relationship scale it was a lot more *teenage crush* than *grown-up monogamy*, so she needed to watch the death looks she gave paying customers.

As she waited for the burgers to be done, she leaned against the inside of the bar and watched a few minutes of the game. Or pretended to, anyway. If she listened hard enough, she could differentiate Aidan's voice from those of the other men, and she liked hearing it. Text messages were quick and fun, but they weren't the same as the in-person conversations she'd been looking forward to having tonight.

When the cook rang the bell to let her know the order was up, Lydia pushed away from the bar and walked down to the pool room. "Somebody come grab a few plates."

Scotty and Rick were in the middle of a pool game,

and the other guys were all seated at the tables, while Aidan leaned against the wall with his arms and ankles crossed.

"I'll help," he said, walking around the pool table. "At the rate they're going, this game won't be over until midnight, anyway."

"It's all about finesse," Rick said. "Something you probably know nothing about."

"Hey, I can do finesse."

He followed her back behind the bar and down the short hallway that led past the restrooms before splitting off to the kitchen area and the office and storage rooms. Every once in a while somebody would frown over carrying food past the bathrooms, but it was an old building and the floor plan predated them by a very long time.

Before they entered the kitchen, Aidan put his hand on her elbow to stop her. "Hey. Hold up a second."

"What's up?"

He chuckled, then cast a glance back the way they'd come. "I've been waiting all day to see you. I couldn't believe it when Danny suggested a trip to Kincaid's."

"I was a little surprised to see everybody. I was looking forward to seeing you, but I should have guessed they'd all be with you. If anybody can wreck somebody's plans, it's a group of firefighters."

He gave her a mock frown and shook his head.

"This isn't a firefighter thing. It's just a group of guys with really shitty timing."

The bell rang several times, and Lydia knew she had maybe a minute before a very pissed-off cook came around that corner to deliver the food himself. "I was kidding. It's fine."

"Not really." The bell rang one more time and Lydia took a step toward the kitchen. He didn't let go of her elbow, but pulled her back so he could kiss her. It was fast and hard and over way too soon, but it left her breathless nonetheless.

"We should get those burgers now," he said, a grin tugging at the corners of his mouth.

She went into the kitchen and, after giving an apology to the cook, put four plates on the big tray. Leaving Aidan to carry the other two plates, she made her way back to the pool room and handed them out.

"Thanks for the hand," she said to Aidan, and then she left them to their meals. Definitely not the evening she'd envisioned.

The women from the table paid and left without even making an attempt to flirt with the guys, which was a relief. Over the next hour, a few other firefighters wandered in and joined the group playing pool. She popped in a few times to bring refills and clear the plates away, noticing that Aidan managed to be busy every time she was in the room.

It looked like one quick, sneaky kiss was all she was going to get.

She heard a burst of laughter again and looked over

in time to see Aidan leave the pool room. He was laughing and took the time to flip off somebody by the pool table, and then he was walking toward her. She watched him scan the barroom and take note of the fact she was just standing there doing nothing, and he tilted his head toward the hallway.

Okay, so it looked like she'd get two quick, sneaky kisses.

But he kept on walking, right past the kitchen and into the storage room, flipping on the light switch. Her pulse quickened, but as soon as she stepped inside and he closed the door, she held up her hand. "I am not making out with you in the storage closet. In case you haven't noticed, I'm running a business."

"Two minutes. I told them I had to take a leak, and customers will assume you're in the kitchen and they'll wait two minutes."

"You put a lot of thought into being locked in a closet with me for two minutes."

"Talking wastes time." He tucked his finger in the front of her jeans and yanked her close.

There was nothing quick or sneaky about this kiss. It was hard and demanding, and she wrapped her arms around his neck so he couldn't break it off. Not that he seemed to want to. His tongue dipped between her lips and she surrendered to his mouth.

When his right hand slid over her ribs and cupped her breast, she sighed against his mouth and struggled to keep their location in the front of her mind. Her desire for him kept trying to overwhelm that important fact, but getting caught kissing anybody in the storage closet would be embarrassing. Getting caught kissing Aidan would be so much worse.

Then his hand slid back to her waistband and she clenched her abs. He wouldn't dare…

He dared.

The button on her jeans popped and she hissed against his mouth. The zipper was harder for him one-handed, but he managed. All the while his mouth was on hers, and she couldn't even think straight. All that mattered was the feel of his lips and the hand he slid down between her stomach and the soft cotton of her underwear.

"Aidan?" she whispered against his mouth.

"About a minute and a half left. I need to feel you, Lydia."

Then his fingertips slid over her clit and she sucked in a breath. His teeth caught her bottom lip and she moaned, shocked by the intensity of her reaction to his touch. She knew it had been a long time, but she was already teetering on the brink. He slid a finger into her and she scraped her fingernails down his back, wanting more.

The heel of his hand pressed against her clit as he buried two fingers deep inside of her. She broke off the kiss, burying her face against his shoulder.

"You have to be quiet," he whispered against her ear. "You are so fucking hot, Lydia."

The orgasm hit quickly and she pressed her mouth to his shirt, willing herself to be silent as it shook her body. He nipped at her earlobe, chuckling softly when she lifted her face to take a deep, shuddering breath.

"That's what I wanted," he said, and then he kissed her again while pulling his hand free from her pants.

"You sure know how to make the most of two minutes."

"I think we still have a few seconds left. Or we can shove all this crap in front of the door and do it again."

"I'm not having sex with you in here. It doesn't seem fair, though."

"All part of my master plan to make sure you owe me a blow job."

"Brilliant plan." She dropped her forehead to his shoulder, still recovering.

"I got what I wanted for tonight."

"I can't believe it happened that fast," she said with a tremulous laugh.

"It's all that finesse I have."

She wasn't sure what it was, but it scared the hell out of her. If him touching her made her feel like that, what would actual sex be like? Explosive. Intense. *Too much.* She needed distance. "I guess so. I mean, you're not even my type."

"I was your type a few seconds ago," he reminded her.

"You're a firefighter, for chrissake. I can't…definitely not my type." She lifted her head and moved out of his arms.

"Don't lump us all together."

The light, teasing tone was gone, but it wasn't

enough distance. She needed more space to figure out what was going on. "You're pretty much all the same. Reckless kids at heart, but with God complexes thrown in."

In the space of a heartbeat, his face completely changed. Gone was the easy, sexy charm, leaving behind hard lines and a jaw that looked as if it had been carved from stone.

He put his hands up in a *see, not touching* gesture and then took a step backward. "Yeah, you're right. I'm not your type."

"Aidan, I didn't mean…I wasn't trying to insult you."

"Sometimes I forget how you really feel about firefighters. All you did was remind me." He opened the door a crack and looked out into the hall. "I should get back before they send out a search party."

He was gone before she could say anything else, and she slumped against the wall, the post-orgasm glow definitely extinguished. What a bitchy thing to say just because she got scared of how badly she wanted him.

She heard the squeal of the men's room door and the water running in the sink. Then, a couple of minutes later, the squeal again and she caught a glimpse of him as he walked down the hall back to the barroom.

Resting her head against the wall, she tried to blink back the tears that threatened to spill over her lashes.

She hadn't meant to hurt his feelings, but it looked like she'd solved the problem of what to do about Aidan Hunt.

EIGHT

THERE WAS NOTHING like a woman panicking, forgetting everything she knew about grease fires and managing to turn cooking bacon into an all-hands fire to start a guy's day off right.

Aidan jammed the Halligan tool into the wall and used the hook to rip it open. Smoke filtered through with the ancient dust and plaster, and he sighed into his mask. This sucker was never going to be fully extinguished. The only good thing about it was the fact it was a single-family and, as soon as the homeowner realized the fire in the pan was now a real fire in her kitchen, she'd grabbed her kid and the dog and run like hell. Her insurance company was going to be pissed, but being able to focus all their attention on the fire and not searching under beds for people meant the structure might not be a total loss. Assuming the practically antique building materials ever stopped smoldering.

Once they were cleared, Aidan set his self-contained breathing apparatus, helmet and coat on the ground and accepted a water bottle from Walsh.

The weather should be starting to turn cooler, but instead it was looking like another scorcher and it was hot as hell in the SCBA.

"I'm glad I'm not the one who has to call her husband at work," Scotty said, taking a seat on the engine's bumper next to him.

"Yeah."

"At least it didn't get the garage. You see the Harley the guy's got in there? What year do you think it was?"

Aidan screwed the lid back on the empty water bottle. "A Panhead. Probably a '56, but since it didn't have a sign on it and I'm not a walking motorcycle encyclopedia, I don't know for sure."

In his peripheral vision, he saw Scott turn to frown at him. "What the hell's wrong with you today? And don't give me any *just tired* shit. You're the relaxed, happy guy. I'm the guy wound tighter than an eight-day clock. That's how it's supposed to work and you're screwing up the vibe today."

What was wrong with him? What was wrong was that he'd given Lydia a pretty decent orgasm, judging by how it looked from his side of the equation, and in return she'd given him a verbal shot to the balls.

"My old man called me at the crack of dawn this morning," Aidan lied. "You know how that goes."

Scotty took a swig of water and shook his head. "I keep telling you to send his calls to voice mail."

"Then I worry something happened and I listen

to it right away, anyway. And then I have to call *him*. It's easier to take the call."

"What did he want this time?"

"Same shit," Aidan said, trying not to dig himself into the untruth hole. He sucked at lying and his best friend would probably know any of his more obvious tells. "Different day."

As pissed as he was at Lydia, he was never going to repeat what she'd said. She'd insulted him on purpose because she was running out of willpower and wanted *him* to do the walking away. In the process of making that happen, she'd not only insulted pretty much everything and everybody he loved, but everybody *she* loved, too.

So, yeah, he might have a hair across his ass at the moment where Lydia was concerned, but he wasn't going to put her in a bad spot with her brother or the old man. Tommy would probably just give her some shit and get over it, but it was the kind of thing that would set Scott off and he'd been known to hold some ridiculous grudges over the years. Kicking off a Kincaid family feud because she'd said something stupid Aidan knew she didn't mean just to get him to back off wasn't his style.

He also didn't want to have to explain the circumstances behind her saying what she'd said. *Well, I had my hand down her pants and...*

So he'd just lied to his best friend and it was a straight-up lie this time, not one of omission. His stomach ached and his head hurt, and he bent forward to prop his elbows on his knees and drop his head onto his hands.

When Scotty clapped a hand to his shoulder, it just made him feel worse. "We should go out. Not to Dad's bar, either. We need to find a club with loud music and hot women wearing short dresses and high heels."

There was a time Aidan might have agreed with him, but the only woman he wanted wore T-shirts, jeans and sneakers. And the fact he still wanted her so badly his body ached just pissed him off even more. On top of all the very valid reasons she was off-limits to him, last night should have been the nail in the coffin when it came to his infatuation with her.

Walsh walked around the end of the truck. "Let's get this wrapped up so we can get out of the way. They want to get the street open again."

"Funny how we become a nuisance as soon as the flames are out," Scotty said before chugging the rest of his water.

When they finally got back to the station, Aidan took care of his gear and then went to drop onto the couch. Leaning his head against the back cushion, he closed his eyes and took a deep breath.

He hadn't slept for shit last night, which of course didn't help his mood any today. And right now he was angry with himself for checking his phone on the ride back, hoping for a text from Lydia. He'd convinced himself he just hadn't felt the vibration, so when he checked and there was nothing, the disappointment had felt bone-deep.

No matter how badly he wanted to talk to her, though, he wouldn't text her. The ball was in her court and she either regretted what she'd said enough to apologize, or she didn't. And if she didn't, there was no sense in them talking.

Aidan felt somebody sit down on the other end of the couch and opened his eyes to see Cobb. "Hey, Captain."

"What's up with you, Hunt?"

"Just relaxing for a minute. What's up with you?"

"Funny. You know what I mean."

Aidan scrubbed his hands over his face, buying himself a few seconds. "I'm in a shitty mood. They happen. It's no big deal."

"It feels like more than that. You've been a little off lately, but I can't quite put my finger on how or why."

And Aidan didn't really want him trying too hard to figure it out, so it was time to lie again. "Having some issues with my old man. The usual."

That seemed to satisfy him. "Just don't let it affect you on the job, son. From where I sit, it looks like you're holding the other guys at arm's length—even Kincaid—and that's not any good for you."

"Just trying to work things out in my head. I'm good. Honest."

Cobb slapped his knee and then pushed himself to his feet. "Good. You let me know if that changes."

Left alone again, Aidan pulled his phone out of his pocket and checked it. Nothing. He even went so far as to pull up their last text conversation and tapped the reply box to say something.

Then he swore under his breath and closed the texting app. Tossing his phone onto the coffee table, he picked up the remote control and turned the television on. Daytime TV sucked, but anything was better than sitting around moping over Lydia Kincaid.

LYDIA WOKE UP on the couch with a stiff neck, a lingering sense of uneasiness from the dream that was already slipping away and sorrow because she knew there would be no funny text messages from Aidan today.

She stretched, wincing a little, and realized she could smell coffee. She'd overslept, but based on the condition she'd found them in last night, Ashley and Courtney probably hadn't been up very long, either.

When she'd gotten home, she'd gone upstairs to find Courtney passed out, fully dressed, on her bed. She'd tiptoed into Ashley's room intending to climb into the big king-size bed with her sister, but Ashley had been sound asleep totally sideways across the mattress. Ashley'd at least gotten most of her clothes off before she passed out, though she hadn't managed to get as far as pajamas. Rather than wake anybody and be forced to make conversation with drunk people in her current mood, Lydia'd gone back downstairs and crashed on the couch.

In hindsight, she probably should have rolled Courtney onto the floor. Sitting up, she gave herself a few seconds to be awake enough not to fall over and then got up. She went to the bathroom first, and then went into the kitchen.

Her sister and their friend looked as bad as she felt, which went a little way toward cheering her up. She poured a coffee and sat down with them. There were no signs breakfast would be forthcoming anytime soon, but she wasn't that hungry, anyway.

Every time she thought of Aidan's face when she'd said those words to him, she felt a little sick.

"Sorry I took your bed," Courtney mumbled. "I was drunk. I might still be. The only thing I know for sure is that, sadly, I'm not dead."

"We got in the cab," Ashley said. "But when I gave him her address, she started to cry because there were ninjas in her closet."

"I was *really* drunk."

"And I tried to tell her ninjas weren't real, but she saw a show about them and…trust me, it was easier just to bring her here."

Lydia nodded. "We get sprayed for ninjas every six months. I can give you the number."

"So funny." Courtney looked like she was going to fall out of her chair until she propped her elbows on the table. "I hardly ever have alcohol other than a glass of wine or maybe even two. There were pretty drinks. They were pink and…I love pink."

"How was work last night?" Ashley asked.

Lydia opened her mouth, then changed her mind

about letting words come out of it. She raised her mug instead and took a hot sip of coffee.

"What happened?" Apparently Ashley wasn't so hungover she missed the hesitation.

"Nothing."

"I bet Aidan happened." Courtney was perking up a little, though she'd definitely be skipping her daily jog.

"Don't you have to work?" Lydia asked. "And who has a bridal shower on a Wednesday night? Nobody does."

"The bride's a police officer and the maid of honor manages one of the fast-food places. And the bridesmaids work in the ER or something. Anyway, they all have to work weekends, so Wednesday's like their Saturday. The rest of us were just so screwed. And I called in sick. I probably sounded convincing."

"I don't know if you convinced your boss you're sick," Lydia said, "but you definitely sound like you're incapable of working."

Courtney beamed, as if that was a compliment. "Good."

"Nice try, Lydia," her sister said. "You should have just hung a flashing neon *changing the subject* sign over that question. What happened last night?"

"Can I finish my coffee first?"

"No," they said at the same time.

"They'd been playing hockey and Danny talked them all into wanting burgers and beer."

"Danny was there?"

"Yeah. I guess he wanted—"

"How did he look?"

Lydia took another sip of her coffee, trying to summon up a memory of Danny's face. "He looked… like Danny, I guess. You know he doesn't give much away emotionally. But he's sad. You can see it around his eyes."

Ashley let that sink in, then waved a hand at her. "Okay, back to Aidan."

She told them the story, not leaving anything out. Halfway through, Ashley got up and went around the table refilling their coffee cups before pulling a package of store-bought blueberry muffins out of the bread box and setting them in the middle of the table.

The hardest part of the tale was, of course, when she panicked and pushed him away by insulting him. She kept her eyes on her coffee and forced herself to get through the entire thing.

"Wow," Ashley said when she was done.

"Wow, indeed," Courtney echoed. "Orgasms turn you into a real bitch."

Lydia would have thrown her muffin at her, but she was too busy crumbling it on the napkin in front of her. "It was too much all of a sudden. I needed some distance and the words just kind of came out."

"They didn't just kind of come out, though," Ashley said. "I mean, I know you didn't mean to insult him, but he also knows how you feel about being involved with a firefighter."

"We're not *involved*."

"If a man could give me an orgasm in two minutes or less, I'd marry him," Courtney said.

"I think you're still drunk. And I don't normally…I think I was just anticipating seeing him so much that I was already a little worked up, I guess."

"What are you going to do now?" Ashley asked.

Lydia shrugged. "I don't know. Part of me thinks I should just leave it the way it is and then we don't have to worry about it anymore. I don't have to worry about finding myself in a relationship with another firefighter and he doesn't have to worry about lying to Scotty anymore."

"But you guys have been friends a long time, too. I mean, not close friends, but friends. And if there's serious friction between you, people are going to pick up on it and wonder why."

"And it hurt him," Lydia added quietly. "I insulted him. I insulted his career and his friends and pretty much everything that's important to him."

"And that hurts you," Courtney prompted.

"Of course it does. Like Ash said, we're friends, too. I should go see him." Courtney nodded, while Ashley shook her head, which made Lydia laugh. She really needed Becca to be there with them because then it was never a tie. "To apologize, I mean."

"You can apologize to him over the phone," Ashley said. "That way you can both put it behind you, but you're safely out of reach of his magical instant orgasms."

Courtney gave another dreamy sigh and Lydia

threw a *really?* look her way. "I'll have to think about it. He's at the station today, anyway. Maybe I'll know what to say by the time his tour ends."

She hoped so, at least, because even if it was in both their best interests to not be speaking to each other, she couldn't stand the thought of leaving things the way they were last night. He deserved better than that.

ASHLEY FORCED HERSELF to eat a bowl of soup at five thirty. Technically, it met the definition of food, but it was light enough so maybe she wouldn't throw it up before Danny stopped by when his tour was over.

She was a mess and definitely second-guessing her insistence on being home when he came by to grab more of his things. But Lydia was right. They needed to start communicating and text messaging wasn't going to cut it. The limbo was playing hell on her nerves and on her sleep, and she wasn't going to be able to take it much longer.

At twenty after six, there was a knock on the front door and the sound made Ashley's heart ache. It wasn't right, Danny knocking on the door of the home they'd made together.

She opened the door and the impact of the mixed emotions made her take a step backward. God, she'd missed him. She wanted to throw her arms around his neck and hold on so tightly he'd never be able to get away from her again.

But his back was almost military straight and

his expression gave her nothing. Ashley could see the sadness in his eyes, like Lydia had said, but she shouldn't have to try to read Danny's face like a coded map. She wanted him to pull her into his arms and hold her as if he'd never let her go.

"Come on in," she finally said, stepping to the side so he could go by her. It was unnatural and awkward, and she cursed herself for not being somewhere else.

"I just need to grab a few things. I have some boxes in the truck."

Boxes, plural? "Okay. Do you want help?"

"I'm all set. But I'll probably be in and out a few times. I'll try to be quick."

She wanted to tell him to take his time. The longer he was in the house, the bigger the chance one of them might say something that would open the floodgates of communication between them. But all she did was nod because he'd already started walking toward the stairs.

Ashley couldn't bear to see him in their bedroom, taking any of his things out of their closet or from his dresser. Throwing some belongings in duffel bags was one thing. Boxes were for moving and moving out seemed so much more permanent than just going to stay with Scott to give her some space.

Danny took four boxes out to his truck while Ashley sat on the couch and stared blankly at the television screen. If there was anything good at all about this night, it was that she wasn't crying. Whether it was because she was all cried out or because things were going so badly she was beyond tears, she couldn't say.

When he came downstairs with his fifth box, Danny hesitated at the bottom of the stairs and Ashley realized with a sense of dread that he was done. He was about to tell her he was leaving.

She stood and walked over to face him. "Is that it?"

"I think I have everything I need for now."

"I mean *is that it*, as in you're just going to grab your shit and leave without even attempting a conversation?"

"I'm not sure what I can say, Ash. I'm the same guy you fell in love with. I'm the same guy you married. I don't know why I'm not enough for you now."

"No, Danny." Her throat ached from the tight ball of emotion wedged there. "That's not…I didn't say you're not enough for me. I never said that."

"I don't know what you want from me."

"I want you to share your feelings with me."

He looked at her for so long, she wasn't sure he was going to answer, but then he sighed. "I thought I was doing that. I've always told you I love you. I don't…I don't know what else there is."

"I want *all* of your feelings. Good. Bad. Loud. Messy. All of it, because I'm your wife and I'm tired of being shut out."

She watched his expression change, as if a shutter dropped to block out a storm, and knew she'd bumped up against something he didn't want to talk about. "I'm not the kind of guy who likes to vent,

Ash. And I don't want to come home and spend my time with you bitching about work. There's freaking piles of paperwork to deal with and one of the guys on second crew is bitching about his share of the house fund because his wife's making him eat vegetarian and packing his meals. Aidan's got a hair across his ass about something, but I don't know what yet. Is that the kind of stuff you want to hear?"

Ashley felt a jolt of guilt, because she had an idea of why Aidan had a hair across his ass. But she couldn't tell Danny because she wouldn't violate her sister's trust. And Danny worked with both Aidan and Scotty, so the entire thing would be a shit show if Danny said something. Which was why Aidan shouldn't have been messing around with Lydia in the first place.

But that didn't matter right now. They were adults and not her problem. "Yes, I want to know if you have a rough day at work. But it's more than that. Maybe it was stupid and childish to try to force you to show you care by telling you I wanted out, but you didn't even try to fight it. You just left."

His jaw flexed several times before he spoke. "You told me you needed space and I'm giving it to you. I'm not the kind of guy who, when asked to leave, refuses to go. That's not who I am."

"You didn't even look upset."

"I was upset." She watched his Adam's apple bob as he swallowed hard. "That was the worst night of my life, Ashley, but I didn't know how to stop it. And I'm ready to come home as soon as you say the word."

It was tempting. She could say the word and he'd sleep in their bed tonight. They'd get up tomorrow morning and go on about their lives as if this marital interruption had never happened.

But Danny hadn't touched her. His hand hadn't even twitched as if he wanted to touch her but wasn't sure if she'd welcome it. He was the same brick wall tonight that she'd grown so tired of beating her head against.

"We need to go to counseling," she said, and that got an emotional response. Just a quick grimace, but she didn't miss it. Of course he'd resist counseling because then he'd have to share his feelings. "I'm not willing to go back to the way it was."

He gave her a quick nod, his mouth tight. "If you find somebody, I'll consider it, but I don't know if it'll help. This is just who I am, Ash, and a few therapy sessions won't change that."

"I hope you're wrong."

Danny hefted the box on his hip and sighed. "Just let me know. And do me a favor. If you decide to file for divorce, let me know. Please don't have me served papers at the house."

Ashley's vision blurred with tears and she squeezed her hands into fists so tightly that her fingernails bit into her palm. "I wouldn't do that to you."

"Thank you. I…so good night, I guess. I'll probably talk to you soon."

"Good night."

Ashley closed the front door behind him and leaned her head against the wood. Gulping in air, she tried to hold back the sobs, but it was too much. She slid to the floor and, wrapping her arms around her knees, cried a whole new batch of tears.

NINE

Prime-time television wasn't any better than daytime TV, Aidan thought. Or maybe, even though he'd eaten and had a hot shower, he still wasn't in the mood to watch anything.

He settled on some kind of historical documentary, hoping the drone of the narrator's voice would put him to sleep. Maybe he'd be sorry if he woke up in the middle of the night with a stiff neck, but at least he wouldn't be lying in bed, staring at his ceiling fan.

An hour later, he was not only still awake, but he knew a lot more about marsupials than he'd ever wanted to know. He picked up the remote control, but rather than get caught up in a cycle of channel surfing, he hit the power button and shut the television off. He'd be better off staring at his ceiling fan because if he got lucky and nodded off, at least he'd already be in bed.

As he stood, his cell phone chimed and he picked it up off the coffee table to look at the screen. The text was from Lydia, and a whole mess of mixed emotions went through him—the desire to see her, and

satisfaction she'd reached out first, and the knowledge patching things up with Lydia would just make
things harder between him and Scotty.

Can I talk to you? In person, I mean?

He wasn't really in the mood to get dressed and
head to Kincaid's at the moment.

When?

I'm outside your door right now.

That was interesting.

Most people knock.

There was a long pause, during which he walked
across the living room and stood next to his door.
He could just open it, but he could tell by the little
dot-dot-dot on the phone screen that she was typing
a reply and he wanted to see what it said.

*I thought it might be more awkward if you were
surprised. This way you know it's me and you can
open the door or you can tell me you're already in
bed. No harm, no foul.*

The way out was right there, as easy as typing in
yeah, I'm in bed, but he didn't. She'd come all the
way over there, so it wouldn't kill him to hear what
she had to say. Plus, they were going to cross paths.
A lot, probably. Better to face the potential awkward-
ness now than in front of somebody else.

He undid the locks and opened the door. Lydia was
leaning back against the opposite wall in the hallway,
staring down at her phone. She looked up when the
door opened, and then her eyes widened.

"You, uh, forgot your clothes."

Aidan ran a hand over his naked chest and glanced down at his black boxer briefs. "People don't call before they come over, they get what they get."

"I texted you. Last-minute, but *before* you opened the door."

He'd probably be annoyed by the lecture, but he knew she was only bitching at him because seeing him almost naked had thrown her off and she was trying to hide it. "If you'd like to make an appointment to visit, I'll schedule in putting on some pants."

Making a huffy sound, Lydia pushed off the wall and—giving him a look as she went by—walked past him into his apartment. "Do you always have to be an asshole about everything?"

"Nice talk." He followed her in and kicked the door closed behind him. "Thanks for stopping by."

"I came to apologize."

"Okay."

She crossed her arms. "Okay? That's it?"

"No, that's not it. *Okay*, you came to apologize. So go ahead."

"I'm sorry."

He arched an eyebrow at her. "Hell of an apology."

"It's not easy being sincere when you're not wearing any pants."

"At least I don't go commando. But really, I don't feel like I'm obligated to make this easier for you."

She blew out a breath. "Can we sit down, at least? It feels so awkward and confrontational, standing here facing each other like this."

Deciding against the couch, because sitting next to her while in his boxer briefs would feel odd, he gestured to his tiny kitchen table. "You want something to drink?"

"Water would be great, thanks."

He filled a couple of glasses from the ice and water dispenser in his fridge, and then set them on the table. She took a sip of hers while he sat down in the chair across from her.

"I'm sorry I called you a reckless kid with a God complex," she said, all traces of annoyance with him gone. "I was losing control and it scared me, what I was willing to do with you in the storage closet of my dad's bar. I needed you to walk away."

"You could have tried telling me to walk away."

"I panicked." She ran a fingertip through the condensation on her glass. "I don't believe what I said, you know. I don't always like your job, but I respect it. You're so easygoing most of the time and you let things roll off you, so I went straight for the cheap shot and I'm very, very sorry."

He wasn't sure how he'd feel if it was somebody else who'd said it, but this was Lydia. She had her own issues with firefighting, including having been married to a guy who'd been ill-suited for the job because he *had* been somewhat reckless and gotten off on being a hero. Knowing the insult came from her life experiences and not her opinion of him made it a lot easier to forgive.

"Thank you," he said. "I accept your apology."

"Just like that?"

He met her gaze across the table and gave her a warm smile. "Yeah, just like that. I'd rather not wallow in it or hold a grudge. That's not really my thing."

The smile she gave him made the bad mood he'd been carrying around since he left her in the storage room disappear. "I'm glad. Beating myself up wasn't a pleasant way to spend the day, so I'd rather not keep on doing it."

"You could have called anytime."

"I never know when you're busy. And there was disagreement on whether I should apologize to you over the phone—which didn't seem good enough— or in person, which might lead to…another moment of weakness, if you know what I mean."

Aidan did know what she meant, but those weren't the words that really caught his attention, as intriguing as they were. "Disagreement? Who was disagreeing?"

Maybe she had a habit of talking to herself and it had escalated into a full-scale argument. He'd never seen her having a solo conversation before that he could remember, but maybe she saved that for when she was alone.

"Courtney—who I don't think you know—thought I should apologize to you in person, but Ashley said the phone would be better."

"Ashley." His fingers tightened around his glass. "So Danny Walsh's wife knows what happened between us."

She tilted her head. "My sister does, yes."

"Yeah, your sister who's married to my lieutenant."

"She won't say anything to him. I get it, Aidan. Danny's her husband and wives tell their husbands things. But not stuff like this. She's my sister and she's not going to share my secrets *or* do anything that might set Scotty off. I promise."

It still made him nervous. But Lydia knew what was at stake and if she trusted Ashley, he didn't really have a choice but to trust her, too. "I guess if I show up at the house one day and Scotty kicks my ass, I'll know why."

She looked startled for a moment, but he smiled and, after a few seconds, she returned it. "What a mess."

"I'm glad you listened to Courtney, whoever she is, and came in person."

"So you could see me squirm?"

"I don't know about the squirming part, but I'm glad to see you."

Her eyes met his and he held her gaze, wondering what was going on behind that mildly amused expression. And he couldn't help but wonder if his own expression was giving away his thoughts. Despite what had happened, and despite the alarm he'd felt when she said Ashley knew about it, he still wanted her.

Maybe his eyes did give it away, because she stood and carried her glass to the sink. After slowly dumping what remained of the ice and water down the drain, she set the glass on the counter and wiped her hand on her jeans. He got the feeling she was composing herself or struggling with something or stalling. He just wished he knew which.

He stood up, thankful he had a little bit of self-control, since he was wearing only the snug boxer briefs and, when she turned around, he noticed she kept her eyes on his face.

"I should go." She opened her arms and stepped forward. "Thank you for accepting my apology."

By the time he realized a hug might be a very bad idea, she had her arms wrapped around his neck and his hands slid over her hips and up to her back.

"Maybe I should have shaken your hand," she said, but instead of pulling away, she dropped her forehead to his chest. Her hands were splayed against his back muscles and Aidan was careful to keep any body contact limited to above the waist. The boxer briefs were growing more snug by the second.

"Do me a favor," he said, "and keep in mind you can't chase me off this time. I live here, and I'm not wearing any pants."

"Trust me, I'm very aware you're not wearing pants. Or a shirt." Her fingertips trailed down his spine.

Aidan lowered his head to kiss her temple, and she tilted her head so he could work his way down her neck. When he got to her collarbone, he put a finger under her chin and tilted her head back. He wanted her mouth.

There was no hesitation in her kiss. She opened

her lips to him, her tongue meeting his. He slid the finger under her chin down to the hollow at the base of her throat before cupping the back of her neck.

There was body contact below the waist now, and it took every ounce of Aidan's self-control not to grind against the front of Lydia's jeans. The hunger he felt in her kiss matched his own, and he wanted to bury himself deep inside of her, right here on the kitchen floor.

She broke off the kiss, resting her cheek against his so he felt the breath of her sigh. "We shouldn't do this."

And there it was. He pulled back so he could see her face. She'd said *shouldn't* not *can't*, and he didn't want to misjudge the significance. "Why not?"

"I don't remember, but I think it was probably a good reason."

"I think you're right, but I'm having trouble caring right this second." He touched his fingertip to her bottom lip, and smiled when she caught it between her teeth. But this push/pull thing they had going on wasn't fun and he'd rather common sense killed the mood now than later, if and when they made it into his bed. "You know what? Let's not do this."

Her eyes widened and she let go of his finger. "What?"

"No, not *this* this. I want to do this, believe me. I just don't want games between us. We both know sleeping together is a bad idea and we both know why. I'd rather we decide together, right now, if we're going to do it anyway."

"Making a decision to not sleep together isn't going to make me not want you, which will make it hard to be around you. I'm going to try too hard not to look at you, and then fail because there's no way I'm not staring at your ass when you walk by. People are going to notice something's up because we're trying unnaturally hard to act natural."

He grinned because he knew exactly what she meant. "So we should get it out of our systems, then. Or try to."

She took his hand in hers, threading their fingers together. "You have more at stake than I do, Aidan. I mean, yeah, they're my family, but I can handle them. They have to come around eventually because I *am* family. But you, they can alienate and it'll matter. You work with Scott. If the other guys think you've done him wrong, you'll suffer for it. My dad means the world to you, and you guys all go to the bar. You play hockey together. It seems like there's no part of your life that wouldn't be affected."

"I'm willing to take that chance." Maybe it wasn't the right decision, but in this moment, it was the only one he was capable of making. "I want you so much, every part of my life already *is* affected."

When she hooked a fingertip under the elastic of his boxer briefs, running it back and forth across his hip, he sucked in a breath and she gave him a smile that promised there was better to come. "There's only you and me in this room. Nobody else."

Aidan shoved everybody and everything out of his mind except for the woman standing in front of him. "Just you and me."

Lydia enjoyed running her finger around the inside of the waistband of Aidan's boxer briefs. He was mostly made up of hard muscle and tough skin, but the flesh under her knuckle was soft and sensitive.

Every time her finger came close enough to *almost* brush the hard length of his erection, which was straining against the cotton, his breathing would change. She changed direction and worked her finger back toward his hip.

When she used her other hand to cup him through the fabric, he hissed and grabbed her wrist. "Gimme a minute to run box scores through my head or something."

"Your hose fully charged, is it?"

He groaned. "If you're going to crack lame firefighter jokes during sex, at least try to be original. But, to answer that ridiculous question, yes."

She laughed as he grasped both of her wrists and pulled her hands up toward his chest. It pulled her closer to him at the same time and he kissed her. She loved the way he kissed. His mouth wasn't gentle or tentative, but neither did he just mash his lips against hers. She thought she could happily spend hours kissing him. Until his hands slid down her arms and sides to the hem of her T-shirt, and then she decided there might be better things than kissing in store for her.

"Keep your arms up," he said, his voice low and firm in a way that made her shiver. He slowly pulled the shirt up and over her arms before tossing it aside. His eyes widened slightly, and then he stroked the lace edging of her bra. "I don't know what this color is, but it's my new favorite."

"I think it's called beige."

"I love beige."

She still had on a lot more clothes than he did, so she tried to give him a little incentive. "The panties are beige, too, and have lace."

When he made a *mmm* sound low in his throat and reached for the button on her jeans, she was never so thankful to have forgotten to switch her laundry over from the washer to the dryer. She usually wore her older, plain cotton underwear sets for work because they were comfortable, but they hadn't dried in time, so she'd grabbed the lace set.

As he popped the button on her jeans open and undid the zipper, she toed out of her sneakers and kicked them aside. She used his shoulders to keep her balance as she hooked a toe in each sock and pulled those off, too. "You have the most amazing shoulders."

"I carry heavy things a lot," he murmured, obviously distracted by the revelation of beige lace as he slid her jeans down over her hips.

When he got them down as far as he could reach,

she wiggled her butt, making them fall a little more until she could stand on the hem of each leg in turn and pull her legs out.

His eyes widened a little. "You should do that again."

"Yeah, I don't think so." She stood on her tiptoes to wrap her arms around his neck, which pressed the length of her almost-naked body against his almost-naked body. His skin was warm and she wondered if hers felt the same to him.

"Maybe later." He kissed her, his hands sliding down her back and under the waistband of her panties to cup her ass.

His erection was pressed against her abdomen, and she wanted the boxer briefs gone, but she didn't want the kiss to end. He was a perfect kisser, with just the right amount of pressure and demand, without being overbearing. She liked a man who could kiss and, in her experience, they were rare.

Another thought occurred to her, and she broke off the kiss. "I know this is not a great time to ask, but do you have condoms? I didn't bring any because I came to apologize and didn't realize it would go so well."

He chuckled. "It's going very well, and, yes, I do. But they're in my bedroom, so we should start moving in that direction."

"Yes, we should." She smiled and then stepped around him to walk toward his bedroom. On the way, she reached behind her and unhooked her bra so it could slide slowly down her arms. Then she caught it and tossed it behind her without looking.

"I love beige," he said again, and she smiled.

His bedroom was clean, which she'd expected based on the rest of his apartment. A lot of blue, with sports memorabilia hung on the walls and on the bureau. The bed was definitely the centerpiece—king-size with lots of pillows.

She lifted the comforter and then slid in between the sheets, surprised by the feel of the fabric against her bare skin. "These are really nice sheets."

"Thank you."

"No, I mean it. Do you know the thread count?"

He looked at her, eyebrows raised. "Really? Is that something most people know? And I feel like I need to try harder or something if you're analyzing fabric in my bed."

She laughed and spread her arms out, running her hands over the sheets. "It feels nice against my skin. Very sensual, actually."

"Oh, sensual is good. You should feel free to spend as much time as you want between my sheets. With me, though. It's kind of pointless for you to roll around in the bed alone."

She held out her hand. "I'm alone in the bed right now."

"Only because the view from over here is incredible. You, almost naked in my bed? I want to memorize this moment."

"Let me know when you're done, because I'm waiting to memorize how you *feel*."

"Okay, got it." He stretched out on the bed over her, and cupped her breast in one hand. "Have I told you how beautiful you are?"

She smiled, knowing it was a little goofy, but unable to help herself. Of course he was going to tell her she was beautiful, but for some reason when Aidan said it, she believed him.

His mouth closed over her nipple and she buried her hand in his hair. He sucked gently at first, but then harder, until she hissed and her back arched off the bed. Then he shifted his attention to her other breast and did it again.

She raked her nails up his back, feeling his muscles twitch under her touch. When his hand slid down her stomach, she held her breath until it skimmed over lace and he cupped her mound.

He turned his face up to hers so she could see his smug smile. "Should we see how fast I can make you come tonight?"

"That's not going to happen again. You're going to have to work for it this time." He probably wouldn't have to work too long or too hard, but he didn't need to know that.

"That sounds like a challenge."

"Only if you're up to it," she said, returning that smug smile of his with one of her own.

He touched his fingertip to the hollow at the base of her throat. "I'm always up to a challenge."

He ran that finger down between her breasts and over her stomach to slip it underneath the waistband of her panties. Because it felt as if she'd been waiting forever, Lydia would have been happy to skip straight to the main event tonight, but when his fingers slid over her slick flesh, she forced herself to relax and enjoy it.

"You feel so good," he murmured before bending to take her nipple into his mouth again.

She buried her hands in his hair as he stroked her, losing herself in the sensation of his hand between her legs and his mouth on her breast. Then he kissed his way down her abdomen and she sucked in a breath.

"I think that's cheating," she said as he settled between her thighs.

Aidan grinned at her before lifting her legs to hook her knees over his shoulders, and Lydia practically trembled with anticipation. His mouth was hot and wet and, with a moan, she fell back onto the pillows.

His tongue slid into her, thrusting, before withdrawing to circle lazily around her clit. Lydia balled his expensive sheets in her fists and tried to fight the intense pleasure his mouth gave her. She hadn't been kidding about making him work for it this time, dammit.

But when he sucked at her clit, two fingers buried deep inside of her, Lydia surrendered to the orgasm. Aidan didn't stop until the tremors passed, and then he nipped none too gently at the inside of her thigh.

"Told you I'm always up to a challenge."

"Oh, you're not done yet," she said, her voice still breathless.

"You're damn right I'm not."

She heard the crinkle of a condom wrapper and then Aidan's hands closed around her ankles. A yelping sound escaped her when he tugged her down the bed to him and parted her legs so he could kneel between them.

"You ready?" he asked, his voice low and ragged.

"I've been ready since you walked into the bar my first night back." When he reached down to guide the head of his cock into her, she lifted her ass off the bed to take him in.

"Nice and slow," Aidan whispered, holding himself still as Lydia rocked her hips to take him a little deeper with each upward thrust.

"Oh yes," she whispered. "I like that."

Aidan took over then, pulling almost all the way out before plunging back into her. Each stroke was hard and fast, and she felt another orgasm building. She came then, her fingernails digging into her palms as he held tight to her legs. Her hips bucked and she moaned as the muscles in her body spasmed with pleasure.

Seconds later, Aidan groaned and pumped against her. His fingers squeezed the cheek of her ass and she fisted her hand in his hair. He gasped her name and then collapsed on top of her.

"Jesus," he whispered. "That was…I needed that."

"You do know how to live up to a challenge."

She stroked his back while he caught his breath, and then he reached between them to secure the condom as he withdrew. When he flopped onto his back, Lydia stretched her arms up over her head, savoring the warm pleasure still resonating in her muscles.

But when Aidan went into the bathroom to dispose of the condom, she sighed and got up. She couldn't stay. If he went for a round two, she might end up staying so long she'd fall asleep in his bed and that was a bad idea.

She went on a scavenger hunt for her clothes, basically putting them on as she found them, in the reverse order that she'd taken them off. By the time she shoved her feet into her sneakers, Aidan was watching her. He'd pulled on a pair of boxer briefs—gray this time—but that was all.

"Leaving already?" There was no judgment in his voice, or surprise, as if he'd expected to find his bed empty.

"I didn't think I'd be here long and it was kind of an impulse thing, so I didn't tell Ashley where I was going. So I should…yeah, I'm leaving." She gave him a chagrined look. There was no sense in pretending she had a good reason for not staying. "You know how it is."

"Always awkward," he said, and they both laughed.

"It was worth the awkward, though."

He grinned. "Definitely."

She took a second to make sure she had everything, including her keys and her phone. "I guess I'll see you around, then."

"I just realized I don't even know how you got here. Did you walk? You can't walk home alone." Before she could respond to that, he lifted a hand. "Don't yell at me. I know you *can* walk home alone. But just because you're capable of doing it doesn't mean I won't worry about you, so I'll walk you home. I'll even put on pants."

"And they say chivalry is dead." When she got to the door, she shoved her feet into her sneakers. "I appreciate the gesture, but I drove. I can get home okay."

"Text me when you get inside."

He pulled her in for one last kiss and she almost surrendered to the urge to stay. She could be naked again and back in his bed in about thirty seconds. But she forced herself to take a step back when the kiss ended.

"Good night, Aidan."

"'Night. Don't forget to text me."

She wasn't surprised when he watched her get into the car from his window, and it wasn't until she was on the road and about to turn that she saw the curtain drop back into place. It was sweet, she thought, and as soon as she was in Ashley's house and had locked the door behind her, she pulled out her phone.

I'm home.

The response came almost instantly, as if he'd timed it and was waiting for the text.

I wish you were still here. Good night.

Me, too. Good night.

She probably shouldn't have admitted that, but she was still feeling that post-orgasm glow. After making sure Ashley had locked the back door before she went up to bed, Lydia crept up the stairs and into her bedroom, wincing when she stepped on a floorboard that squeaked. She'd have to remember that one for next time she had to sneak in to avoid questions from her older sister.

Somehow she got the feeling there would definitely be a next time.

TEN

AT TEN THE NEXT MORNING, Aidan leaned against the counter in the kitchen area, drinking coffee and trying to stay out of everybody's way. He was in his dress uniform that thankfully he always kept clean, pressed and ready to go since he'd been too busy last night to worry about creases in his pants or the shine on his shoes.

The memory of why he'd been late made him grin again and, dammit, he needed to stop doing that. Walking around all day with a goofy look on his face would attract attention and then questions, and he was determined not to dig his hole any deeper.

And that was why he was hiding in the kitchen. There were too many guys in the station who could pick up on his new and improved mood, and Aidan hoped like hell that Scott and Danny showed up soon. Gullotti and Porter were already there, hanging out down in the bays. The five of them were going to represent the firehouse at a promotion ceremony and, since they'd all ride together, they were meeting here. Since E-59 and L-37's second crews were doing the day tour, there were too many people and they were tripping over each other downstairs.

When Scotty walked in, also in his dress uniform and carrying a bag from the market down the street, Aidan straightened his expression out and lifted a hand in greeting. "Good morning."

When his friend did a little bit of a double take, he wondered how he'd managed to screw that up. All he'd said was two words. "Good morning?"

"It's a general greeting often used by two people the first time they see each other on any given day if it's before noon."

"Usually you say 'hey.'" Scotty set the shopping bag on the counter and pulled out two smaller bags of green grapes.

"I got up early today, so I've already had enough coffee to muster two words instead of one." He drained the last of his coffee as if to prove his point.

"No, you're definitely in a good mood today." Scott stared at him for a few seconds before opening the fridge and put the grapes in the fruit drawer. "Did you finally tell your old man to pound sand?"

"Uh…" Aidan had no idea what to say to that, since he couldn't explain the reason for his good mood but also didn't want to say he'd booted his old man out of his life because that lie would easily come around and bite him in the ass.

Another guy walked into the kitchen and saw the open fridge. "Hey, are those grapes?"

"Those are *my* grapes," Scotty said.

"Sharing is caring, Kincaid."

Worrying about his grapes served as a good distraction for Scott, though, and Aidan took the opportunity to wash out his coffee mug without answering the question about his dad. He was just finishing up when Walsh walked in, looking a little tense.

"Hey," Aidan said, not wanting to reintroduce the one-word versus two-word greeting conversation.

"Are you guys ready to go?"

Aidan and Scotty exchanged a look, and then Scott closed the fridge. "Sure. We're ready."

On his way past, Aidan grabbed the shopping bag and shoved it into the fabric sleeve hung on the wall so somebody could reuse it, and then he followed the others to Gullotti's truck. He had a four-door, short-box Chevy, but it was still a little cramped with three of them in the backseat. Gullotti drove, of course, and Porter automatically got shotgun because he was too big to shove into the backseat, which left Aidan, Scotty and Danny getting very cozy in the backseat. They forced Scotty into the middle since he was the shortest by maybe an inch.

"I'm going to get wrinkled," Scotty complained, lifting his butt to try to straighten his dress pants.

"Next time we'll order you a limo," Danny snapped.

"Ouch. Aidan's in a strangely good mood and you're in a particularly bad mood, and I'm sandwiched in the middle. What a fun day this is going to be."

"You know I had to go by the house this morning," Danny said after a few minutes of silence, "since I had my uniform but forgot to grab the shoes. It's the second time I've had to knock on the door of my own house and it sucks."

Aidan guessed that was understatement, which was Danny's style. "How was talking to Ashley?"

He really wanted to ask if Ashley had said anything about Lydia, like maybe she'd been out late the night before, but he didn't. Not only because her brother was sitting between them, but because his first instinct should be sympathy for a friend, not worrying family gossip might reach Scotty.

"It was awkward," Danny said. "I feel like when she looks at me, she's *willing* me to say the right thing, but I don't know what the hell the right thing even is."

"I've been married twelve years," Porter said from the front seat, "and I can almost guaran-damn-tee you the right thing to say is 'I love you.'"

"She knows that." All four of them made a *you might be wrong about that* sound of some sort, and Danny shook his head. "How could she *not* know that? I married her. I go home to her—or I did before this—and I don't run around on her."

"When it comes to expressing emotions," Gullotti said, "you're kind of like…a stone wall. There are some cracks and gaps here and there, but mostly it's just rock."

While he was talking, the phone vibrated in Aidan's hand. He couldn't wear its holster with his dress uniform and the pants pockets were so shallow it had a tendency to fall out when he was sitting, so he was holding it for the ride. As soon as it went off, he tilted it so Scotty wouldn't be able to see the screen.

Busy?

Making a mental note to change her name in his contacts to anything but Lydia Kincaid—and feeling like a douche bag for thinking of it—he looked out the window to get his bearings. Then, using just his right thumb because of the screen angle, he tapped in a response.

Hold on 10 mins.

"Who's that?" Scotty asked, because of course he would. They were buddies and he was easily bored, so he always asked. He kept his voice low, though, because the other guys were still talking about Walsh being a stone wall.

"A woman I met at…the corner market. She was buying sour cream and onion ripple chips and I like those." *Sour cream and onion ripple chips?* He needed to stop talking.

"And you didn't tell me you met somebody? Is she from around here? What's her name?"

"I, uh, forgot her name."

"Didn't you put it in your phone when you put her number in it?"

"No. She said her name and wrote her number on my hand with a pen. By the time I put her in my contacts, I forgot it."

"You're an idiot. How did you list her?"

"Blonde from market."

Scotty snorted. "She'll be really impressed if she sees that. You should put a passcode on your phone if you haven't already, so she can't snoop in it while you're in the shower."

"It'll be a while before she's around while I'm in the shower. We're just in the 'hi, remember me?' phase." That might buy him a little time before Scotty would expect to meet her or run into her at the bar.

When they finally arrived at their destination and climbed out, Aidan was relieved to see a crowd of firefighters milling around outside. Letting the others go ahead to say hello and talk with guys they didn't get to see all the time, he stayed by the truck and pulled up the contacts on his phone. He felt like an idiot, but the first thing he did was change Lydia's name to *Blonde from market* because if they were sitting around and Scotty wanted to look something up or get a score check, he'd just grab whichever phone was closest, no matter who it belonged to.

I have a few mins, he typed into the reply box of her last text.

Alarm?

No. Promotion ceremony.

It took her a while to type her reply.

So you're wearing your dress uniform. I like that look on you. You should model it for me sometime.

He chuckled, trying not to laugh loud enough to attract attention.

I think it's against regulation to use my uniform as a sex prop.

Even for me?

We can talk about it while you give me that blow job you still owe me.

He could almost picture her eyebrow arching as she read that, and the way the corners of her delicious mouth would turn up in a smile.

If you're ever lucky enough to have my mouth on your dick, you won't even manage a coherent thought, never mind making words into a sentence.

Even though he was on the other side of Rick's truck from the crowd and his coat was probably long enough to conceal the instant hard-on, Aidan turned his back to them.

This will be the most uncomfortable ceremony ever.

She sent back an emoticon that was sticking its tongue out, and then *Oops, sorry.*

"Hey, Hunt, let's go," he heard Porter yell.

They're calling me in. Talk to you later.

Have fun.

These shindigs were his least favorite part of the job as it was. Suffering through it without thinking about Lydia and blow jobs was going to be almost impossible, which meant it would be an exercise in having enough self-control not to squirm in his seat.

Sure, it was going to be all kinds of fun.

LYDIA FELT BONELESS, trying to catch her breath with her head hung over the side of Aidan's bed. The man *really* knew what he was doing between the sheets.

When he came back from the bathroom, she heard him chuckle before he lifted her up and slid her around so her head was on the pillow. Then he climbed in and spooned himself around her.

"I needed that very badly," he murmured into her hair. "I swear today was endless. And sitting in that ceremony thinking about blow jobs didn't help, just so you know."

"You're the one who brought them up."

"I just don't want you to forget that you owe me."

She laughed. "Someday, when you least expect it…"

He was rubbing her hip with his left hand, but then he draped his arm over her body so he could hold her hand. Their fingers slid together and she smiled. They fit well together in a lot of ways.

"I told Ashley I wouldn't be home tonight," she said. "Is that okay?"

"Admit it. You just want to sleep on my sheets."

"I was hoping you wouldn't figure that out." She squeezed his fingers. "I don't think I've ever met a single guy with sheets like this, though."

He laughed. "They were a gift from my mother. I can ask her the thread count or whatever if you want."

"That's okay. I'll just enjoy yours."

"Consider this a standing invitation to enjoy my sheets anytime."

She closed her eyes, enjoying the feel of his warm body cupping hers and his soft sheets and his breath in her hair. It was nice, she thought, to not rush out as soon as the glow faded. Not all the time, of course, because that would be a bad precedent to set. But once in a while.

It was probably stupid, spending the night. It was bad enough she thought about him every waking moment, watching the clock and waiting until she could see him again. The whole *burning off the excess chemistry* excuse was wearing thin and falling asleep in his arms wasn't going to help.

But one time probably wouldn't hurt, she told herself as Aidan's breathing deepened into soft snores.

Later in the night, something woke Lydia and she blinked in the dark, trying to figure out why she was awake. It took her a few seconds to remember she was in Aidan's bed, and she squinted at the clock until the red blur formed numbers. 3:19. She *definitely* shouldn't be awake.

Aidan kicked the back of her heel and she realized he not only wasn't snoring, but he was breathing funny. Folding back the sheet, she rolled over and pushed onto her elbow. He was on his side, facing away from her, but in the moonlight she could see the slight sheen of sweat just below his hairline. His leg jerked again and the hand she could see clenched into a fist.

He was having a nightmare.

Lydia wasn't sure what the best way to handle it was. Maybe she should move away and call his name, in case he came up swinging. That probably wasn't likely, though. It was more likely his dream involved fire than violence.

When he made a keening sound low in his throat and his head twitched on the pillow, she couldn't stand it anymore. She stroked his hair, making a *shh* sound. He stilled, but his breathing was still quick and his hand didn't relax.

"Aidan?" He rolled onto his back without waking up, and she saw how deeply a scowl had drawn his eyebrows together. Pushing his hair back from his clammy forehead, she tried again. "Aidan, wake up."

He opened his eyes and then took a deep, shuddering breath. It took him a few seconds to shake off the dream, and she smiled when his gaze finally focused on her.

"Hey," she said softly. "Bad dream."

"Yeah." His voice was hoarse, and he cleared his throat to try again. "I couldn't find Scotty. I can never find Scotty."

She stroked his hair, smiling down at him. "Scotty's fine. Do you want some water?"

"No." He lifted his arm and she ducked under it to lay her head on his chest and throw her arm across his body. He held her close and kissed the top of her head. "I'm sorry I woke you up."

"I'll go back to sleep." She could hear his heartbeat, and it was slowly returning to normal. "Once you're okay."

He pulled the sheet back over her and then gave her a squeeze. "I'm okay now. Sleep."

She didn't right away, though. *I can never find Scotty.* She squeezed her eyes closed, trying to imagine anything except Aidan and her brother in a fire gone wrong. And, besides the fear that was constant when you loved firefighters flaring up, Lydia felt guilt rising above it.

To her, brotherhood meant people who were as— if not more—important to her father and ex-husband than she'd ever been. But to Aidan and Scotty and the rest of them, it was more than just a word. They lived together and worked together, but they also risked their lives together. They depended on each other in a way most people could never understand. Aidan and Scotty weren't only best friends. They trusted each other with their lives.

And there was a possibility her choosing to be here in Aidan's bed might break that bond. No amount of telling herself Aidan was a big boy and could make his own choices could ease the knot in her chest at the thought of he and Scotty not having each other's backs, and it was a long time before she drifted back into a fitful sleep.

AIDAN WOKE A FEW hours later with the weight of Lydia's head on his chest, half her body flung over his, and an arm he couldn't feel and simply had to hope was still there. He didn't care. Having her there to comfort him when that damn dream got hold of him again had been worth any price.

He closed his eyes again, knowing he wouldn't go

back to sleep, but content to hold her and listen to her breathe softly. She had to work later, but she could sleep another hour and still get home in plenty of time to get ready for her shift at Kincaid's.

"Coffee," he heard her mutter against his chest.

"Good morning," he said, kissing her hair. "I thought you'd sleep a little longer."

"Coffee."

"I'd be happy to make a pot of coffee, but I think it'll be at least two hours before I get feeling back in my arm."

She rolled away, taking the sheet with her, until she was back on the other side of the bed. He grimaced and tried to make a fist, but was pretty sure he failed. The pins and needles were going to suck.

"How'd you sleep?" he asked Lydia. "Other than me waking you up, of course."

"Coffee," she growled into her pillow.

Laughing, he rolled out of bed and pulled on a pair of sweatpants. "I'll go make a pot of coffee."

"Make some for yourself, too," she called after him.

In an act of impeccable timing he assumed must be her secret superpower, Lydia walked into the kitchen just as the coffeemaker gurgled and shot the last bit of liquid into the carafe. He turned to tease her about it, but whatever he'd been going to say died on the tip of his tongue.

She was rubbing her face, and having her arms slightly raised also slightly raised the hem of his

T-shirt so he got a tantalizing glimpse of the tops of her thighs. The shirt appeared to be the only article of clothing she was wearing, which was ample reward for the pain of the blood flow returning to his hand and arm. Her hair was what the younger crowd probably meant by "hot mess," and she'd never looked more beautiful to him.

"Coffee's done brewing," he said.

"Those are my favorite words in the whole world." She kissed him, leaving behind the minty tingle of his mouthwash, and then took a mug out of his dish rack. After fixing herself a cup of coffee, she went to his couch and curled up on one end.

He usually sat at his kitchen table with his first coffee, watching the news and scrolling through headlines and the Facebook account he mostly ignored on his phone. He'd signed up for that at the urging of a former girlfriend and, since everybody else had one, he'd given in to the peer pressure. Now he skimmed through, looking at pictures, but he never posted and rarely commented.

But if Lydia wanted to sit on the couch, he was okay with that, too. She hit the power button on the TV and pulled up the on-screen guide to change the channel to what he assumed was her usual morning news show. Not the one he usually put on when he bothered with the television, but he didn't really care. He listened to the chatter of the people on the screen and read the constant scroll across the bottom, leaving Lydia to drink her coffee in peace.

She was about halfway through when she turned her head to face him. "Have you had that nightmare before? Or is it new?"

A vague sense of embarrassment crept over him. Not super smooth, having a nightmare the first time she stayed over. "I've had it before, but it's not usually so vivid. And I've had it twice in the last couple of weeks. That's different."

"I think that makes sense, though."

He laughed. "Yeah, a firefighter having a nightmare about being lost in the smoke and separated from his company probably makes sense."

"I meant your dream about Scotty being more vivid and more frequent. You feel like you're distanced from him. Because of me."

"No." *Maybe.* As much as he didn't want to admit it, that theory might not be totally off base. But he wasn't going to let her take the blame for it. "When it comes to my friendship with Scott, that's between him and me, and I own the choices I've made."

She reached over to slap his shoulder. "We made the decision together, remember?"

"Either way, I've had the nightmare before—many times—so don't read too much into it. It's probably the fire version of that stress dream where you're at school or in front of a crowd and you realize you forgot to put on pants."

"If you say so. Are you making me breakfast?"

He laughed. "I made the coffee."

"Okay, I'll make breakfast, but only because of the storage closet. I still owe you for that."

It took him all of two seconds to shake his head. "Oh, no you don't. You *know* what you owe me for that and it's not scrambled eggs."

"So you're making breakfast, then?" she asked sweetly, though the look of impending victory on her face gave lie to that.

No way in hell was he giving up a blow job IOU to save himself a few minutes of cooking. "I'll make breakfast."

He made them scrambled eggs and melted a couple of slices of American cheese on top. A few slices of toast and microwave sausage links and it was done. It was nice, he thought as he sat down across from her at the kitchen table, having somebody to eat breakfast with. And to watch television with.

Not only had giving in to his need to sleep with Lydia not scratched that particular itch to his satisfaction—and he wondered if that was even possible—but new little, nagging itches seemed to be popping up now.

Like the one that wished they could spend the entire day doing nothing but watching television and making love and maybe taking a walk to the deli for lunch. Couple stuff.

He wanted to take her out on a date. Make out with her in a movie theater. Kiss her without looking over his shoulder to make sure nobody was watching. His brother could sometimes get him decent tickets to a ball game, and he wanted to buy her a chili dog.

But he'd known this was how it was going to be when he made the jump, so he ate his eggs and made up his mind to enjoy every minute he had with her. He'd worry about the minutes he *didn't* have with her some other time.

ELEVEN

LYDIA WAS GOING to be late if she didn't get a move on. The good news was that she'd already showered. The bad news was that Aidan had been in the shower with her, so it had taken longer than it should have. A *lot* longer.

Because she was rushing, she swung the door closed behind her with a little more force than she'd intended and it slammed. Wincing, she headed for the stairs. She may have showered, but she needed a fresh set of clothes and some hair product before it totally dried that way.

"Lydia?"

Dammit. "Yeah, it's me. I have to get ready for work."

Ashley walked out of the kitchen, and Lydia could see she'd been crying. "Danny stopped by again last night."

And she was still puffy-eyed and red-nosed. "You should have called me. I would have come home."

"I don't know what to do, Lydia."

On the inside, she let out a long, resigned sigh.

Outwardly, she offered a supportive smile. "Go pour us each a cup of coffee. I've got to get this hair into a pony or it'll drive me crazy."

Once she was upstairs, Lydia took a few seconds to send a text to her dad, telling him she might be a little late and he needed to head to the bar or let the cook open. It shouldn't have surprised her when her phone rang in her hand a few seconds later. The man hated texts.

"Hi, Dad."

"Why are you going to be late?"

It was tempting to tell him she was having lady problems. Nothing made her old man bail from a conversation faster than bringing up menstruation. But she needed to hold that in reserve for if and when it was actually an issue. "Danny stopped by last night and Ashley's upset. I'm going to talk to her for a few minutes and then I'll be in."

"Why didn't you talk to her last night? Or earlier this morning? You gotta wait until it's almost time to open the bar?"

Lydia froze, making an *ouch*, *busted* face she was thankful he couldn't see. That's what she got for trying to multitask. "I was out. I just got home."

Maybe it would be enough. If menstruation held the number one spot for things Tommy Kincaid didn't want to hear his daughters talk about, sex was definitely a close runner-up.

"You went out after the bar closed last night? Where did you go?"

Lydia sighed, but quietly so he wouldn't hear it, and lied. "I had to stop by Becca's and we got talking and it was late enough so I just crashed on her couch."

"Fine. Go see what's up with your sister. I swear, those two really need to get their shit together, so talk some sense into her, would ya?"

Once the call was over, she changed into some clean clothes and put her hair up, muttering unflattering things about her father the entire time. She knew as dads went, others had worse. Hers didn't drink more alcohol than he could handle. He'd never laid a hand on his wife or kids in anger. But he was also gruff, emotionally hands-off and—perhaps worst of all—not exactly progressive when it came to his thoughts about women and family. The implication Ashley should just get over whatever her problem was made Lydia want to dump a full mug of ice-cold beer over his head.

Ashley, who was leaning against the counter, gestured to the mug on the table when Lydia walked into the kitchen. "I made you a coffee, but you don't have to drink it. I know you have to get to work, and I'm okay now. I just had a moment, that's all."

"Why were you crying?" Lydia pulled out the chair and sat in front of the coffee. "What happened?"

"Nothing happened. He texted me and asked if he could stop by again, and I said yes. When he stopped by in the morning, he only grabbed his dress shoes, so this time I thought he was ready to talk. But when he got here, he just wanted to talk about the financial situation. We have joint accounts, of course, and he said he didn't feel right taking money out of them without talking to me, but he was running low on cash."

"That's better than him taking the money out and screw you if you don't like it." Ashley stared into her coffee mug, looking like somebody had just kicked her favorite dog. "I asked the wrong question. You told me what happened, but what were you expecting to happen?"

She knew she'd hit the right button when her sister's eyes filled up with tears. "I want him to fight for me—for us. I want him to tell me he loves me and that he doesn't want our marriage to be over, and not sound like he's reading it from a script or something."

"When you told him you weren't sure you wanted to be married anymore, you were testing him, weren't you? Pushing him into a corner so he'd have to give you some kind of emotional validation."

Ashley took a deep breath and then shrugged. "I don't know. I honestly *wasn't* sure if I wanted to be married to him anymore, but I saw it as some kind of wake-up call that we needed to work on it before it got worse. I guess he saw it as my way of saying I wanted a divorce."

"And you don't."

"I love Danny. I don't want a divorce."

"You need to tell him that."

"No," Ashley said, and Lydia sighed. She really wanted to go to work. If somebody was having a bad day, you set a beer and some pretzels in front of them and put a game on the television. "If I tell him that and he comes back home, nothing's changed. Maybe we won't be divorced, but the problems that drove me to that point will still be there. I need for him to show me he loves me. I'm not going to let him keep assuming I know."

Lydia wrapped her hands around her mug and took a long drink of her coffee to give herself time to think of how to phrase what she was thinking. While Ashley was the most even-tempered of them, she could be pretty stubborn.

"Just say it," Ashley snapped. She was also perceptive.

"Have you told *him* any of that, or are you expecting him to read your mind?"

"A guy doesn't have to be psychic to know if his wife says she's so unhappy she's not sure if she wants to be married to him anymore, that he should sit down and talk to her about it."

"You've told me yourself Danny doesn't like emotional confrontations. That his parents are always screaming at each other and that he'll walk away before he'll lose his temper. Maybe it's not just his temper he keeps a tight hold on. And you told him you needed space. Maybe he's just trying to give you that and doesn't realize you're expecting him to push back."

"I should have let you go to work."

Lydia laughed and got up to rinse out her cup. "You know I always have your back, even if that means telling you something you don't want to hear. And let me ask you one more question. Have you asked him straight-out if *he* wants a divorce?"

Ashley's long silence was telling, but she waited her out and made her say it. "No, but he's made it sound like he doesn't. He's putting it all on me."

"Your communication problem is not all on Danny, love."

"You should go to work now," Ashley said, and Lydia kissed her cheek and made a break for it.

Kincaid's Pub felt like a drama-free oasis after her sister's kitchen, and Lydia quickly settled into the rhythm of the bar. Even though the basic job description was the same, it was amazing to her how much different it seemed than the job she'd quit in New Hampshire. Granted, an old neighborhood bar and a nice restaurant weren't the same, but serving customers was serving customers.

At some point, she was going to have to decide what she wanted to do when Ashley was ready to return to Kincaid's. Going back to her old job wouldn't be an option, even in the unlikely event they were willing to take her back. Being here behind her father's bar again had reminded her how much she loved bartending. But it didn't make a lot of sense to go tend bar for strangers somewhere—and for less money—when she had Kincaid's. At the rate her sister and Danny were going, Lydia had plenty of time to start making decisions, but the question of her future was definitely simmering in the back of her mind.

About nine o'clock, Scotty walked in and Lydia tried not to be disappointed he was alone. In fact, it might even be for the best, since it was hard to know how awkward it would be to see her brother and Aidan at the same time. Hopefully it wouldn't be too bad, since it was inevitable that moment would come, but at least it wouldn't be tonight.

"Hey, sis." He draped his hoodie over the back of the seat and hopped up onto the stool. After waving to Fitz a few seats down, he turned back to her. "Where's Dad tonight?"

"He said he was going out with a friend."

Scotty jerked his thumb toward the end of the bar. "Fitz is here."

She shrugged. "I assume he has more than one friend. I don't know. Maybe he's got a special lady friend."

"No." He took the beer she handed him, scowling. "He can't have a special lady friend if I don't. That makes me feel really inadequate."

They laughed together, because it was hard to believe their old man could find a woman who'd put up with his crap at this stage of his life, and because there wasn't much that would make Scott feel inadequate.

"You eat already?" she asked.

"Yeah, I made a couple of sandwiches at home, but then I got bored so I thought I'd come have a beer with the old man and see who all was here." He looked around the bar, which wasn't too full of familiar faces tonight. "I probably should have looked for some infomercials and nodded off to promises of all things new and improved."

Lydia opened her mouth to tell him that was almost as bad as Aidan's confession he used animal documentaries to the same effect, but then realized she'd have to explain how she knew that and closed it again. And then she felt stupid because if Scott asked how she knew that, she would just say that Aidan told her. She'd known him as long as Scotty had and, though they'd never spent a lot of quality alone time together, Aidan had spent many hours leaned against the bar over the years.

She couldn't imagine how Aidan was dealing with this. He probably had the same incidents of almost casually mentioning something about Lydia and having the same conversation with himself that she'd just had. Only it would happen to him more often because he spent a hell of a lot more time with Scotty than she did. No wonder the poor guy was having stress dreams.

She was delivering cheese fries to the table by the door when the old scanner by Fitz squeaked out some noise. It was usually quieter than that, which meant he'd turned it up. Looking over her shoulder, she saw him leaned as close as he could get to it.

"Somebody's hurt," Fitz said in a voice that carried over the small talk going on around the bar.

The hush was immediate and all heads swiveled in his direction. He had his ear to the scanner, which was ancient and barely worked anymore. Everybody tended to use text messaging and social media for updates nowadays, so they'd never gotten around to replacing it with a newer model. It was practically antique, too, and her dad liked the novelty of it.

Fitz said the engine company's number, but it wasn't familiar to Lydia. Saying a quick and silent prayer for whoever was involved, she made her way down the bar, checking on her customers.

Scotty leaned closer to Fitz, though. "Have they said who? Or what happened?"

"This piece of junk," Fitz grumbled, slapping the side of it. "I get more static than anything."

Scott pulled out his phone and there was a sense of urgency about his movements that alarmed Lydia. They all worried about each other because that was how the community worked, but it looked like more than standard worry on his face, so she walked over to him.

"Do you know those guys?" she asked.

"I know them all," he said, scrolling through something on the phone. Then he paused. "Hit by a car? Jesus."

"Who?"

"I don't know yet. They're not going to release his name and the last thing they need on-scene is a shit-load of texts asking who it is."

"Hopefully you'll know something soon." That was how it went. Waiting for news. Waiting to find out who was involved. She'd always hated that part.

"Jesus, I just hope it's not Hunt."

The room seemed to spin for a second and Lydia placed her palms on the surface of the bar to steady herself. No. She'd left Aidan that morning and he'd said nothing about working. He would have told her. But she couldn't tell her brother any of that. "Aidan's out with those guys?"

Scotty nodded without looking up, intent on his phone's screen. "One of their guys is out because his wife just had a baby, and then another guy called in sick, so Aidan picked up a night tour with that company."

Lydia felt the chill slowly taking over her body and her lips parted as she tried to breathe normally.

Aidan might be hurt.

She didn't know if it was him. She didn't know how badly, if it *was* him. Frustration rose like a scream in the back of her throat and she forced it down. She'd been here before. Waiting for news on her dad. On her brother. More than once for her husband.

When she'd packed up and moved to New Hampshire, it was supposed to mean she'd never do this again. She wasn't supposed to be standing behind the damn bar, waiting to find out if somebody she cared about was going to make it home.

"Anything?" she asked, and even though it was only one word, she must have sounded funny because he looked up at her. His brows were knit together in concentration and her stomach sank even further when he shook his head.

"Screw this." He stood and grabbed his hoodie. "I'm going to go outside and call the house. Maybe they know something."

"Let me know, okay?" she said, wanting more than anything to go outside with him. "If it's Aidan or not."

"I will."

She felt helpless. That was the worst thing. Knowing there was nothing she could do but wait was hell on her nerves. She wanted to *do* something. Drive to the scene. Drive from hospital to hospital until she had the answer she was looking for. But that wasn't how it was done.

All she could do was wait. And pray.

AIDAN SAW IT coming and there wasn't a damn thing he could do to stop it. The engine company was helping the police officer trying to clear traffic so the ladder crew could get the outriggers down and the aerial ladder up, but it was dark. It was the third alarm, so apparatus clogged the street. And though it wasn't raining hard, it was enough to refract the bright lights of the engines through windshields.

One asshole in a luxury SUV was in a hurry and Aidan saw a guy named Jones stepping out from behind the ladder truck's outrigger. He shouted a warning and waved his light at the firefighter, but the guy in the SUV saw nothing but an opening and gunned the engine.

Aidan was running, yelling into his radio before Jones rolled off the hood of the SUV and hit the pavement. Within seconds, he was on his knees beside the firefighter and he said a quick prayer of gratitude when Jones looked up at him, his eyes focused on his face.

"Ow."

Aidan smiled and placed his hand gently on the man's forehead. Jones had had his helmet on, but Aidan had no idea where it was now. "Don't move. They're bringing the board."

"I remember reading that Chapter in the book," Jones said, the humor not quite masking the pain in his voice.

"He ran right out in front of me," SUV guy was yelling, and Aidan realized the man had gotten out of his vehicle.

He did his best to ignore the asshole until the EMS guys took over on Jones and then Aidan pushed himself to his feet. A police officer Aidan vaguely recognized was talking to the driver, who was gesturing with his hands.

"It wasn't my fault! He ran out in front of me."

The officer saw Aidan coming and there must have been something on his face that alarmed the guy because he held up a hand. "I'll take your statement later."

"What the hell kinda moron are you?" Aidan yelled at the driver, whose mouth dropped open. "Huh? What were you thinking?"

"Hey," the police officer shouted to somebody behind Aidan. "Come get your guy."

"Hunt," he heard, recognizing the voice as that of the incident commander. "Let's go. Striking fourth alarm, so we've got more companies incoming and we need to get this shit under control."

He itched to get his hands on the asshole whose time was more important than their safety, but that wouldn't help Jones and it sure as hell wouldn't put the fire out. He started to walk away, but turned back to speak to the officer. "You make damn sure you get a statement from me when this is over."

As the ambulance carrying Jones pulled away, Aidan double-checked his gear and went to do his job.

His phone vibrated a few times, but it was almost two hours before he had the opportunity to dig under his gear and pull it out of its holster. There were a few from Scotty, asking him if he was dead.

Not dead, which you probably know by now. Jones has concussion & waiting on hip X-ray, he texted back.

And there was one from Lydia sent not too long ago.

I swore to myself I'd never do this again.

It might have been short, but it said a lot. He tried not to picture her waiting for news. He hadn't even told her he'd picked up a tour for another guy, and he wondered how she'd found out he was there. He didn't know that, but he did know she'd probably spent the past couple of hours kicking herself in the ass for getting involved with another firefighter.

I'm sorry, he typed. *It was crazy, but I'm okay.*

She immediately texted back.

I want to see you later.

Tour doesn't end until 0600.

I'll be asleep on your couch when you get home. Wake me up.

He smiled, but he wasn't sure how that was going to work.

Door's locked.

I stole the key from Dad's office. See you in the morning.

He'd forgotten about that key. When he moved into the apartment, he'd given Tommy a key to keep in the office in case anything happened to him. And if he ended up in the hospital at a weird hour and wanted something from home, he didn't want Tommy having to drag his landlord out of bed in the middle of the night.

After securing his phone, he took a deep breath and looked around. The scene was a mess. The fire had gotten in the pipe chase and, from there, it had free run of the three-decker building. They were still finding hot spots and checking the integrity so the investigators could get in there and determine the cause and origin.

There were three families in the street, getting some help from the Victims Assist Team, and there were hoses and tools all over the damn place. It was going to be one long damn night. But as he hefted an axe and went back inside with his temporary company, he found himself smiling.

When it was over, he was going home to Lydia.

LYDIA OPENED HER EYES, her sleep-fuzzy brain trying to figure out what was going on and why she was awake. The realization she was on a couch came first, followed quickly by the fact it was Aidan's couch.

She jerked upright and saw him standing at the kitchen island, putting his keys in the wooden bowl he kept there and plugging in his cell phone. A small duffel bag was at his feet and she knew it held some toiletries and a change of clothes for when he was going to a firehouse besides his own. He'd showered, though he hadn't shaved, but he looked exhausted.

He looked over at her and smiled when he saw she was awake. "Sorry. I tried to be quiet."

"I told you to wake me up."

"It's pretty early. I figured I'd let you sleep another hour, at least."

"By then, you'll probably be asleep."

He shrugged and turned on his coffee brewer. "I never go right to sleep when I get home. I'm having decaf, but do you want a coffee?"

"Sure." She got off the couch and stretched her back. "Just let me run in the bathroom real quick and then I'll help you make them."

She probably should have skipped looking in the mirror. At least her hair wasn't too insane. Though she hated sleeping with it in a ponytail, she'd left it when she crashed on his couch so it would stay reasonably contained. But her face was slightly puffy and her eyes a little bruised-looking from not sleeping well.

She'd known Aidan was okay for quite some time before she got a response to the text she'd finally given in and sent to him. Scotty had reached out to somebody and gotten the word on who was injured and how badly. But even once she had that information, her mind hadn't settled.

What the hell was she doing messing around with a firefighter again?

Sex was one thing, and she would have said even that was off-limits if she'd been asked before seeing Aidan again. At least with casual sex she could pretend she was leaving her emotions out of it. But there was no denying her emotions had gotten all tied in a knot when she heard Aidan could be hurt, and the need to see him—to see for herself that he was okay—had driven her to curl up on his couch and wait for him to come home.

After washing her face and using his mouthwash, Lydia went back to the kitchen. She must have beat herself up in front of the mirror longer than she thought, because he was already done making their coffees and had set them on the coffee table. He looked exhausted, she thought, taking a seat on the couch.

"You okay?" he asked, which she thought was

ironic. "I know you probably didn't sleep well on the couch, but you look like something's bothering you, too."

She shook her head, not wanting to talk about it. And even if she did want to talk about it, now wouldn't be the time. Picking up her coffee mug, she drank while looking at the television screen. He'd turned the news on, but the volume was muted so she had to read the subtitles.

"I guess it probably has something to do with your text from last night," he said, pushing the issue.

"*I swore to myself I'd never do this again.*"

She should have sent something simple. *Let me know you're not hurt.* Or maybe just *you okay?* Instead, in a moment of emotional weakness, she'd shown her cards. "It was no big deal. You know how written words are. Without inflection and facial expression and stuff, it probably sounded a lot heavier than it was meant to."

"I should have sent you a text. I should have known that, once the code went out, you'd worry. But the fire was getting away from us and…I'm sorry."

"I didn't even know you were working. When Scott said you were with those guys, it scared me."

"It was a last-minute thing." He had his hands wrapped around his coffee mug, but he wasn't drinking it. "I'm not used to having people worry about me, I guess. The people who care about me the most tend to be with me when shit happens, you know?

Last night was different, but in the heat of the moment, I didn't think."

"You don't owe me any explanations," Lydia said sharply, not wanting to dig any deeper into feelings at the moment. "Or a text or a phone call."

He looked at her for what felt like forever, his eyebrows furrowed. "Are you mad at me or yourself here?"

"That's a stupid question."

"Not really, because there's no good reason for you to be this pissed off at me, so I'm thinking you're mad at yourself and taking it out on me. And I'm happy to be a shoulder to lean on, but I'm a little tired right now and not in the mood to be a whipping boy."

"Last night was just one of the reasons I never should have slept with you in the first place." She set her mug down on the coffee table and wrapped her arms around her knees. "I'm not cut out to be a firefighter's wife again."

"If anybody knows how to live with a firefighter, it's you. I mean, you grew up surrounded by them, for chrissake."

"Okay, let me clarify that. I don't *want* to be a firefighter's wife again." She used both hands to push her hair back from her face. "I have to stop using the word *wife*. Not wife. I swore I'd never get involved with another firefighter."

"I hate to break it to you, but you're always going to be involved with firefighters. Your brother, your brother-in-law, your friends."

"My brother-in-law? I think we can see how well that's turning out for Ashley."

"I think that's more about Danny's personality making it hard for them to talk to each other than his job." He took a sip of the decaf, watching her over the rim of the mug. "My point is that you're going to worry no matter what. I bet even when you were in New Hampshire, if there was a fire in Boston on the news, you had to know which companies were involved."

She couldn't deny that was true, but it was different. "There's a difference between being worried about a member of the larger community and waiting for the guy who's supposed to put you first to remember to let you know he's not dead."

"Well, I'm never going to be a guy who says 'I'm gonna save your life, but hold your breath and try not to inhale any smoke for a minute so I can text my girlfriend a status update,' and I don't want to be." He shrugged. "I responded to your text as soon as I could."

The word *girlfriend* stuck in her mind. Was that how Aidan saw her, or was he just making a point? "Now I sound like a self-centered bitch."

"You're not a self-centered bitch. You have some issues, like with your dad and your ex-husband, and right now those issues are making you a little unreasonable."

She stood and looked down at him. "I'm going to

go now, because this just seems to be getting worse and we're both tired."

"I don't want you to go, Lydia."

"And I don't want to sit here and talk about how my issues are making me unsupportive and unreasonable."

"That's not fair. Look, you married an asshole. That sucks, but that guy being an asshole doesn't mean I'm an asshole, too, just because we do the same job." He set his mug on the table. "I'm not carrying some other guy's baggage."

"It's *my* baggage," she snapped. "And don't worry about it. I can carry it myself."

"Stop," he said when she headed for the door. "Lydia, please. Just wait."

Something in his voice broke through her anger, and she turned back to face him. "What?"

"I'm not asking you for anything, Lydia. Just a little company for a while." He held up his hands. "Maybe we could watch a movie or something. I just don't want to be alone."

"You really should get some sleep."

"I will later. But I always come home to an empty apartment and last night sucked, but once you told me you'd be here, that was all I could think about. That you'd be here. And now we're arguing and I don't want you to leave like this." She hesitated, torn by the sincerity in his voice. "For no other reason than I'm a friend who had a shitty night and could use some company."

"Even shitty company?"

He smiled, and the weariness in his eyes tugged at her. "I don't care what kind of mood you're in. I always want your company. And if you get too bitchy, I'll just turn the TV up to drown out your voice."

She laughed and sat back down on the couch. "You're not as funny as you think you are, Aidan Hunt."

"You still laughed." His slid his hand across the sofa cushion and laced his fingers through hers before using his other hand to unmute the television. "I'll even let you pick what we watch."

TWELVE

Two DAYS LATER, Aidan kept his gaze on the yellow reflective tape on Scotty's jacket and helped support the line as they tried to beat the flames back. The smoke was thick and the world seemed to be crackling around them, but the woman was still screaming, pleading for somebody to save her.

That was good. As long as she was still screaming, she could be saved. They pushed forward, their world reduced to each other, the fire and the woman's voice.

They knew she was the only person left in the house and they had an idea of where she was. Her husband thought he might have fallen asleep in his recliner while smoking a cigarette because he woke up with his sweatpants on fire and had to roll on the grass to extinguish the flames after throwing himself out the window. As they'd put him in the ambulance, he'd begged for them to find his wife, who'd been in the master bathroom.

"I see her," Aidan shouted. He reached over Scotty's shoulder to point to the doorway, and waited for his nod. As his friend turned the hose to keep the water spraying toward the flames that kept popping out at them, Aidan went by him with Grant Cutter on his heels.

She'd almost made it out. The fire, along with the water they had to throw at it, had weakened the structure and the ceiling had partially collapsed on her, pinning her legs. Her pleas for help were hoarse now—barely audible and broken up by coughing— but she was moving.

Aidan spared a second to grasp her hand and squeeze it while he looked over the situation. It wasn't too bad, and if she'd been younger and stronger, she might have freed herself.

"Get ready," he yelled to Grant. Then he wedged the Halligan tool under the beam across her legs, looking for leverage and taking the precious seconds to play out the cause and effect in his head. If he moved that beam, those ceiling panels would fall and another joist might shift, but nothing catastrophic. "On three."

He counted, and then put his weight on the end of the bar until it lifted the beam. The mask blocked his peripheral vision, so he couldn't see the woman, but he heard Grant shout that she was clear.

He slowly released the tension on the Halligan and let the beam back down into place. He didn't see or feel any shifts in the structure, so he pulled it free and turned. Grant had the woman in his arms and they got the hell out of there as quickly as they could. They had to stop a couple of times and turn the hose on hot spots that flamed up, and Aidan could hear

Grant yelling to the woman the entire time. He told her over and over she'd be okay, and he tried to keep her face tucked toward his coat.

The woman had stopped coughing and was limp in Grant's arms when they cleared the building, and the kid ran straight to the ambulance with her. They were ready because of the constant radio contact, and Aidan watched Grant back out of the way, his gaze never leaving the woman.

Stepping forward, he pulled off his helmet and mask before putting a hand on the younger man's shoulder. There weren't really any words that would help. Aidan and most of the others had been there. They'd pulled a lot of people out of harm's way. They'd been too late more often than he cared to dwell on, retrieving bodies instead of rescuing victims.

The worst, though, was getting to a person on time and racing to the ambulance, only to have EMS sadly shake their heads. It had happened to Aidan only twice, and both times he'd been torn up. Could he have run faster? If he'd gone down one hallway instead of another, would it have made a difference? He'd lain in bed, staring at the ceiling and trying to count off the seconds every action and decision had taken him in an effort to convince himself he couldn't have saved the victim by making a different choice.

Suddenly the woman was coughing and Aidan felt Grant's shoulder sag as the tension left his body. "Good job, kid."

Walsh, who'd stood by to kill the water pressure, gave them a nod. "Nice job. I heard the EMS talking about her husband. He's going to be fine, obviously, but all he could talk about was how his wife had been nagging him to fix the smoke detectors."

"If they'd been working, she wouldn't have gotten pinned down," Aidan said. "That would have been a shitty thing for him to live with the rest of his life."

"Yeah. I guess one kept going off in the middle of the night and he couldn't figure out why, so he ripped them all down." Walsh shook his head. "And then fell asleep smoking a cigarette. Okay, get a drink, you guys, and then we'll see what's up."

Once he'd drained a quarter of a water bottle, Aidan pulled out his phone to text Lydia.

Fire today. I'm not hurt. Just FYI.

He grinned and hit Send. Yesterday, she'd threatened to run his phone over after he sent her constant updates, like *had to help a roofer get off a roof because he sprained his ankle on a loose shingle, but I'm okay.*

He was deliberately being a pain in the ass, he knew, but she had it coming. In the three days since they'd had their less-than-pleasant discussion about her not wanting to be a firefighter's wife, they hadn't mentioned it again. But he hadn't forgotten about it, either.

You can forget that blow job I owe you.

Ouch. She wasn't playing nice anymore.

This was a big fire. We saved a woman, so we might be on the news. I was only thinking of you.

You're only thinking of being a pain in my ass.

There was a pause, and then a second text came through.

But I'm glad you saved the woman and that you're okay.

So the blow job?

I'm working. Gotta run.

He chuckled and snapped the phone back into its holster. He should know better than to play games with a Kincaid. They weren't above playing dirty if it meant they won.

"Still the blonde?" Scotty asked, sitting next to him on the bumper.

Aidan was totally blank for a second, and then he nodded. "Uh, yeah. The blonde from the market."

"She have a name yet?"

"No. I haven't seen her again. We've just been texting here and there, but it's gone on too long to ask her at this point."

"Maybe you'll get lucky and she'll send you a Facebook friend request or something before you get together and she figures out you have no clue what her name is." Scotty shook his head. "Women don't like that too much."

Aidan downed some more water so he didn't have to answer. The less he said to Scott at this point, the fewer lies he was forced to tell. He hated it, more than his best friend would probably believe if he ever found out, and sometimes it literally made his stomach ache.

"I guess we should see if those guys need a hand," Scotty said, nodding toward the men still working on making sure the fire was totally out. "But let me know if you and the blonde from the market want to go out sometime. I've got a few women I could call so I'm not the third wheel, and it could be a group thing. And, since I've got your back, I can find a way to introduce myself so she has to tell me her name herself. Problem solved."

Shame burned like acid in his stomach. Scotty had his back. He always had. And now Aidan was going *behind* his back. "Yeah, I'll let you know."

"THIS IS GOING to blow up in your face. And in his. It'll be bad, Lydia."

Lydia knew Ashley was right, but she didn't want to hear it right now. She had only a couple of hours before she had to open the bar and, since Aidan was home, she wanted to spend those hours with him. They were trying to limit the late nights after the bar closed because, as they'd both agreed, they were too damn old to stay up half the night, even for sex, and still function the next day.

"Nothing's blowing up in anybody's faces," she said.

"Look at you. You're like a teenager going to the prom and all you're going to do is hang out for a couple of hours before you go to work. You can't tell me you're just having some hot sex to get it out of your system now."

"Sure I can. I just haven't gotten it out of my system yet."

"Whatever." Ashley yanked the vacuum cleaner's cord out of the wall. "It'll be no big deal for you. You'll just run back to New Hampshire. Aidan will be the one left here with a broken friendship and, honestly, he'll probably end up having to transfer to a different house."

"He's a grown man, making his own choices," Lydia responded, but the words made her feel a little sick inside. Under the bitchy tone, what her sister said was probably true.

The words stayed with her on the way to Aidan's, and she sat in her car for a minute after parking it on the main street where there were plenty of businesses offering excuses for being there.

It was hard to tell how Scotty would react if he found out Aidan and Lydia had been hooking up. They were both assuming he'd be pissed, but maybe he wouldn't care. Hell, maybe he'd even be happy, thinking the relationship might go the distance and Aidan would be his brother-in-law. Lydia didn't think so, though. Or at least she wasn't willing to bet on it, with the stakes being so high for Aidan.

She walked down the street and turned the corner to Aidan's building. After jogging up the back stairs to the third floor, she gave a quick knock and let herself in. Aidan walked out of the bedroom when she called for him, looking annoyed.

"Hey," he said. He gave her a quick kiss, but his mind was elsewhere. "I can't find my damn phone. And I can't call it because I don't have a landline anymore."

"You didn't do any laundry this morning, did you?"

"No. And I checked the hamper to make sure I didn't leave it in my pocket, even though I've never done that. Send me a text so I can listen for the ding."

Lydia grabbed her phone and sent a happy face emoticon to his phone and listened for the notification. "I think it came from the couch."

"I already looked there."

"I have smaller hands. I can reach farther down in the cushions."

A quick search turned up nothing, so Lydia typed *dumbass* into the box and hit Send again. This time they were ready and she shoved her hand down behind the cushion, feeling around until she came up with his phone. She started to hand it to him, but then she noticed the text previews on his lock screen and pulled her hand back.

"Who is *Blonde from market*?" She looked at the screen again, then shook her head. "Wait. I'm the one who called you a dumbass. You have me saved in your contacts as *Blonde from market*?"

"It's a long story."

She crossed her arms, his phone still clutched in her hand. "If you want your phone back, you should probably make the time to tell it."

He grinned. "You know I can take that phone away from you if I want to, right?"

"Maybe you can, but you'll need bandages and Bengay later."

"I believe you." He sat down on the couch and

laced his fingers together on top of his head as he leaned back against the cushion. It was a favorite position of his and usually she liked the effect it had on his biceps and chest, but she wasn't going to be distracted right now. "Remember the day you texted me while I was on my way to a promotion ceremony?"

"Yeah."

"When you sent that, I was mashed up against Scotty in the backseat of Rick's truck and my phone was just kind of in my hand. I turned it before he saw your name on the screen, but I realized he grabs my phone sometimes. So I changed your name in my contacts."

"Because you didn't want him to know I was texting you."

"He might think it was a little weird, and some of the texts you've sent…no, I don't want him reading them."

Lydia wasn't sure how she felt about the depths Aidan was going to in order to keep their relationship a secret. It made her feel as if she was doing something wrong and she really wasn't. But Aidan obviously thought *he* was, and so he was lying to his best friend. Then it got weird because Scotty was her brother and she knew his best friend was lying to him, which should make her angry on his behalf.

All of that on top of what Ashley had said was too much, and she wanted to kick a garbage barrel or something to let off steam. The entire situation was seriously messed up and obviously a huge part of why you didn't sleep with your brother's best friend.

"Why *Blonde from market*?" she asked, because that seemed a little random. "You could have at least left me a brunette."

"Scotty asked me how I saved her in my contacts since I couldn't remember her name and it just came out of my mouth at the time," he replied. When he shrugged his shoulders with his hands on his head like that, it made his biceps flex, which she liked. "I'm not a good liar, so it's been a challenge."

"Or you could just tell him."

His mouth tightened as he considered her words. "You really think that's a good idea?"

Lydia tried to imagine what her brother's reaction would be if Aidan told him he'd been sleeping with her, and it wouldn't be pretty. "I don't like that you have to lie to him. I know that bothers you."

"You're right. I hate lying to him and the more I lie to him, the worse it'll be if I tell him."

She mentally flailed for a solution. "Maybe we can pretend we haven't been seeing each other and you can bring it up to see how he reacts. If he freaks out, then we're still a secret. But if he's okay with it, then we go out on a date and pick up where nobody knows we left off."

"If he freaks out, that would be the end of it. What I'm doing now is shitty. If I kept seeing you after he said no…I couldn't do that to him."

She could see in his eyes how much it tore him up, and she hated it. "I think Ashley's starting to get bored and she'll need to start making money again, so pretty soon I'll probably be back in New Hampshire and you won't have to."

That didn't seem to make him feel any better. If anything, his mouth got even tighter and his eyes more troubled. He dropped his hands to his lap and then held one out to her. "I don't want to think about that right now."

She thought he was reaching for his phone and, since he had told her the story as requested, she put it in his hand. But he just dropped the phone into his lap and reached out again. "Come sit with me."

When she took his hand, he pulled her down so she was sitting next to him. Lydia wanted to change the subject to pretty much anything other than her brother and New Hampshire, and she had a good idea of how to do that.

Turning sideways, she leaned her head against his shoulder and ran her hand over his stomach. His abs tightened in response, making her smile. "Sometimes the fact you're always running around in just your boxer briefs is very convenient."

"Oh yeah? How so?"

She slid just the tips of her fingers under the elastic waistband. "Easy access."

He moaned when her fingers stroked the length of his erection, and closed his eyes for a moment. She wasn't surprised when he opened them again, though. He'd want to watch.

"I should see if I can make you beg," she told him.

"Nope." He lifted his hips so his hot, hard flesh

brushed her palm. "I didn't make you beg for my hand down your pants in the storage closet, did I?"

She closed her fingers around his hard length and smiled when he groaned, deep in his throat. Then she stroked him with long and slow strokes, watching his face. "But we're not talking about my hand. We're talking about my mouth."

"I'd beg for your mouth."

It was tempting to make him, but she wasn't in the mood for games. She moved over on the cushion so she had room to bend down and then very slowly circled her tongue around the head of his cock.

Her hair fell forward and she shoved at with her free hand, but it wouldn't stay. She was debating on how much it would kill his mood if she paused to throw an elastic in it when she felt his hands gathering it.

He held it all in one fist, and she knew it was as much so he could see her face as to keep her hair out of the way. She licked her lips, making him groan in anticipation, and then closed her mouth over him.

With the same slow, lazy rhythm he liked to torment her with, she drew him into her mouth and then raised her head again. When his hand tightened in her hair, she stopped and closed her lips only around the head of his cock. She swirled her tongue around the tip and resisted when he gave her head a little nudge.

He muttered a mix of curses and pleas under his breath, and she closed her hand around the base of his dick. Squeezing gently, she worked her hand up to meet her mouth and then back again.

His breath grew ragged and she took him fully into her mouth again, until her lips met her curled fingers. Then she worked them together—her mouth and her fist—in fast, deep strokes. He groaned her name, his fist in her hair tightening almost to the point of being painful, and then he was coming. She stroked him until the orgasm passed, swallowing without losing the rhythm.

When he was finished, she ran her tongue over the tip and then pulled the waistband of his boxer briefs back into place. Aidan hauled her up and into his lap, holding her close and kissing her hair.

"Gimme a few minutes," he said, still catching his breath, "and then we'll see if I can make *you* beg."

Now that was a game she could get behind.

DANNY TOOK A LONG and slow breath before he opened the front door of his parents' house and walked inside. It felt weird to just walk in, even after years of doing it, but his old man had gotten pissed about having to get off his ass to answer the door, only to find out it was his son.

Neither his brother nor sister was around, which suited Danny just fine. He loved them, he supposed, and would always be there for them if they needed him. But he didn't like them very much and all of them in the small house at the same time could be a bit much.

"Ma," he yelled from just inside the door, since he still felt a need to announce himself.

"In the kitchen!"

Of course she was. It was a room her husband rarely ventured into, preferring to have his wife deliver anything he wanted to his recliner that had been parked in the living room for as long as Danny could remember.

His mom looked a lot older than the last time he saw her, even though it had only been five or six months. Or maybe she just looked that way to him because she'd lost some weight. He kissed her cheek, noticing she still smelled like cigarette smoke even though the doctor had warned her to quit at least a year ago.

"It's good to see you," she said in her raspy, chainsmoker's voice.

"You, too, Ma. Where's Dad?"

She sneered. "He went upstairs because he's a moron and he had a frappe for lunch even though the doctor told him he's lactose intolerant."

Danny wasn't sure why his parents even bothered seeing doctors. He couldn't think of a single time either of them had ever listened to the advice they were given. "What is it you need me to do?"

He realized after he asked it that the question probably sounded abrupt, but he didn't care. His mother had asked him for a favor and he'd do it, but he didn't want to be in this house any longer than necessary.

"I need you to change the lightbulb in the laundry room," she said. "I've been asking your father to do it for two months, but you know how he is. The only light I have is what shines in from the hallway."

Danny just walked to the high cabinet over the

fridge without saying a word. If there was anything that pissed his father off more than the existence of his youngest son, it was his youngest son having to come over and do the chores the old man should be doing himself. That meant this visit was going to be especially fun, he thought as he took a box of cheap lightbulbs down. Maybe if his mother spent more on the damn things, they wouldn't need to be changed so often.

He was almost done when he heard the thump of his father's feet on the stairs, and he sighed. He'd almost made it.

After flipping the switch to make sure the new bulb worked, Danny took the burned-out bulb into the kitchen to throw in the garbage. His dad was standing in the doorway, his arms folded across his chest.

"Fire department changing lightbulbs now?"

As greetings went, it wasn't exactly warm. "I stopped by. The light needed changing."

"So you're here taking care of my house, but you can't keep your own in order?" Danny clenched his jaw, refusing to rise to the bait. "Heard Ashley threw you out. Guess you fucked that up."

"Guess so," he agreed in an emotionless monotone. His old man fed on emotions like some kind of mythological monster, and the more you fed him, the more ravenous and ruthless he got.

"I like Ashley," his mother said. "I hope you didn't cheat on her."

"I didn't."

"Her old man's an asshole," his dad declared, even

though the only time he'd met Tommy Kincaid was at Danny and Ashley's wedding. "You're better off without them."

"I'm not better off without my wife," Danny responded. He knew it was a mistake, but his dad dismissing his marriage so easily didn't sit right.

His dad snorted. "So you'll go crawling back to her, then, like the little pussy you've always been. You probably let her keep your balls in a jar instead of standing up for yourself like a real man."

And that was his cue to leave, but before he could say so, his mother made it worse. "Shut up, Lou. What do you know about being a real man? We been married forty-five years and you still don't know shit about how marriage is supposed to be."

"Maybe if I wasn't married to a bitch, always yapping at me. *Yap, yap, yap,* like a fucking Chihuahua."

Danny felt himself shut down inside. He'd been listening to this his entire life, and he knew nothing he could say would make it stop. And, if he tried, they'd probably turn on him.

He was done. "I'm leaving."

"You just got here," his mother protested, as if he was skipping out on a fun family afternoon.

"Let him go," his father said. "He's probably going to go lick his wounds, like a little bitch."

"Stay and have some coffee cake."

If he hadn't grown up in this house, he might have found her offer of coffee cake in the face of his father calling him a little bitch jarring, but this was how they communicated and always had. But this time, he couldn't lock his emotions down like he'd always done.

He didn't like these people. He felt absolutely nothing for them except disgust and a vague sense of obligation because they were, after all, his parents. They were toxic, and every time he was in this house, they poisoned him a little bit more.

After glancing at each of them, he shook his head and walked to the front door. And when he passed through it and felt the rush of fresh air as he walked down the stairs, he swore it was the last time he'd ever step foot in that house.

It was time to make some changes in his life. He wasn't sure yet how he was going to fix his marriage, but instinct told him letting go of his toxic past was a step in the right direction.

THIRTEEN

LYDIA'S CELL PHONE ringing jerked her out of a really nice dream and she wanted to sink back into it, but it was already sliding away from her. A pickup truck, a dirt road and she and Aidan holding hands were all she could remember now.

Maybe she shouldn't have let some friendly, money-spending customers talk her into changing the radio to a country station the night before, she thought as she reached for her phone.

The caller ID showed it was Shelly, her roommate in New Hampshire, and she groaned. She'd paid her rent in advance and Shelly hadn't been upset, so hopefully this wasn't an *I'm evicting you* phone call. It was too early. "Hello?"

"Hey, did I wake you up?"

Shelly was not only an incurable morning person, but one of those really chipper morning people that not-morning people wanted to smack upside the head with the toaster. "I'm awake. What's up?"

It was almost thirty minutes before Lydia was able to extricate herself from the call because Shelly wanted to catch up. Lydia just wanted coffee. She would have gone down to the kitchen, since cell phones were nothing if not portable, but she really needed the bathroom before she had coffee and she couldn't pee while on the phone.

When she finally made it to the coffeepot, Ashley had the fridge door propped open with the garbage barrel and was cleaning it out. Lydia was surrounded by morning people.

"Did I hear your phone ring?" Ashley asked her. "Everything okay?"

"Yeah, but I need to go back to Concord for the weekend. Shelly wants to go see her sister's new baby and she can't take the cat."

Ashley gave her a sideways look. "It's a cat. You put down extra food and water before you leave and make sure the litter box is clean. A cat can handle a couple of days without a human. Knowing cats, it's probably their version of a vacation."

"Oscar's kind of Shelly's baby. She won't leave the cat alone and she can't find anybody else to stay with him because most people reacted like you did and she doesn't trust them now."

"Okay." Ashley was quiet for a long moment, and then she took a deep breath. "So you need me to work for you? It's okay if you do. I mean, I guess I have to go back sometime, but you know they like to play pool on Saturday nights and—"

Lydia held up a hand to stop her. "I already sent a text to Karen and she's going to cover for me."

Her sister's relief was almost palpable. "Okay. Didn't she and Rick break up, though? I thought I heard that from one of the other wives, who called to tell me about some sale at the secondhand store, but really just wanted to get the latest gossip about my marriage."

"They're not seeing each other anymore, but I don't know if I'd say they broke up. They were *really* casual, I guess. She met somebody less casual and told Rick the dinner, movie and sex part of their relationship was over, but they're still friends."

"I'm glad to hear it. Not just because she'll still cover your shifts at the bar. I like her, so I'm glad she'll still be around."

"I'll probably grab some different clothes while I'm home," Lydia said. "I'm getting bored with my very limited rotating wardrobe. I mean, half the time I'm wearing a Kincaid's T-shirt anyway, but I miss my favorite fleece hoodie when it's chilly."

"You'll come back, right?"

Lydia looked at her sister and saw the very real concern on her face. It worried her, because it wasn't like Ashley to hide away like this and Lydia was starting to wonder if she should be enabling her. Maybe she needed to shove her sister back into the real world and tell her to suck it up.

But she also felt like things would be coming to a head between Ashley and Danny soon. They weren't going to be able to keep on the way they were and there was either going to be an emotional breakthrough that brought them back together or an emotional breakdown that ended the marriage for good. Either way, Lydia couldn't imagine not being there for Ashley.

"I'm coming back," Lydia promised. "You know what would be awesome? If Aidan could go with me. We could get away from here and go out for dinner or something—like a real date—without worrying about anybody seeing us and telling Scott or Dad."

"You should invite him. He can work it out with the other guys. I know he's always willing to cover for them, so a bunch of the guys probably owe him a favor."

"You don't think both of us disappearing at the same time will be suspicious at all?"

"I guess if somebody picked up on it, it might seem a little weird. There has to be a way, though."

Lydia gave her a hard look. "Weren't you the one worried about this blowing up in everybody's faces?"

"Yeah, but you're an adult and you can do what you want. And I owe you big-time, so if you want to get out of town with Aidan for the weekend, I'll help you make it happen."

Lydia frowned. "So where could he say he was going? If his family lived farther away, he could say it was a family emergency, but he can take the T from his place, so disappearing wouldn't make much sense. And he's not close with them."

"Maybe we're looking at it the wrong way," Ashley said. "Have you told anybody else at all you need to go back to Concord? Did you tell Karen why you need the time off?"

"No. Shelly just called a few minutes ago so I haven't talked to anybody else yet, and I didn't tell Karen why because it was a text and I can't type that much before coffee."

"So don't tell anybody what you're doing. We'll say you're wicked sick. Your car will be in the driveway and you'll be in bed, right? You start laying the groundwork tonight, like you don't feel so hot."

That might actually work. "But where's Aidan going to say he's going? It would have to be something that came up suddenly, since all they do when they're not on a run is sit around and yap at each other and he wouldn't have big plans they don't know about."

"I don't know. He could still use his family as an excuse. Maybe they want him to remodel the bathroom or something and it's easier if he just stays there. If he says his dad wants to use him for manual labor because he's too cheap to pay a professional, the guys will believe that."

"And probably offer to help."

"His mom doesn't want a bunch of firefighters running around in her house. She can barely tolerate the one she gave birth to, from what I've heard." Ashley grinned. "It will totally work. And I'm excited for you. It'll be fun."

"I should probably ask *him* if he wants to go."

"Hell yeah, I want to go," Aidan told her several

hours later, when he had a chance to return her call. "I can get the time off, but won't it look a little weird if we both disappear at the same time?"

"There's a plan," she said, and she filled him in on the scheme she and Ashley had concocted. It was brilliant in its simplicity, really. Nobody was going to insist on going up the stairs and into her bedroom to see if she was really sick in bed, especially her dad or brother. They wanted nothing to do with sick women. And if anybody sent her a text, she could just text them back.

"You really thought this through." There was a short silence, and then she heard him blow out a breath close to the cell's microphone. "God, I hate lying."

Lydia felt a pang of guilt. "I know you do. Look, it's no big deal if you don't want to—"

"I want to," he interrupted. "I definitely want to."

The eagerness in his voice made her smile. He sure was good for a girl's ego. "I'm glad. I'm looking forward to it."

"So did you and Ashley come up with a plan for a secret handoff in a parking garage with your hood pulled up, or will I just pick you up at her house?"

She laughed, trying to picture that scenario. "I think you can just pick me up at Ashley's. Let me know when you've worked out your schedule and we can figure out a time."

"Okay. Are you going to stop by after work?"

She shouldn't. They were becoming too much like

a real couple as it was, and now they were going on a couple's weekend getaway. Their casual fling was in danger of becoming a lot less casual. But she wanted to see him. She *always* wanted to see him.

"I'll be there," she said, mentally kicking herself in the ass. "But I can't stay long."

"I don't care if it's only long enough so I can give you a hug and a hello. And a kiss. I'd stop by Kincaid's for the hello, since I just want to see you, but the kissing would be awkward."

"I'd rather kiss you without an audience."

"I'll be waiting."

To GET THE ENTIRE weekend off, Aidan worked the day tour on Friday, but it was a blessedly quiet day outside of some routine calls. At 6:30 Friday evening, he parked on the street in front of Ashley's house and got out of his truck.

He'd warned Lydia he hadn't been able to get out of his commitment to dinner at his parents' house on Sunday, since he hadn't been in a while, but she'd told him they could be back in plenty of time. The roommate would be back by Sunday night and Oscar the cat could survive a few hours of solitude.

He made it as far as stepping around the front of the truck and onto the curb when the door opened and Lydia walked out. She was walking fast, with a duffel bag in her hand and the hood of her sweatshirt pulled over her head. She gestured for him to get back in the truck, which made him laugh, even though he did it.

"You're kidding, right?" he asked when she'd hopped into the passenger seat and closed the door.

"Just go."

He pulled away from the curb and started making his way toward the highway. Friday evening traffic could suck, and it would be a longer than usual drive north. "I was going to go inside and say hi to Ashley. I didn't realize this was a covert mission."

She pulled her hood down and smoothed her hair. "Ashley was on the phone with Danny. And you know how neighbors are. This way, if anybody says anything, Ashley can claim it was her and you were helping her out with something that required a pickup truck."

Her neighbors must be idiots, then, because she and Ashley didn't look alike, even with their heads covered. "You guys sure covered all the bases."

She laughed, leaning her head back against the headrest. "I think we were bored, so we amused ourselves with this little adventure. The hood might have been too much."

They stopped for coffee and a drive-through dinner once they were out of their neighborhood, and they made small talk as the miles passed. She always had funny stories about Kincaid's over the years, and he shared a few sibling tales from his childhood. He didn't dip into work stories because he wanted to keep Scotty and the fact he was a firefighter on the back burner this weekend, at least as much as possible.

"I haven't seen a single cow yet," he said when

they were about twenty minutes into New Hampshire. "Where do they keep all the cows?"

She laughed, but when he didn't, she quieted and looked over at him. "You were kidding, right?"

"I heard there were cows."

"They don't keep them in the highway median strip, dumbass." When he grinned, she realized he was joking and slapped his arm. "And you've been here many times. You've been to Hampton Beach a few times, and you've been up here four-wheeling. And there was a big paintball thing you guys did. I remember Scott having a wicked welt on his face because one of the other guys accidently shot him when he had his face shield up."

So much for leaving her brother on the back burner. He supposed it was natural, since they were all tied together so closely, but he wanted it to be just him and Lydia this weekend.

She finally gave him the heads-up that they'd be getting off at the next exit and he moved out of the fast lane. A few turns, stoplights and stop signs later, she told him to turn into a small lot beside a huge square, brick building and to park in one of the two spaces marked for unit three.

"Nice building," he said as he killed the ignition. "It looks old."

"It is, but it was rehabbed inside about ten years ago, so it's not too shabby."

He slung the strap of his bag over his shoulder and grabbed her duffel before locking up his truck and following her inside. The apartment she shared with Shelly was half of the second floor, and he couldn't help being curious as she unlocked the door to let them in.

He'd seen her at the bar and at Scotty's and her dad's. He hadn't seen Lydia at Ashley's place, but he'd been there a few times because of Danny and could picture her there. And, obviously, he'd seen her at his place, but he couldn't remember ever seeing the inside of the house she'd shared with Todd. He'd waited in the vehicle a few times when Scotty stopped by for something quick, but had never gone inside.

So, even though she shared the apartment with a roommate, this would be the first time he got to see a space Lydia had made for herself.

"Everything you see pretty much belongs to Shelly," she said, stepping aside to let him in. "She's been here for years, but I'm her third roommate. So we split the rent, but it's mostly her place, if you know what I mean."

It was neat, without a lot of clutter. The furniture was on the feminine side, covered in floral fabrics, and there were lace doilies under the lamps. But there were some cool art prints on the walls, and he looked at them while she said hello to a tortoiseshell cat that sauntered out of a bedroom to see what they were up to.

"I have to text Shelly a selfie of Oscar and me, so she knows I'm here. She had to leave by noon to get to the airport and she was a nervous wreck about leaving before I got here."

Aidan snorted. "Should I go buy a newspaper so you can make sure the date shows in the photo, like a proof of life?"

"She didn't mention that, but probably only because she didn't think of it." He watched her pick up the cat and carry it to the couch. "We actually get along really well—me and Shelly, I mean—which is nice. She has a lot of anxiety about her cat, but I can live with that. Right, Oscar?"

Once she'd texted a photo of her and the cat to her roommate and had a brief text conversation, Lydia grabbed her bag. "Come on and I'll show you my room."

Unlike the rest of the apartment, her bedroom showed a little bit of Lydia's personality. There were no floral fabrics or doilies in this room, but there were some family photos framed on the bureau and a Red Sox throw blanket tossed over a plain wooden chair in the corner. The bedding was a light blue, with darker blue throw pillows. Instead of art, there were sports posters hung on her walls, and when he peeked into the bathroom, he saw a lot of hair stuff and almost no makeup. Definitely Lydia's bathroom.

"This is it," she said, sitting on the edge of the bed. "Welcome to my very humble abode."

"I like it," he said, sitting next to her. He bounced a little on the mattress and then nudged her with his elbow. "Doesn't squeak. I like that in a bed."

"I like *you* in a bed," she said, nudging him back, and that was all the invitation he needed to make himself at home.

Lydia stretched, then froze when her leg kicked something hard. Aidan's shin, she realized when she opened her eyes. They were in Concord, far away from prying eyes and gossip, and she had the entire day—and Aidan—all to herself.

"Ow."

"Good morning," she said, rolling to face him. "What do you want to do today?"

He blinked because she'd forgotten to close the blinds last night and the sun burned through the thin, decorative curtains. "I'd say spend the day in bed with you, but these sheets are really abrasive."

She laughed and tried to hit him in the shoulder, but he caught her hand and kissed her knuckles instead. "You're a sheet snob."

"Blame my mother. And this is your weekend. What do *you* want to do? Does it have to be something the cat can do with us?"

"No, Oscar won't be joining us."

"Are you sure? I feel kind of bad we locked the poor guy out of the bedroom last night."

"You would have felt worse if we'd let him in and he'd buried his claws in some soft, vulnerable part of your body." He winced. "And yes, I once had to hide in here and try not to laugh at a guest of Shelly's swearing while she put first aid cream on the gouges Oscar left on his right ass cheek."

"Ouch. That's worse than scratchy sheets."

"Keep it up and you can sleep with Oscar tonight." She sighed and snuggled closer to his chest. He threw his arm over her and kissed her hair. "I want to go out today. I don't even care where. I want to walk around holding your hand and you can kiss me in public and then we can go to a restaurant and have a nice dinner together."

"Sounds like a perfect day."

After they'd showered and made sure Oscar had enough food, water and affection to last him a few hours, they went to Lydia's favorite breakfast restaurant. It was too far to walk, so she gave him a mini tour of the city after they'd eaten.

"And that's the restaurant I worked at until Ashley called me and asked me to help her out," she said, pointing to the building that was probably meant to look elegant, but looked stuffy and overblown to her.

"Do you miss it?"

She laughed. "Not even for a second. I hated that job."

"Why didn't you get a different one?"

"The money was good." She shrugged. "I hated it and I found out I'm not very good at serving fancy dinners or being formal with those kinds of diners, but when the check is high, the tip is, too."

"Were you saving for something?"

"What do you mean?"

"To be worth being unhappy at work, it seems like you must have had a goal. Something you wanted to do or buy."

"Not really. I guess I would have liked to get my own apartment at some point but, like I said, Shelly and I get along really well. And my car runs fine. I thought about doing some college courses, but there's nothing I really want to do that's worth the money, time and work. I like what I do, just not where I was doing it."

"How does it feel being back at Kincaid's?"

She sighed, looking out the window. "That's a tough question. I've always loved working there. I just haven't always loved working for my dad and being surrounded by…everybody we know."

"Like firefighters," he said, but he turned his head to give her a quick grin as he said it.

"Yeah. I don't know anybody here. I'm nobody's daughter or sister or ex-wife."

"Speaking of which," he said, yanking the truck into an open parking space. "There are all kinds of neat shops on this street and I'm tired of driving around. Let's walk for a little while."

They spent several hours walking down one side of the street and up the other, ducking into any of the shops that interested them. She bought a couple of books, and a few storefronts later, she had to talk him out of spending way too much money on a cool guitar he didn't know how to play. They walked hand in hand, enjoying the sunshine and the lazy nature of not having anywhere to be.

"I can see why you like it here," he said after a while. "Plenty to see and do, but there's a little more room to breathe."

"It's nice. It's different, but not *too* different."

"So you're going to come back here, then? When Ashley's ready to take over the bar again."

Lydia didn't stop walking, but something froze inside of her. "That's the plan. This is where I live now, which you know since you slept in my bed with the crappy sheets last night."

He chuckled at her joke, but it sounded forced to her. "I didn't know if things had changed. You quit your job, so the only thing actually tying you here is a bedroom. And you told me you like working at the bar."

She'd also told him there were things she *didn't* like about working at Kincaid's, and he knew how she felt about the community as a whole. They might be family, but she wanted out of the goldfish bowl. "There are bars in Concord. There's actually a sports bar in walking distance I might check out when Ashley's ready to go back to work."

He nodded, but fell silent for a few minutes. It was an awkward silence, but Lydia wasn't sure how to fill it. As dismaying as the thought was, maybe this weekend getaway had been a bad idea because she couldn't have it both ways. She'd wanted to spend some time alone with Aidan, but the more they did things like a real couple, the harder it was to remember they actually weren't.

"Hey." Aidan squeezed her hand and she looked up to see him smiling at her. "Stop overthinking things and enjoy the day. Is there some place on this street we can get some ice cream before we go check on Oscar?"

A dish of black raspberry drowning in whipped cream and jimmies went a long way toward saving the weekend. And when Aidan let her have a lick of his soft-serve twist and then kissed her with a sweet, sticky mouth, Lydia decided to stop worrying about tomorrow and just enjoy the hell out of today.

FOURTEEN

AIDAN WAS STRETCHED out on the floral couch, having a stare-down with the cat perched on his chest like a Sphinx. Oscar was purring so hard they were both vibrating. "I can't decide if this cat really likes me or if he's trying to keep me pinned down so I can't do anything nefarious."

"It's probably some kind of subliminal mind control," Lydia told him. "Cats are like that."

"You gave him food and water, and now you're scooping his shit out of his box so it's all fresh and clean. What else could he possibly need?"

"To rule the world. Obviously you haven't spent a lot of time around cats."

"My sister's allergic to them and I've always been a little afraid of them. I dated a girl in high school—do you remember Nicole, uh…do you remember Nicole's last name?"

She laughed. "No, I don't remember your high school girlfriend *or* her last name. I was probably too busy doing adult things since I was already an adult and didn't have time for you and Scotty's little-boy doings."

"Funny. Four years, Lydia. It's not like you were my babysitter or anything. Although that could have been hot."

"You're digressing," she said, and he heard the kitchen faucet run as she washed her hands.

"Anyway, this girl Nicole had a cat and I remember they were always complaining because it would try to trip them on the stairs. Who keeps pets that want you dead?"

Before she could answer, his phone chimed and he stretched his arm out to pick it up off the coffee table. Oscar refused to move and just continued to stare intently at him and vibrate.

How's it going?

It was Scotty, and Aidan sat up, using his hand to gently nudge Oscar down so he didn't try to hold on by way of sheer cat will and very sharp claws.

Ok. What's up?

Bored. Need a hand?

He sighed and thought back to the lie he'd told the guys to get this time off with Lydia. He was helping his mom replace and fix a few things around the house because the other Hunt men weren't as handy as they were cheap.

Probably not. It's one-guy stuff and I think she just wants to visit with me while Dad's on biz trip.

It was one more believable lie, made possible by

the fact Scotty knew how screwed up the Hunt family dynamics were.

Don't you have family dinner tomorrow night?

Oops. There was that small detail.

He'll be back for that.

That's too bad. Probably more fun without him. I'll see you Monday morning, then.

Aidan set the phone back on the table with a sigh. He was getting better at lying, which was a skill he'd never wanted to improve on.

"I'm guessing that was my brother," Lydia said, and he looked up to see her leaning against the kitchen counter, her arms crossed.

"How did you know?"

"Because you look like you're beating yourself up about something and it seems to me the most likely reason is that you had to lie to Scott."

He *really* didn't want to put a damper on this weekend. "Yeah, it was him. He's bored and wanted to know if I needed a hand at my mom's house."

"I guess it's a good thing he didn't just show up there."

Aidan shook his head. "He's only met my parents a few times, at ceremonies and stuff, and they've never been particularly warm to him. We always hung out at Tommy's and never at my parents'."

But it did go to show there were so many ways they could get tripped up when it came to lying and hiding their relationship from the people who knew them better than anybody else.

"I'd rather talk about Nicole-from-high-school more than my brother right now," she said.

He stood up, brushing cat hair off the front of his shirt. The stuff was everywhere and the more he tried to brush it off, the more it seemed to multiply. "I'd rather take you out for a nice dinner somewhere than talk about either of them."

When Lydia grinned and shoved away from the counter, Aidan felt his spirits rally. "Yeah, you're the one who told me to stop overthinking things and just enjoy this day."

"Yes, I did. So let's go enjoy the hell out of it."

They decided they didn't want to go anywhere *too* nice, because they were both comfortable in their jeans, though they traded the T-shirts for nicer shirts with buttons. While she brushed her hair and put on a little makeup, he sat on the edge of the bed and used his phone to pull up possibilities.

"Pasta," he said. "I could go for pasta."

"Carbs. Yay." He laughed and looked at her. Since she was facing away from him, he had a perfect view of her ass and legs, which he thought were perfect the way they were. And, since she was looking in a mirror, she saw him looking and rolled her eyes. "I could do pasta, but you have to help me work it off later."

He met her gaze in the mirror and his blood rushed from his brain to his dick. "Maybe you should have seconds, too."

"You keep looking at me like that and you'll be

lucky if I let you out of bed long enough to make a sandwich."

As threats went, it wasn't a very strong one. He thought about it for a minute because it was tempting as hell to drag her into bed right that very second and stay there. But having her in bed wasn't something he lacked, although at times he wished he could have her there all night and every night. But taking her out for dinner in a public restaurant was a pleasure he hadn't experienced yet.

"I've been waiting for days to take you out on a date," he said. "You're not talking me out of it now."

"A date, huh?" She flipped the bathroom light off as she walked toward him.

"Yeah, I figure it's probably about time we have a first date."

She laughed and offered her hand to help him up. Once he was on his feet, he kissed her, but didn't allow himself to get lost in the moment. Date first, then they could revisit this moment.

The restaurant they went to was a chain place, but they didn't care. At least they knew the pasta would be good. There was a wait, so they sat on the tailgate of his truck in the parking lot, holding hands. She swung her legs and they made small talk, watching people walk by, until their table was ready.

An hour later, he knew he'd made the right choice in not sacrificing this date for sex and sandwiches. Lydia was relaxed, especially after a couple of glasses of wine, and free with her laughter. It was warm and deep, occasionally attracting the attention of nearby diners.

She told him stories about the restaurant she'd worked at before returning to Boston, and he had to laugh, too, at some of her misfortunes in fine dining. He'd like to get in his truck, drive over there and hand the sous-chef a beating, but at least she wouldn't be going back there.

But she'd be coming back here, to Concord.

He shoved the thought down as firmly as he could. When the subject had come up earlier, she'd seemed almost surprised that he would question whether or not she'd leave Boston again. Maybe, on some level, he'd started believing they were building something together and it would be enough for her.

"Hey." Lydia covered his hand with hers, frowning. "You okay?"

"Yeah." He forced a quick laugh. "I was thinking about what a douche bag that sous-chef was."

"Yeah, he had his moments. Some of the regular customers might be a pain in the ass, but at least I don't have to put up with that crap at Kincaid's."

He just smiled at her in the dim lighting and kept his mouth shut. He knew her well enough to know if he pushed, she'd push back twice as hard. But if he kept quiet and just enjoyed one day at a time, she might just realize all on her own that Boston was where her heart was.

"I SHOULD *NOT* have had that dessert," Lydia said, pushing her empty plate away with a groan.

"I think it might take more stamina than I have to work this meal off," Aidan agreed, rubbing his stomach.

"You won't have to expend a lot of energy getting me to take my jeans off."

"This is my kind of first date," he said, and she laughed.

When the server brought the bill, Lydia didn't bother making a show of reaching for her wallet. She knew Aidan and, while she could out-stubborn most people without breaking a sweat, she knew there was no way he'd let her pay for her half of the meal. Not this time, anyway.

He stood when she did and held her hand while they walked to his truck. It was sweet, and she loved that he opened her door for her. And she knew this wasn't a show for their so-called first date, either. Aidan was always polite and over the years, she'd seen him hold the door or pull out chairs for women all the time at the bar, whether they were with him or not. She liked that about him.

Hell, she liked a lot of things about him.

They rode back to her apartment in easy silence, listening to the radio. Once he'd pulled out onto the road, he'd reached over for her hand again and laced his fingers through hers. He seemed to enjoy touching her like that—holding her hand or rubbing her shoulder—and she never got the impression he was trying to put any moves on her. He simply liked touching her.

When they got back to her place, Oscar came walking out of Shelly's room to meow at her. He was presumably voicing his displeasure at being abandoned yet again, but she crouched down and rubbed the top of his head. After a few strokes, he decided he'd had enough and stalked over to Aidan.

While the male human sat in one of the chairs at the kitchen table so the cat could jump on his lap and be the center of his attention, Lydia stopped into the bathroom and then plugged in their phones to charge. "I'm putting mine on Silent. Shelly's probably missing Oscar badly by now and I wouldn't put it past her to want me to video chat with him or something."

"You can put mine on Silent, too."

She looked over at him. "Are you sure?"

"Yes, I'm sure." Still, she hesitated. "I promise I'm sure. Nobody *needs* to talk to me right now. And Cobb knows I'm not at my mother's."

That surprised her. "He does? What did you tell him?"

"I did *not* tell him I was running away with Tommy Kincaid's daughter." He winked at her. "I told him I needed some personal time and that I was telling the guys I'd be at my mom's, but that I would actually be out of town so I can't be called in, no matter how many alarms they strike."

"Oh. Okay, then." She flipped the switch on the side of his phone and plugged it in next to hers.

Oscar got bored and jumped down to twitch his tail at them before sauntering back into Shelly's bedroom. Lydia watched him go, feeling the familiar mash-up of affection for this particular cat while wondering why people wanted to live with cats in general.

"He was keeping my lap warm," Aidan said. "He's good at that, I guess. Like a furry, purring hot water bottle."

"Are your legs getting cold?"

He leaned back and sighed, giving her a sad look. "So cold."

Lydia laughed and straddled his lap, bunching the front of his shirt in one hand. With the other hand, she ran her fingertip over his bottom lip. He tried to catch it between his teeth, but she snatched it away. Then she ran her hand up his neck and curled her fingers into his hair to pull his head back.

Lydia kissed him, enjoying the sensation of having the upper hand, in a way. He was the one tipping his head back and she was in control. She dipped her tongue between his lips, running her nails over his scalp because it made him squirm.

"One more kiss," Aidan said, his voice low. His hands were on her hips and his fingertips pressed into her jeans to keep her from moving.

"It's the sheets, isn't it?" she teased. "You're dreading being naked on them."

He laughed. "I'd happily be naked on burlap or on a sandy beach if you're naked with me."

Warmth flooded her, and she told herself it was

simply physical desire. It wasn't the way that, despite the laugh, she could see in his eyes that he meant that. And, even if she wouldn't admit it, she felt the same.

"One more kiss," Lydia said. "And then we should go to bed."

He tugged her hips forward, seating her more snugly against his obvious erection. "I kind of like this chair. And the couch is closer."

"I wouldn't mind the couch, but I'm not the one with dangling body parts that could be easily mistaken for cat toys."

"Oscar," he hissed, looking around. "Damn cat. Where did he go?"

"He's hiding, waiting for you to drop your pants so he can pounce."

He grinned at her, shaking his head. "Burlap sheets or sand in the crack of my ass, I'm willing to risk for you. Castration by cat claw? A guy's gotta draw a line somewhere."

"One more kiss," she said just before she touched her lips to his.

She kissed him until the ache between her legs was so intense, she caught herself grinding against him. Aidan caught her lower lip between his teeth, biting down until she sucked in a breath. His hands rocked her hips, sliding her back and forth along the length of his cock.

"Let's go get out of these jeans," Lydia whispered against his mouth.

"Don't forget to close the door."

A few minutes later, her bedroom door was closed and she was naked on her scratchy sheets. Aidan, who'd stripped and put on a condom in record time, stretched his body over hers. Propping himself on an elbow, he smoothed her hair away from her face, tucking a few strands behind her ear.

Lydia ran her hands across the smooth, hard planes of his chest. No matter how often she got to touch him, she never tired of exploring the muscles of his chest, shoulders and arms. She knew they had exercise equipment at the station, but his physique was the kind that came from a lifetime of doing physical work and she loved running her hands over his body.

"You get this look on your face when you do that," he said. "It's hard to describe, but it makes me feel like the hottest guy on the planet."

"I like touching you."

When he grasped her behind her knees and opened her legs, she sighed with sweet anticipation. But then he slid into her with exasperating slowness, obviously trying to torture her. Every time she tried to lift her hips, he pulled back the same amount. But she could see by the way he was clenching his jaw that he was tormenting himself just as much as he was her.

"Are you in a hurry?" he teased, but the husky rasp of his voice told her he was suffering. She put her hands on his ass and pressed her fingernails into his skin, just enough to give him a nudge, but he resisted.

"No, I'm not in a hurry," she said, changing tack.

She tucked her hands under her head, as if she was totally relaxed. "Take your time."

He looked down and grinned. "That makes your boobs look amazing."

That made her laugh. "I'll keep that in mind if I ever pose for naked photos."

"No." His expression turned fierce and she put her hands back on his body, running them over his shoulders and biceps before stroking his back. "I don't want anybody else seeing you naked."

Aidan drove into her, burying his cock so deep within her she almost came immediately. She cried out, but he covered her mouth with his. The muscles of his back worked as he fucked her slowly and with long, deliberate strokes—almost pulling out completely before burying himself deep again. When she moaned his name, hovering on the brink, he quickened his pace.

"Come for me," he said, his voice raspy.

And she did. Her muscles spasmed, tightening and releasing as he drove into her, not letting up until her fingernails bit into his back and they were both breathless and trembling from their release.

After a minute, he rolled to his side and kissed her shoulder. Then he went into the bathroom for a minute and Lydia rolled onto her stomach, stretching muscles that were still deliciously warm. She couldn't help remembering the possessive look that had taken over his face when she joked about having naked photos taken, and she smiled.

"That kind of smile's good for a man's ego," Aidan said as he slid back into bed. He pulled the sheet and blanket up over them and then lay on his side so he could throw his arm over her back.

"I don't think your ego's in any need of fluffing," she said, and then she giggled when he slapped her on the ass through the covers.

Then she rolled onto her side so he could spoon her, and her smile changed to one of contentment. It was nice, she thought, curling up with Aidan with no thought of anybody or anything else lurking like a shadow elephant in the room.

Tomorrow they'd go back to Boston and those elephants would start closing in again, but for now she was content to nestle against Aidan's body and feel his breath in her hair.

FIFTEEN

AFTER DROPPING LYDIA off at her sister's and making a quick stop at his place, Aidan made his monthly trek to his parents' house in East Cambridge for a family dinner. The rest of them were there every Sunday, but he'd managed to convince his mother that his work schedule only allowed for one Sunday with the family per month.

During football season, that Sunday usually happened to coincide with the Patriots having the early game, so he could see the whole thing before suffering through the meal. And sometimes he was able to stretch it to six weeks or even two months, though he was expected monthly.

Unfortunately, everybody was already seated around the big dining room table when he walked in, though nobody had food on their plates yet. His father sat at the head of the table and Bryan was at his left, both of them in crisp dress shirts and ties. Bryan's wife, Deborah, sat next to her husband, looking very put together and vaguely unhappy to be there. Aidan's sister, Sarah, was on his father's right, and his mom sat at the foot of the table. The empty chair between Sarah and his mom was for him.

"I'm sorry I'm late, everybody," he said, bending down to kiss his mother's cheek.

She wrinkled her nose. "You smell like gas. And your shirt is smudged. Is that dirt?"

Aidan looked down at sleeve and saw that, yes, there was a small smudge of dirt on it. "I stopped to help a woman who was out of gas, and I must have rubbed against the car trying to get the gas can nozzle into it. I'll go wash up."

"And unroll your sleeves and button the cuffs properly while you're in there," his mother said.

"Honestly, Aidan," his father said, "just once you could keep driving past, you know. Let somebody else stop and help for a change."

It was probably a good thing his old man couldn't be bothered to look up at him, since Aidan figured his expression was probably something like *are you fucking kidding me right now?*

"Helping people is what I do, Dad."

"Yes, we know. Higher calling and all that. But gas delivery boy is stretching it a bit, don't you think?"

Aidan bit down on whatever words might come out of his mouth should he open it and instead walked in silence to the guest bathroom. His old man was pretty damn dismissive for a guy who'd had his head split open by colliding with a tractor trailer and laid in the middle of the road while his wife sat by the guardrail in shock.

And whether he'd grown up to be a firefighter or an investment advisor, Aidan liked to think he was the kind of guy who wouldn't drive by a woman broken down on the side of the road with her kids.

Maybe he shouldn't hold it against his dad. He'd been raised by a family with some money and he'd made even more for himself. John Hunt wouldn't know which end of a wrench to use, and he'd never even changed his own tire. He wouldn't have the slightest idea how to help somebody in trouble, unless it was a financial issue. Aidan knew that. What he found hard to forgive, though, was the implication his father found him somehow *lesser* because of his job.

It was a matter of respect, and his dad not only disrespected him, but pretty much everybody he cared about. It was tough to swallow sometimes, but he washed his hands with the flowery soap and, after a few futile swipes at the dirty streak, fixed his shirt sleeves. He could get through dinner and then he'd be off the hook for another month.

After taking his seat between his mom and Sarah, they started passing the serving dishes. The food, at least, would be amazing. He considered it his consolation prize for doing his duty as a son once a month. Today it was roast beef with garlic mashed potatoes and roasted asparagus, which happened to be one of his favorites of his mother's meals.

"So, Aidan, are you dating anybody?" his mother asked, once they'd all begun eating. She usually held up the bulk of the conversation since his father rarely knew what to say to him. They didn't have a lot in common and neither went out of his way to find something.

Whether or not he was dating anybody was a complicated question, but he suspected it was asked more to be polite and offer expected conversation than out of genuine interest. "I've been seeing somebody lately, but it's very casual and I haven't been seeing her for very long."

"Oh, that's nice. Deborah has a lovely friend I'd thought perhaps you might like, but it seems I'm too late."

Aidan glanced at his brother's wife and she gave him a tight smile. He suspected she was mentally sighing in relief, though. She didn't look thrilled about the idea of hooking one of her friends up with a guy like him.

Conversation continued around the table, but Aidan didn't pay a lot of attention. And they wouldn't even notice. Once, when he was about thirteen, he'd gone through his father's office and his mother's closet, certain he'd find adoption papers. At the time, it had seemed the only possible explanation for why he not only didn't fit in, but seemed to be actively disappointing to his parents. As he'd aged, though, the resemblance to his father had become unmistakable, and his brother looked like them both.

And this feeling of being the odd man out at the dinner table was exactly why Tommy Kincaid meant so much to him. The man "got" him, and he'd taken Aidan under his wing and taught him everything he knew. The guilt hit him again, harder this time, and put a damper on his appetite.

Aidan wasn't so old-fashioned that he believed he was dishonoring Tommy's daughter. She was a grown woman and she was entitled to a sex life, and none of that was her father's business. It was the lying that ate at him. He was lying to Tommy and to Scott, and that was a betrayal in itself.

"Aidan?" He realized his mother had spoken to him and looked up. She was looking at him intently. "Are you feeling all right?"

"I guess. Why?"

"You look a little flushed and you're pushing your food around on your plate."

"I'm fine. Maybe not as hungry as I thought, though."

"I hope you're not sick. I have to fly to South Carolina in two days for business and I'd rather not fly sick," his father said. "It's bad enough you smell like gasoline, but germs, too?"

Aidan took a deep breath. One of these days he was just going to get up and walk out and not come back. There were a whole lot of people who liked and accepted him just the way he was. Why he cared about people who did nothing but judge him and find him wanting just because they shared DNA was beyond him.

But today wouldn't be that day. He knew if he did

that, it would be a long time before he saw his family again, especially since they'd blame him without taking a look at their own possible shortcomings. And, even though there were countless reasons why it shouldn't matter to him, he couldn't quite bring himself to cut ties completely.

He made it through dessert, which was carrot cake with cream cheese frosting. Just like the meal, it was one of his favorites, and it went a long way toward making him feel better. She might not be any better than her husband at making him feel like a valued member of the family, but this wasn't a coincidence. Maryanne Hunt had little ways of making her son feel loved, even if she wasn't good at the words.

After an hour of listening to his dad and Bryan recount their recent business triumphs, though, he'd had enough. "I have the night shift, so I should get home and get ready for work."

It was a lie. He wasn't assigned the night tour, but he did want to get home. Not only because he was tired of investment talk, but because Kincaid's Pub closed at nine on Sundays—except when the Patriots had a Sunday Night Football game—so he'd have an extra couple of hours to spend with Lydia tonight.

"Honestly, Aidan, I think it's barbaric the way they just flip from day to night at will like that."

"It's not that bad, Mom. There's usually enough time between the changes and you just sort of get used to it. We learn to sleep when we need to sleep, for the most part, whether it's day or night."

"Be careful," she whispered, squeezing his hand when he bent down to kiss her cheek.

"Always."

He kissed Sarah on the cheek, wishing they were closer. He'd tried over the years, partly because he envied the relationship Scott had with Lydia and Ashley, but his sister had the personality of a wet paper bag and absolutely no desire to return the effort. Then he said goodbye to Deborah and Bryan from across the room, stiffly shook his father's hand and got the hell out of there.

LYDIA WASN'T SURE what to expect when she showed up at Aidan's after he got back from his parents' house. She knew he had a contentious relationship with his family and his father had a way of putting him in a bad mood.

When she'd texted him to let him know she'd thrown his phone charger in her bag and then forgotten about it and offered to drop it off, she'd expected him to tell her not to worry about it. He probably had more than one, and he could get it another time.

If you don't mind bringing it by, I'd like to see you.

She'd laughed, getting a curious glance from Ashley, who'd been watching some afternoon talk show she was hooked on now.

It's only been a few hours since you saw me.

You can help me forget I spent the evening with my family.

There had been a pause while he typed more.

Unless you're tired or don't want to. I have another charger.

Of course he did. But she didn't mind.

I'll be over later.

"Really?" Ashley asked a few hours later, when Lydia told her she was heading out for a while.

"Yeah, really. I accidentally stole his phone charger."

"Yeah, because I'm sure he only has the one."

Lydia frowned at her, not liking the attitude she heard in Ashley's voice. "What is going on with you? One second, you're giving me shit. Then you're helping me plan a weekend alone with him. Now you're all snippy again."

"I'm sorry. I guess I can't decide how I feel about it. And maybe if my life was settled, I'd be better at knowing how I feel about yours, but everything just seems so messed up."

Lydia sank onto the couch next to her with a sigh. "That's because everything *is* so messed up."

"I'm going to work with you tomorrow night."

"Really? Are you sure?"

Ashley shrugged one shoulder. "I'm not sure. That's why I'm going to work *with* you and not telling you I'll work instead of you. If I need to leave, I'll be able to."

"You have to brace yourself for some comments, though. Because you've been away, people are going to want to say something about you being back."

"I know. I think I'm ready. Danny and I are...I

can't hide here until we figure it out. It shook me and I didn't know how to act, but I'm turning into a hermit afraid to face the world and that is *not* me."

Lydia's heart ached for her sister. "It's not. You're stronger than this, but it's not something anybody can push you into."

"Dad and Fitz are going to something at the VFW for a friend of theirs, so it seems like a good night to get my feet wet again."

Lydia reached over and squeezed her knee. "Good thinking. And you'll be fine. I'll be there, so if you need a break, you can hang out in the office for a breather. And if you need to leave, you can do that, too."

She didn't think Ashley would leave, though. Once she made up her mind it was time to get back behind the bar, she'd probably stick with it.

"Thanks." Ashley picked up the remote control and gestured at the paused television screen. "Go bring Aidan his phone charger. I'm going to finish watching this show."

Aidan was in his boxer briefs when he opened the door again, but Lydia was used to that now. She wasn't sure if it was just his nature, or if it had to do with wearing almost seventy pounds worth of gear at work, but the guy hated wearing clothes in his own apartment.

He let her in and kissed her as soon as the door was closed behind her, as if he hadn't just kissed her goodbye a few hours ago. "Hey, stranger."

"Funny. Here's your cord." When he took it and tossed it on the counter, she caught a whiff of something odd and frowned.

"What's wrong?"

"You smell like a cheap hooker." She wrinkled her nose, amused by his look of outrage. "I'm serious."

"What the hell are you talking about?"

She moved closer, sniffing at him. Then she grabbed his hands and inhaled deeply. "It's your hands. Seriously, it smells like you've been rubbing them all over a cheap hooker."

Aidan laughed. "I'll pass that compliment on to my mother. She'll be thrilled to know the soap in the guest bathroom smells so nice."

Lydia winced. "Ouch. If you pass that compliment on, tell her Ashley said it. So, how did dinner with the family go?"

"Same as usual. My dad's an ass and my mom tries to pretend he's not. My brother needs my father's permission to breathe and my sister's turning into my mother. But the food was good."

"I can put up with a lot for good food. Especially if it's free and I don't have to cook it."

"It'll be at least a month before I have to do it again. Six weeks if I can come up with some good excuses." He dropped onto the couch and patted the seat next to him. "Sit with me. Unless you're running right off."

"I can stay for a little while. Didn't you save an

episode of that show you want me to watch on your DVR?"

"Oh, yeah." He grabbed the remote and pulled up the menu. "And it's not just an episode. They had a marathon, so I saved the whole first season."

"Aren't you way past that? You've already seen the first season."

"I'll watch it again. It has zombies. Trust me, you'll like it."

Once he hit Play, he lifted his arm and she snuggled against his side as the show started. She'd heard a lot about the show, but working nights meant having to save or stream prime-time shows to watch during the day and she was lazy when it came to television.

But as he tried to drum up her enthusiasm—he was one of those *watch this* and *oh, this next part's cool* kind of people—a part of Lydia's mind was hung up on Ashley going back to work at the bar the next night.

She wouldn't leave Boston until Ashley had resolution one way or the other with Danny. Not for the entire process, if it came to divorce, but she'd be there to hold Ashley's hand when she filed the papers. But if Ashley was feeling strong enough to go back to work, the clock was ticking on her making up her mind about her marriage.

Lydia didn't want to say anything to Aidan and ruin the mood, but there was a very real possibility she wouldn't be around to watch the entire season of this show he'd saved to share with her.

ALMOST A WEEK LATER, Lydia took another slice of pizza out of the box and slid it onto her paper plate. "This pizza was worth pissing my dad off for. Every time I have pizza in Concord, I think of this, but I haven't had it since I got home."

"How pissed is he?"

She shrugged. "He's not happy, but what is he going to do? He could cover me for three hours while I had a fake appointment, or I can quit and he can cover Ashley every night until she returns to work."

Aidan laughed and snagged a third slice for himself. "You've pretty much got him over a barrel, since you're the one doing him a favor."

"So true." She bit into the pizza, savoring the spicy pepperoni and gooey cheese while a giant robot got its ass kicked in the ocean on television.

When Aidan had texted her that morning and wondered what the chances were she'd be able to stop by for pizza and *Pacific Rim*, she'd told him she'd make it happen. They'd both seen the movie at least a half dozen times, but they hadn't yet seen it together. And it had been three days since she'd seen him, so she wasn't missing this opportunity.

After a second bite, she realized that Aidan was looking at her instead of the TV screen. "What?"

"I just think it's funny how you call the place you have an apartment *Concord* and here *home*. I don't even know if you're aware of it."

She hadn't been, actually, but when she replayed

her words in her head, she realized he was right. "Old habits die hard, I guess."

"Or maybe that's just a place you happen to live, but this is still home to you."

"Most people probably refer to their hometown as home, especially if they still have family there."

He shrugged. "Or maybe you needed some time away after your divorce, but your subconscious knows your heart is here."

Lydia didn't want any part of a conversation about her heart. "I doubt that."

After setting the half-eaten slice on the coffee table, Aidan turned sideways on the couch so he was facing her. "Would it be so bad?"

"Would what be so bad?"

"Staying here. You love Kincaid's Pub. Anybody who spends an hour in the place can see how much pride you take in the place, and the customers love you."

"Of course I love Kincaid's. It like...part of the family, as weird as that sounds. But I didn't leave Boston because I wanted a different job."

"I know that. It just seems like you're different now. You've proven—to yourself and to your dad— that you can do what you want and make your life whatever you want it to be. So, this time, if you stayed in Boston and tended the bar, it would be your choice."

It was on the tip of her tongue to deny she had any interest in staying, as if by reflex, but she didn't. What he'd said kind of made sense to her, and the sudden uncertainty threw her off.

But there were a lot of bars like Kincaid's Pub in the world, even if they didn't bear her last name, and she could make a place for herself at any one of them. The difference between the Boston she left behind and the Boston she'd come back to was the man sitting on the couch with her.

The firefighter. The man hiding his relationship with her from the world so his best friend wouldn't find out. The man so worried about what her father and brother would think that she was sneaking around and lying like a teenager just to have pizza with him.

"Did you really become a firefighter because of my dad?" she asked, deciding if he could push a little, so could she.

He seemed startled by the question, but he recovered quickly. "I guess the easy answer is yes, but I don't know if that's true. Maybe it's more accurate to say I became a firefighter because of the accident. Or maybe I would have anyway, even if that never happened."

"What was it about the accident, though? I mean, you'd seen firefighters on TV and in movies, I'm sure. Why did seeing them in person make a difference to you?"

He shook his head. "It's really hard to explain, but it wasn't about them at all. It was about me. I was always trying to be who my family expected and failing, and then the accident happened and I took charge.

I was confident and somehow, even without knowing what to do, I was in my element. It was like for the first time, I was my true self. Does that make sense?"

It did, Lydia admitted to herself with a sinking feeling. She'd known a lot of firefighters in her life, and they chose the job for a lot of reasons. Some because it was family tradition. Some, like her ex, wanted to be heroes. Luckily, there weren't a lot of those guys around because they washed out pretty quickly. Most wanted to help people and serve their communities.

For Aidan, it was obviously a calling. Putting on that bunker coat and running toward what others ran away from was a part of who he was.

These feelings she was developing for him—feelings that made her think she might rather keep doing what she was doing than go back to her apartment in New Hampshire—didn't pick and choose which parts of him to like. But her head had a say, too, and it still shied away from allowing her to love another firefighter.

And then there was the fact that, even if she managed to reconcile herself to his job, there was no way their relationship could progress until it was out in the open.

"You're thinking about something wicked hard," Aidan said, giving her a questioning look. "Something bothering you?"

Something like both of them dancing around the fact they weren't just burning off the excess chemistry anymore but neither of them could admit it because that would raise a whole lot of questions they couldn't answer.

"Nope." She smiled. "I was just curious how you ended up with Boston Fire, I guess. Scotty's fourth generation, which you obviously know. It's what the men in my family do. But you come from a totally different background."

"I don't remember if I was into fire trucks or anything before the accident, but I know from the time I was eleven on, there was nothing else I ever wanted to be."

And that was the hard part. The firefighter community drove her nuts, but that didn't mean she didn't have a deep, lifelong respect and admiration for the men and women who did the job. And because of that, and the look in Aidan's eye when he talked about it, she knew she couldn't ask him to give it up.

"Oh, I like this part," Aidan said, and she realized she'd lost him to the movie again. The two main characters—a man and a woman—were sparring with staffs as part of a training and selection process, and after a few minutes, Aidan turned back to her. "Do you know how to use one of those?"

"I'm not sparring with you," she told him. "That's not my idea of foreplay at all."

"Bummer."

"But if I *did* spar with you, I'd totally kick your ass."

He grinned, his eyes lighting up at the challenge.

"They don't have sticks like that at my gym, but they've got gloves. We could go a few rounds and give each other a workout."

Even as she thought that sounded like a fun date, his expression dimmed and she realized he was thinking of Scotty. Obviously they went to the same gym, and there was also no way Aidan could take Tommy Kincaid's daughter there without every guy in a five-house radius hearing about it.

"We don't need to use gloves for a workout, you know," she said, not in the mood to watch him beat himself up about her brother.

It worked. "Are you asking me to choose between sex and *Pacific Rim*?"

Good point. "We can fast-forward through the science guys and still have time for a quickie workout before I leave."

"I do love the way you come up with a plan." He picked up the remote control and turned his attention back to the TV, his thumb hovering over the fast-forward button.

Lydia laughed and moved closer so she could snuggle with him now that they were done eating. If only she could come up with a plan for having a real relationship with him as easily as she came up with plans for a secret fling.

SIXTEEN

A FEW NIGHTS LATER, Aidan sat at the bar, sipping Sam Adams out of a cold bottle and watching Lydia work. And he watched with the awareness he could happily do this forever.

He'd finished up his shift and hit Kincaid's for a meal—the grilled chicken sandwich tonight because a man couldn't live on burgers alone—and a beer. After visiting with Lydia and the other regulars for a while, he'd head home. Maybe do some laundry or clean the bathroom. And then Kincaid's would close and Lydia would show up. She usually didn't stay more than an hour or two, because of Ashley, but they made the most of that time and it was enough.

Almost. The few occasions she'd stayed over and he'd slept the entire night with her butt pressed to his hip before waking up to her sleepy face made him want more of them.

If he pressed her to stay, she always defaulted to Ashley. If her sister got up in the middle of the night or early morning and she wasn't home, she'd worry.

And she'd already gone to bed, so it was too late to text her and tell her *not* to worry.

Aidan knew that was a bunch of crap. He was pretty sure if Ashley woke up in the middle of the night and Lydia wasn't there, Ashley would assume she was at his place. It was more likely some boundary wall Lydia had built to keep up the pretense they weren't really having a relationship. If they weren't having a real relationship, she didn't have to worry about the fact he was a firefighter or that some apartment in New Hampshire she shared with a virtual stranger and a cat was her future.

He still believed, however, that the best way to convince Lydia otherwise was not to try to convince of her anything. If he pushed too hard, she'd dig in.

"How long you going to make that beer last?"

He tore his gaze away from Lydia to look at Ashley, who was standing in front of him in a green Kincaid's Pub T-shirt identical to her sister's. He wouldn't say she looked happy, but she looked better than she had the last time he saw her and it was good that she was getting out again. She needed to step back into her life and reclaim her space.

"When the beer's gone, I'll head home." He flicked a glance at Lydia. "So it might take me a while to drink it all."

She smiled, but her eyes were sad and he wondered if that sadness was for her or for him. "Take your time."

He wasn't stupid. Ashley felt a little sorry for him

because she could probably see he was mooning over her sister and she would know better than anybody that Lydia wanted nothing to do with another firefighter.

A few minutes later, Lydia freed herself from a group of guys who were convinced they'd play pool better if she went in the alcove with them and blew on their cue sticks. He'd been watching them, making sure they didn't step out of line, but he knew Lydia had it under control. She'd been doing this for a lot of years and she was really good at it. She knew how to keep them in check while also making them think she was the most wicked cool bartender ever, knowing they'd tip accordingly.

That didn't make it any easier to watch them hit on Lydia with their cheesy innuendos, but if he went Neanderthal on them, she'd throw him out along with them.

"You are seriously rocking the scowl tonight," she said.

"I feel like those guys could be a problem."

She laughed. "They're amateurs, trust me. If cracking jokes about touching their balls and blowing their sticks makes them happy, more power to them. If it changes from corny shit to personal, or one of them touches me, then they'll be leaving."

He watched her face change as she looked over his shoulder. "What's up?"

"It's not a big deal. Scotty and Danny just walked in."

His muscles tensed and he sat up straight, as if he was putting distance between him and the woman on the other side of the bar. "Okay."

"Will you relax? Jesus, Aidan, how many years have you known me? There's nothing weird about you sitting here at the bar talking to me."

He knew that, but he also knew he'd been sitting at the bar talking to her while counting the minutes until he could have her in his bed, which was the problem. "Yeah. Did Ashley see Danny?"

"She's out back. I'll let her know he's here, though, so it's not a surprise."

"Hunt!" Scotty slapped him on the back and then hopped onto the stool next to him. Danny leaned against the bar on the other side, and Lydia set two beers in front of them. "What the hell, dude? You don't call and invite us anymore?"

"I was driving by and stopped spur-of-the-moment. Thought you might be here." The lies came so easily now. Finding the balance between watching Lydia like a man anticipating having sex with her and *not* looking at her so deliberately it was awkward wasn't as easy as lying, though.

Before Lydia could go out back, Ashley emerged from the hallway to the kitchen and stopped dead in her tracks when she saw Danny. "What are you doing here?"

"Thought I'd have a beer. It's what I usually do here."

He said the words calmly, like he said every damn

thing, but Aidan saw the flush of anger across Ashley's cheeks and thought maybe droll smart-ass wasn't the way he should have gone. "You don't think you should find another bar out of respect for me?"

"I like this bar. It's where I proposed to you."

The bar had fallen quiet, so everybody heard her quiet, sad words. "You say that like it means something."

"What the hell is that supposed to mean?" Danny stopped slouching against the bar, and Aidan looked at Lydia, wondering if they should intercede somehow. Neither Danny nor Ashley would want to play this out with an audience, even if they were currently caught up in the heat of the moment. They'd be embarrassed later. "You think it doesn't matter to me where I met my wife?"

"I don't think it matters to you whether or not I'm your wife."

"You told me you didn't want to be married anymore. You said you needed space. So I gave you space and now I'm an asshole."

"I wanted you to care. I wanted you to be *upset* that I thought our marriage was in trouble and show me that you were willing to fight for it."

"You think I wasn't upset? Is there some Kincaid standard of showing emotion? Do I have to yell? Break things? Is that how I show I care?" He threw the glass against the lower part of the bar and it smashed. "Is that what you want, Ash? You want me to lose control?"

"Yes! I want you to care enough to get pissed off and throw a goddamn glass."

Danny shook his head, crossing to the wall with a few long, angry strides. After kissing his fingertips, he slapped Bobby Orr's picture so hard, Aidan was afraid the glass protecting it would shatter. He wasn't sure what would happen, jinx-wise, if *that* glass broke. Maybe that's how the apocalypse would start.

"Is that upset enough for you?" Danny wasn't finished yelling, and Aidan had no clue what to do. He glanced sideways at Scotty, who just gave him an *I don't know, either* shrug. He wasn't sure he'd ever seen Danny yell before. "Or do I need to cry? Do you need to see me cry, because I can do that, Ashley. I usually do it in the shower so nobody knows, but if me in tears in front of everybody is what it takes, I'll do that."

"No." Ashley's voice was hoarse and choked. "That's not what I want."

"I love you. I'm sorry I don't always express things the same way you do, or the way I guess you want me to. But I do love you."

Tears were running down Ashley's face, and Aidan watched Lydia untie her sister's apron strings and take it off her. "You guys need to go somewhere and talk. Like right now while it's all out there in the open."

"I drove," Danny said, looking at Scotty, who then looked at him.

"I'll bring this guy home," Aidan said, recognizing his cue. "You and Ashley should go talk."

Once they'd left, Aidan moved out of the way so Lydia could clean up the broken glass and beer. "You want some help with that?"

"No thanks. I've had a lot of practice, and it's totally worth the cost of the glass if it breaks through whatever's been between Ashley and Danny."

"Yeah. Hopefully they'll keep talking until they get it all sorted out."

He and Scotty watched the sports news scrolling across the bottom of the television screen, occasionally making a comment on a trade or an injury. It was stilted, though—at least it seemed so to Aidan—and he could feel the tension in his shoulders.

When Scotty was finally ready to leave, and had paid for Aidan's beer in exchange for the ride, Aidan caught Lydia's gaze and gave her a regretful smile. She shrugged slightly, like *what are you gonna do?* and he knew he wouldn't be seeing her tonight. It was for the best since, even if she did stop by, he was currently being overwhelmed by guilt.

It just got worse when Scotty slapped him on the back as they headed for the door. "Married people sure do have a lot of drama. Thank God I still have you, though. You never have female drama."

If only he knew, Aidan thought, casting a quick glance back at Lydia before he went out the door.

Danny pulled into Ashley's—into *his*—driveway and put the truck in Park, but he didn't open his door. "I should go."

"No, you should *not* go. We're finally getting somewhere and now you want to shut me out again?"

"Losing my shit and smashing a glass is getting somewhere?" His chest felt tight when he thought about how much he must have looked and sounded like his father at that moment.

"You told me you love me." Her voice was so quiet, he could barely hear her over the truck's engine.

"I tell you I love you all the time. If it only counts when I'm yelling and smashing things, then…I don't know what's happening here, Ashley. I can't keep doing this."

The color drained from her face and he watched her rub at the narrow white strip on the finger where her damn wedding rings were supposed to be. "I can't, either."

Before he could say anything else, she got out of the truck. He said her name, not wanting her to go, but she slammed the door and walked toward the house. Anger and desperation and confusion and love were still churning inside of him, and he almost let her go. He was too worked up to have a conversation.

But Danny had a gut feeling if he drove away right now, his marriage was over.

He killed the engine and got out. Ashley had closed the door, but she probably wouldn't lock it since Lydia wasn't home yet. And if she had, he'd use the key that was still on his ring.

This time he didn't knock. It was still his house

and she was still his wife until she looked him in the eye and said it was over.

When he closed the door behind him, Ashley stopped. She'd been on her way into the kitchen, and he could tell by the way her shoulders shook that she'd started crying. But he watched her take a deep breath, swiping at her cheeks, and she lifted her chin before turning to face him.

"I'm not leaving yet," he said. "It's not ending like this."

"Is it ending?" she asked, the look in her eyes tearing at his heart.

"I don't want it to. I don't want a divorce, Ashley. God, that's the last thing I've ever wanted."

"Then why did you leave?"

"I thought we had a good thing going. You'd even stopped taking your birth control pills, so I was looking forward to starting a family. And then, bam, just like that, you told me you didn't want to be married to me anymore."

"I said I *wasn't sure.*"

"You said you needed space. All I knew was that our marriage might be over and it was like this... freezing cold nor'easter swirling inside me and I didn't know what to do with that. I was afraid I'd explode with it if I tried to change your mind, so I gave you the space."

"And *that's* the problem! You shut down. It's like you don't even care. If you cared, you'd at least say something. I wanted you to fight for me. I wanted you to look the way you do right now."

"That's when people say bad stuff, Ashley," he said, hating the way his voice was getting loud, but he was running out of chances to make her understand. "When people lose their cool, that's when they say stuff they can *never* take back. Hurtful stuff. Name-calling. Words designed to cut to the bone. I don't ever want to hurt somebody I love because I said something awful and hurtful in the heat of the moment."

She stared at him for what felt like years, and then her face softened. "I'm not your mother, Danny. And you are most certainly not your father. We would never say things like that to each other."

"You don't know that."

"I *do* know that. We love each other. And you know my family, Danny. You've seen us go off on each other. Sometimes we even call each other names and it gets loud and crazy, but we're not mean. There's a difference."

"People say things when they lose control of their emotions." Shame made his face feel hot when he realized his voice was choking up. "Great. Now I'm going to cry like a girl because I'm weak. I guess you're going to get all those emotions you want."

"Bullshit. You're allowed to cry when your life's coming undone, Danny. It's not weak." He was surprised when she wrapped her arms around his waist and pulled him close. "God, I hate your parents. I'm sorry, but I really hate them."

All Danny knew was the feel of his wife in his arms and he held her as tight as he could without hurting her. He pressed his face into her hair and fought to control his raging emotions. Not because he didn't want to express them, but because he wanted to talk and he couldn't right now.

Ashley was trembling, her fingernails pressing into his lower back, and he kissed the top of her head. "I'll go to counseling."

"Do you mean it?"

Even muffled against his shirt, he could hear the tears and the hope in her voice. "I do. I'll go with you and maybe I'll go alone, too. I'll do whatever it takes to make you happy. To make *us* happy."

She squeezed his waist and he closed his eyes, letting himself believe everything would be okay. He wouldn't stay tonight, no matter how much he wanted to. They were both too raw and the night had been far too emotionally exhausting. He needed to think about the fact that, in his effort to not be his parents, he'd gone too far and suppressed too much. They were, in that way, still affecting his marriage despite his vow long ago their relationship would never touch his. It was a lot to process, and he knew she'd finally understood why he'd built that wall she hated. There were still a lot of deep, personal conversations in their near future.

But the important thing was there *was* a future.

Ashley was his again and that was the only thing that mattered to him. "I love you."

"I love you, too, Danny. I always have and that's never going to change."

LYDIA HAD BEEN at work for only half an hour the next day when Scotty walked through the door. He looked agitated, but she didn't think anything of it because it wasn't an usual look for her brother.

He sat at the end of the bar, rather than down where their father was loitering, which *was* unusual. Lydia set a coaster in front of him. "You want a soda? It's a little early for a beer."

"Day off, so I can have a beer if I want."

She raised her eyebrow, not caring for his tone. "A beer it is, then."

After she set it in front of him, she started to walk away, intending to get the order sheet so she could start figuring out what they needed from their distributors in the near future. While Danny and Ashley had had a good talk, according to her sister, they still had a ways to go in the communication department. But at least they both knew now that neither of them wanted a divorce.

"I wanna know what's going on between you and Hunt."

Lydia jerked her head around, eyebrows arched. He'd said it quietly, so maybe she'd heard him wrong. "Excuse me?"

"You and Aidan. What's going on with that?"

"You seem to have me confused with somebody who answers to you."

"It was bugging me last night, but I couldn't figure out why. Then, this morning, it hit me. Aidan's been acting weird for a while, like there was something wrong. I haven't seen as much of him. I haven't seen a lot of you. And there were some looks between you last night."

It was something of a crossroads, she thought. She could tell him he was crazy and, if she tried hard enough, she could make him believe that. Then they'd laugh at how stupid he was and she'd give him another beer.

But this was a head-on confrontation, right here, and she knew that in this situation, Aidan wouldn't lie to Scotty. He would see a distinction between lies of omission and lying straight to her brother's face, and it would matter to him.

"It's not really any of your business," she said, because that wasn't a lie, either.

"Like hell it's not."

She leaned across the bar so their faces were level. "Leave this alone, Scott."

"How long has he been screwing you behind my back?"

The fuse lit and she jabbed her finger at his chest. "If you don't watch your mouth, I'll slap you so freakin' hard, you'll fold like a cheap paper napkin."

He glared back at her. "You're sleeping with my best friend. My *best* friend, Lydia. You're not supposed to do that. And he sure as hell knows better. How long has it been going on?"

"Since shortly after I came back."

"Are you serious?" He dropped his head into his hands, then looked up at her again. "Did you have the flu? When Aidan was at his parents' doing whatever, which made no sense because his family just pays people to do that kind of shit."

"I wasn't sick. I had to go back to Concord to baby-sit my roommate's cat for the weekend and Aidan went with me so we could be away from nosy-ass people who can't mind their own business."

"So Ashley's lying to me, too. I can't fucking believe you two."

"What are you two carrying on about?" their dad called from the other end of the bar. "I heard what happened with Danny and Ashley last night and, I swear, the next member of my family to raise a ruckus in this bar is getting my boot up the ass."

"It's Hunt who needs a boot up the ass," Scotty said before Lydia could say anything. She would have preferred keeping their father out of it.

"What does he have to do with it?" he asked, scowling at Aidan.

"Maybe you should ask Lydia."

When he turned to look at her, she wondered if her dad might actually be happy to hear she and Aidan had been seeing each other. In his mind, it would bring her back into the fold and—more importantly— back into the bar for good. But since that probably wasn't going to happen, he was going to end up having a problem with it one way or another.

"It's none of anybody's business what Aidan and I do," she said firmly, looking him in the eye.

It took a few seconds and then she saw the understanding dawn in his eyes. "Ah, damn. That kid."

So much for being happy about it. He shook his head and looked at Scotty. "You just find this out?"

"Yeah. You think I'd have bought him a beer last night if I knew?"

"Why shouldn't you buy him a beer?" Lydia demanded. "Your friendship with him is no different now than it was yesterday. This has *nothing* to do with you."

She could see that he wanted to say more, but then he shook his head and got off the stool. After knocking back a long swallow of beer, he started toward the door.

"Where are you going?" she called after him.

"I'm going home." He stopped to turn and glare at her for a second. "Don't worry. I'm not going to go kick the shit outta your boyfriend."

"He's—" She sighed and waved a hand at him, not wanting to get into the semantics of whether or not Aidan was her boyfriend. "Just leave him alone until you've cooled off."

Lydia watched him leave, wincing when he opened the door by slapping his hand on the glass and shoving so hard, she was surprised it didn't break. She hoped like hell he was telling the truth when he said he was going home.

"I really hate to butt in here," a guy at the counter said, "but can I get another beer?"

"Yeah, sorry about that." She got him a beer and looked around to see if she could sneak a few minutes more out back, but she really needed to take care of the customers. They'd probably finished their drinks while watching her family's circus sideshow performance.

She pulled out her phone to send Aidan a text. A phone call would be better, but she'd have to go out back to have any privacy and it would take too long. She'd be lucky if anybody tipped her as it was. And she didn't want to wait until after the customers were taken care of just in case Scotty changed his mind about going home. She couldn't leave Aidan to be blindsided.

Scott & Dad know about us. Not thrilled.

It was a bit of an understatement, but she knew he'd get the picture.

Should I lock my door?

He said he was going home. Wanted you to know in case he changes his mind.

Thanks for the heads-up.

There was a lot more she wanted to say, but she could almost feel the impatient stares drilling into her back.

Busy now. Talk to you later.

Coming over?

She hesitated, but somehow it didn't feel right tonight.

Not tonight. But I'll text you.

Good night.

As she put her phone away and plastered a smile on her face, Lydia wondered how upset Aidan would be that their secret was out. And she wondered if, like her, he'd feel a good amount of relief along with everything else. She had no idea how this was going to turn out for any of them, but at least the lying was over.

SEVENTEEN

AT LEAST THE lying was over, Aidan thought as he walked toward the front door of the ice rink. He wasn't sure what his reception would be today, but at least he wasn't hiding anything anymore. Maybe they could work through it and salvage their friendship.

They didn't have a tour scheduled for several days, which would have been nice as a cooling-off period before they had to work together again. But they'd already scheduled this ice time and Aidan wasn't going to back out at the last minute, if for no other reason than Scotty would see it as a sign of weakness.

He was running a few minutes late, though, having sat in his truck for a few minutes in his driveway, debating on whether or not showing up was the right move, so he anticipated the locker room being empty when he went in.

Scotty was sitting on one of the benches, obviously waiting for him. "I wasn't sure if you were gonna be here."

"I said I would be."

"Ah, that's right. You're a man of integrity, right?"

Aidan looked him in the eye. "I never wanted to lie to you. I hated every minute of that, but…"

"But what? I think you owe me complete sentences, at least, after all these fucking years."

"If I talked to you about her and you told me to keep my hands off her, it was going to be worse because I couldn't do it. I tried. At least this way, I didn't outright lie to your face."

"You're not too ugly, you're a firefighter and you don't live in your mother's basement. You could bang any chick in Boston, but you gotta mess around with my sister?"

"It just happened, Scotty. It's not like it's something I planned to do. But when she came back…it was just different somehow. I don't know if I was different or if she was different, but there was chemistry."

"She's *not* different. She's still my sister." Scott scrubbed his hand over his face, shaking his head. "You've been lying to me this whole time. There wasn't any blonde chick at the market whose name you didn't remember. That text was from Lydia."

"Yeah."

"And you don't have the balls to just come and talk to me like a man about it?"

Normally, Aidan wouldn't take well to a comment like that, but he forced himself to accept that, in this case, he had it coming. And the only way his friendship with Scott Kincaid would survive was if he took whatever venting his best friend needed to do without escalating it.

"It wasn't supposed to be a big deal. It was just going to be...hell. I don't know. We knew you'd be pissed, even though she's an adult and can make her own choices."

"That sounds like a douche bag way of saying it's none of my business."

"I don't know." Aidan dumped his bag and stick on an empty bench. "Part of me wants to say it's not, but I know I crossed a line."

"Yeah, no shit."

The door to the locker room banged open and Jeff Porter stuck his head in. "You two girls start your periods or are you gonna play some hockey?"

Scotty, who was dressed and ready, stood and grabbed his stick. "I'm coming."

"I'll be right there," Aidan said. When Scotty followed Porter out without another word, he unzipped his bag and popped open his locker.

It sucked. He and Scotty had been tight since they were teenagers and, though they'd had some disagreements over the years, this was a bad one. Scotty hadn't swung on him, which was good *and* bad. He didn't want to fight his best friend, but Scotty being quiet often meant he'd decided something wasn't worth his time or effort anymore.

By the time Aidan hit the ice, the others were warmed up and they fell into an easy rhythm. They'd all been playing hockey together a long time—

whether just for fun or for the league—but they'd decided this year they were going to step up the practices. They'd had their asses handed to them by the police department's hockey team in their last charity matchup and that shit couldn't happen again.

There was a lot of trash-talking and name-calling, along with a lot of laughter, and for a little while Aidan almost felt as if everything would be okay eventually. It would take a while. But he and Scotty were practically brothers and, like brothers, they'd find a way to get through this and maybe even come out stronger on the other side.

Then he and Scotty reached the puck at the same time and Aidan realized at the last second that Scotty wasn't slowing down. He barely had time to turn his body before his best friend checked him into the boards so hard he dropped to his knees, sucking air.

For a few seconds, he let himself believe it was an accident. But then Scotty slapped the puck and skated away without offering him a hand up and he knew the hit had been deliberate.

He shoved himself to his feet and, leaving his stick on the ice, took after Scotty. His friend watched him come, a sneer twisting his mouth, and then he dropped his stick and gloves onto the ice. Aidan flung his gloves to the side and led with his right.

Scotty jerked his head back so it was only a glancing blow. They grappled, and Scotty tried to come up underneath with a blow to his ribs. Aidan shoved hard against him, looking for room to get a swing in. He connected with Scotty's cheek, but Scotty's left grazed the corner of his mouth and Aidan tasted blood.

Enraged, he hit Scotty in the gut and then threw him down on the ice. With his practice jersey clenched in his left fist, he cocked his arm back, ready to drive his right fist into Scotty's face. Somebody caught him from behind, dragging him backward.

Scotty scrambled to his skates, still coming, but Gullotti wrapped his arms around him from behind and held tight.

"What the fuck is wrong with you guys?" Gullotti bellowed. "Cut the shit."

Aidan strained against whoever was holding him, but he wasn't breaking free so it was probably Porter. "I got more, Kincaid, if you wanna keep going."

"Fuck you, Hunt."

"That's it." Gullotti shoved Scotty away. "We're done here. You guys give us a few minutes to get this one outta here and then he can change."

Aidan relaxed, but Porter didn't release him. "I'm good. You're breaking my freakin' arms, dude."

"And you ruined my hockey time, so be thankful it ain't your kneecaps, too."

He sat on the players' bench and waited until Gullotti sent a text to Porter telling him the locker room was clear. Porter showed him his phone's screen.

Tell Hunt to go directly to the house. This shit will stop.

Aidan snorted. "You ladder guys can be real pushy."

"Walsh isn't here and somebody's gotta keep you guys in line. It's gonna be Cobb that reams your ass, anyway, not Gullotti."

Porter wasn't wrong about that. Cobb was waiting for him in the second-floor office, and Scott was already seated in one of the two chairs on this side of the paper-covered desk.

"Sit down," Cobb said. "And if either of you two morons even thinks about throwing a punch in my office, I'll knock you both senseless with a five-pound sledge. Tell me what's going on."

Both men sat silently, arms folded and gazes fixed on spots over Cobb's head. He was the equivalent of the school principal and no matter how pissed off they were, neither Aidan nor Scotty was a rat.

"So now you put up a united front. Idiots. Look at you." He gestured to their faces, which probably weren't pretty. "You two are brothers. Not just on the job, either."

"Makes it even more fucked-up that he's banging my sister, then, don't it?"

His eyes widened. "I hope like hell you don't mean Ashley or I'll need to contain Walsh. Jesus, Mary and Joseph, tell me that's not why they separated."

"He'd be dead already," Scotty said quietly.

"Lydia, huh?" The captain leveled a look at Aidan. "That true?"

He thought about his answer for a few seconds. He

wasn't going to lie, but he wasn't going to let anybody disrespect Lydia, either. Even her brother. "I object to that description of our relationship."

"Oh, excuse me," Scotty said, his voice dripping with fake sincerity. "It's fucked-up that he's having sexual intercourse with my sister. Is that better?"

"You need to have some manners if you're talking about Lydia, asshole."

Scotty scooted to the front of his chair, ready to stand. "Oh, really? You gonna give me a lesson on my own family, Hunt?"

"Enough!" Cobb leaned back in his chair and threw his pen onto the desk with so much force it slid across the paper planner and off the other side. "I won't have this bullshit."

Aidan sank back against his chair, shaking his head. "I don't want to fight with you, Scotty. I never meant to hurt you and I'm sorry I lied."

"I'm not going to swing again," Scott said after what seemed like forever. "I'll work with you. I'll have your back when we go through the door. But you and me? I don't know if we can be friends again."

LYDIA CLOSED THE FRONT door quietly, in case Ashley was sleeping. They'd had a late rush at the bar and it had taken her forever to get out of there, so the house was dark. She flipped on the light switch as she walked into the living room, but the television being on struck her as weird. Her sister usually shut it off when she went upstairs.

Usually Lydia would watch it for a few minutes, relaxing after being at work, but tonight it would take a lot more than the television to relax her. She had no idea what was going on with the guys, and it was giving her a stress headache. When she'd called Aidan earlier in the night, he'd been quiet and when she asked him about Scotty, he'd said they were still working some stuff out. Then he'd told her he was going to catch up on sleep and he'd talk to her tomorrow.

Then she'd sent a text to Scotty asking him to stop by the bar, but he said he was busy, and didn't respond at all to her text asking him to make time to talk to her. She didn't appreciate being shut out of whatever was going on, as if it had nothing to do with her.

On her way to shut off the TV, she tripped over something and swore in a low voice, before realizing it was a man's shoe. That was even weirder than the television being on, she thought.

"Oh, shit," she heard Ashley say, and she realized her sister was on the couch. She hadn't seen her because the furniture was in some kind of conversational arrangement, whatever that meant, and the back of the couch faced the entry. "Don't come in."

Lydia froze, not sure what that meant. "Are you okay?"

"Yeah. But I'm…not fully dressed."

"So?"

"I'm not fully dressed, either," a male voice said, and Lydia realized it was Danny.

"Oh." Ashley and her husband were partially un-dressed together on the couch. *Okay.* "I'll, uh…be upstairs for a while. Or for a long time. Actually, I'll just go to bed, so good night."

"Lydia," Danny called, "you don't have to go up-stairs. Just give us a second."

"I don't want to be in the way."

Ashley's head popped up over the back of the couch, and Lydia smiled at her. Her sister's hair was disheveled and her face was flushed. Then Danny sat up, looking much the same. Obviously her sister and her brother-in-law were finding a way to accel-erate working through their communication issues.

"You're not in the way," Ashley said. "And you can stay down here. We'll go upstairs."

Danny turned around so he could give her a reas-suring smile. "Don't worry about us."

But she had been worried about them, and right now Ashley looked happy and in love and she needed some alone time with her husband. "You guys want to be alone."

"I took some time off, so she and I have plenty of time to catch up," Danny said. "If you can spare a little more time for the bar."

"Sure, no problem. And give me ten minutes and I'll be out of here. I'll go stay at Dad's."

Ashley grimaced. "You don't have to do that, Lydia. You know that."

"I want to. Really. Nothing's more hideous than being the third wheel to two people acting like new-

lyweds." She grinned at them. "Trust me. Ten minutes and you guys can go back to making out on the
couch like teenagers."

She went upstairs and pulled her bag out of the
closet. Taking just what was clean and necessary, as
well as her toiletries from the bathroom, would save
her some time. She could come back for the rest another time.

"You aren't really going to stay at Dad's are you?"

Lydia closed the top drawer of the bureau and
dropped the handful of undergarments into the open
bag. "We grew up in that house. It's Dad. I can handle staying there."

"You're making me feel guilty."

"Don't." Lydia straightened and gave her sister a
warm smile. "I'm happy for you. I really am, and you
two need to be alone right now."

"Can't you stay with—" Ashley broke off, looking
over her shoulder, and Lydia realized Ashley didn't
know the secret was out. Danny must not, either.
Then, in a lower voice Ashley continued, "I'm sure
you could find somebody else to stay with."

"That's not really…" Lydia let the words die away,
not sure what to say. Playing house, even temporarily, with Aidan was a recipe for disaster as far as her
emotions were concerned. "We're not really heading
in that direction and it's probably best not to muddy
the water."

"I think you guys are a great couple."

"That's based on what, exactly? We haven't been

running around doing the couple thing where every-body can see us."

Ashley shrugged. "No, but I've seen you together a couple of times at the bar, and I know you both well enough to know you're probably great together."

"Yeah, we are, I think."

"So…what's the problem?"

Lydia threw some more clothes in the bag, figur-ing they would be enough for a couple of days, and fell back on her standard excuse. "I don't live here anymore, Ash. I just came here to help you out and now you won't need me much longer."

"You could live here again. Just don't leave."

It was that easy and also that hard, but she didn't want to open that door with her sister. If Ashley knew Lydia was even considering staying in Boston, she'd never hear the end of it. "You're missing the point, which is that I don't *want* to live here anymore. The reasons I left are still valid reasons to leave again."

"But now there's Aidan."

"He's a firefighter."

Ashley walked over and sat on the edge of the bed, trying to make Lydia look at her. "It wasn't Todd's job that destroyed your marriage. It was Todd."

Lydia really wasn't in the mood for an impromptu therapy session. "And then there's Dad. Tell me it wasn't hard being his daughter and I'll tell you you're full of shit. And Scotty. And everybody's in every-body else's business and the brotherhood and blah blah blah."

"You see it as drowning you and I see it as buoying me and helping me float."

Lydia gave her an arch look. "I seem to recall they were buoying you so much I had to come down here and fill in at Kincaid's so you could have a minute of privacy to worry about yourself."

"Touché." Ashley stood and looked at the bag. "You really don't have to go to Dad's. You know he's already in bed."

"I still have my key. I'll leave a note in his chair so when he gets up, he'll know I'm there."

"He'll be cranky as hell if you wake him up."

Lydia snorted. "He's going to be so thankful to have Danny back in the family fold, he wouldn't care if I showed up with a mariachi band."

And she was right. Leaving the two lovebirds to get back to what they'd been doing before she interrupted them, Lydia drove to her dad's house and parked behind his car. She'd leave her keys on the table in case he needed to move it, but owning a bar had trained the morning person out of him.

She thought she was quiet, but she was only halfway to her old bedroom—which had stayed a guest room—when her eyeballs were seared by a flashlight so bright, she wondered if he had it hooked to a car battery.

"Jesus, Dad, it's me," she said, trying to shield her eyes behind her hand. It clicked off and she blinked at the spots she'd probably be seeing for days.

"What the hell are you doing? What if I'd clocked you upside the head with a bat?"

"You think I'd just stand here and let you come at me with a bat? And I'm temporarily—very, very temporarily—going to stay in my old room."

"You don't call and ask? Maybe I turned it into a craft room."

She snorted. "Yeah, you're crafty, all right. And if you don't want me staying here, that's fine. An hour and a half from now, I can be back in my own bed in my own apartment and you can tend your own damn bar."

"You always did have a fresh mouth."

"Gee, I wonder where I got that from."

"Your mother," he grumbled. "I'm surprised you're not staying with your boyfriend."

Lydia shook her head and started walking toward the bedroom again. "I'm not talking about Aidan with you, Dad."

"I thought you knew better than that."

"Better than what?"

"To come between them. Aidan and Scotty, I mean. You got no business there, and you probably ruined their friendship."

"I haven't done anything to Scott. Nothing about my relationship is any of his business. Or yours, for that matter." And she didn't know what their relationship even was anymore, if anything, since she hadn't seen him.

"That ain't how it works, and you know it."

"If you mean that I know you consider your brotherhood of firefighters more important than your actual family, then yes. I do know that."

He recoiled, as if she'd physically struck him. "That's not true, Lydia."

"It *feels* true. And it always has." They could stand here and argue until they were blue in the face and it wouldn't make a difference. "That's why you're standing here telling me I've done something wrong instead of telling your son it's none of his damn business who I sleep with and to grow up and get over it."

"I'm going back to bed. Maybe tomorrow you'll be more reasonable."

"If by being more reasonable, you mean I might admit you're right tomorrow, I wouldn't count on it." She went into the spare room and closed the door behind her. She didn't slam it, but she wanted to.

The room she'd shared with Ashley had been made into a true guest room, with no debris from their childhood scattered around. What they hadn't taken with them when they moved out but didn't want to throw away was boxed up in the cellar, and the bunk beds had been replaced by a queen mattress and box spring on a plain metal frame.

The bedding was clean and she was too tired for a little dust to bother her. After changing out of her clothes, she crawled in between the sheets and tried to rein in the thoughts racing around her mind.

First and foremost, of course, was the hope she and her old man both survived this forced cohabitation.

She also hated fighting with Scotty, though this was not the first time and it probably wouldn't be the last. And then came Ashley and Danny. Lydia genuinely hoped they were on the path to saving their marriage and getting back on track.

Which brought her to the point where her runaway train of thought ran off the tracks. Ashley putting her life back together meant Lydia would be free to go back to *her* own life. The one in New Hampshire, where she chose who to be friends with and there were no bar patrons who'd known her since she wasn't old enough to be in there, and no firefighters.

And no Aidan.

She'd made her peace with being involved with him because it was only temporary. But now that the clock was ticking and that temporary time was running out, she wondered how she'd make peace with not having him in her life anymore.

She'd fallen in love with a freaking firefighter.

Rolling onto her side and curling up, she tried not to think about that. She'd gotten used to having Aidan around and now she wasn't sure how temporary she wanted their relationship to be. At the same time, she didn't see how it could be anything else.

Sighing, she drew the covers up over her face and started counting beer brands she could name in place of sheep. She'd think about Aidan tomorrow.

EIGHTEEN

LYDIA WAS GOING to throw everybody out of Kincaid's Pub, hang the Closed sign in the door and go find her brother. Once she was done slapping some sense into him, she'd find Aidan and give him a piece of her mind, too. They were both idiots and the next time she saw either of them, it wasn't going to be pretty.

No fewer than seven different people had asked Lydia if she'd heard about the fight between her brother and Aidan Hunt, and it pissed her off to no end. Not being asked about it—she was expected, as bartender, to be gossip central—but because she had to hear about it from her patrons rather than one of the idiots in question.

She managed to piece together a bare minimum of information. They'd gotten into a fistfight while playing hockey and then been called onto the carpet for it. If the customers had any balls, she knew the real question would be *how long have you been sleeping with Aidan Hunt* because nobody would be able to imagine anything else that would make them exchange blows. And depending on how discreet everybody was, they might not have to imagine.

But did *she* get a heads-up? It might have been nice if one of them warned her the bar might be a hotbed of speculation that night, especially since it involved her. But apparently this was going to be a *guy* thing, despite both of them knowing that would send her over the edge.

When she couldn't take it anymore, she sent a text to Aidan.

Are you home?

Yeah, but I might go do some stuff.

Stay home. I'm coming over.

There was a long pause before the reply came through.

Aren't you working?

Dad's here. If he can't handle it, he can call Ashley. I'm on my way.

"I'm leaving," she told her dad, reaching behind her to untie her apron.

He paused in his conversation with Fitz, scowling at her. "What do you mean you're leaving? You're working."

"It's your bar. You tend it. Or call Ashley in. But I'm leaving early tonight."

"You're going to see Hunt."

"Yeah." She put her hands on her hips, glaring at him. "Did you know about the fight?"

"I heard about it."

"And you didn't tell me?"

He shrugged. "This is between them."

So many words ran through her mind and she wanted to shout them all at him. Both Scott and Aidan had so much respect for him and, if he'd be reasonable about her relationship with Aidan, he could help them be reasonable, too. But that was too much to expect from him, and the disappointment he'd never change was almost as keen as her anger.

But there was a line and if she unleashed her temper on her father, she had no doubt she'd cross it. So she just stowed her folded apron on the shelf under the cash register and walked out of the bar without saying another word.

When she finally reached Aidan's apartment and he opened the door, she stood there staring at his face for a few seconds before walking past him into the living room. His lip had been split and it looked like he had a bruise on his cheek. She wasn't sure what Scotty looked like, but he'd obviously gotten in a couple of good shots on Aidan.

"Tell me what happened," she said. It took her a second to realize he was shirtless, but had on a pair of jeans. She wasn't sure what that meant.

"What do you mean?"

She tried to keep her cool, but she wasn't in the mood for him to play stupid. "Don't bullshit me, Aidan. What happened with you and Scotty? Everybody's giving me the side-eye and I heard you guys dropped gloves on the ice. I heard it from pretty much *everybody* who came into the bar tonight. You guys fought?"

"Something like that."

"And everybody who came in the bar knew, but neither of you told *me* about it?" She held up a hand. "And if you tell me it's between the two of you and not my business, I swear to God, I'll finish what he started."

"I just needed a little time, I guess," he said. "Maybe I thought you wouldn't find out, which is stupid, and you wouldn't feel like you're being pulled between us. When push comes to shove, he's your brother."

"And you're my...I don't know." She blew out a breath, crossing her arms. "I don't answer to my brother, you know. And I certainly don't live my life to make him happy, so it's none of his business what we do."

"He's my best friend." Aidan sat on the edge of the couch, resting his elbows on his knees. "He's like my brother, you know. And we're supposed to have each other's backs. We *have* to."

And there it was. The brotherhood. The bond that held them together and was protected above all else. Sometimes even above spouses and children, forcing families to put on a brave face and accept the fact they came in second because it had to be that way.

"So if you have to choose which one of us you piss off," she said, "I lose."

He rose to his feet, anger coloring his cheeks. "Who said anything about choosing?"

"You and Scotty threw fists at each other because you're with me, and now you're sitting here beating yourself up because you're supposed to have his back. It sounds to me like you feel a need to choose."

"What do you even care? You've made it pretty clear you want nothing to do with a firefighter. If you're looking to get laid, I'll do just fine, but I can't ask any more of you than that because your ex-husband was a dickhead."

"It's not just Todd," she shot back at him, her voice louder. "You wanna put Tommy Kincaid on some kind of pedestal, that's fine. But I'm his daughter. I grew up in this brotherhood of yours. I married into it. I've done my time waiting for somebody to remember to call and tell the family everybody's okay. I've done my time losing sleep and putting on a brave face and making casseroles while the guys sit vigil in a hospital waiting room. And in return, what do I get? I get to be an afterthought. I get to be understanding and supportive and make sure the fridge is fully stocked with beer. Screw that."

"I told you I won't carry some other asshole's baggage, Lydia."

"Fine. But you know how I feel about coming second to the brotherhood and you had an opportunity to have enough respect for me to tell me what happened, and you didn't. You let me get blindsided at the bar rather than include me in a situation that involves me, which means you're no different."

"I guess I don't have to make a choice, then," Aidan said, his deceptively quiet voice at odds with his flexing jaw and the tightness around his eyes. "Sounds like you've already made it for both of us."

She looked at him a long time, her heart slowly breaking. It had been inevitable, this moment, but she hadn't imagined it would hurt so much. She hadn't realized how very badly she'd been hoping that, if it came down to it, he would choose her.

"I'm sorry it turned out this way," she said in as steady a voice as she could manage. "I hope you and Scotty can find a way to be okay again, without me in the middle of it."

"Lydia, I don't want it to be like this between us."

"It won't matter because I'll be back in New Hampshire." She forced a shaky smile. "But I might see you around sometime, if I come to visit Ashley."

Before he could say anything else, she left, closing the door quietly behind her. She made it all the way to the ground floor before the tears started falling. She'd actually thought he might choose her.

A LONG, LONELY week passed for Aidan, and he figured it was just the first of many long, lonely weeks in his future.

He'd lost Lydia. In trying to keep her out of the ugliness between him and Scotty so she wouldn't feel torn, he'd inadvertently disrespected her in a way she wasn't going to forgive. Now every minute of every day—even times he wouldn't have seen her anyway—he missed her.

He and Scotty had worked a few day tours together without any problems. The day after the fight and the chewing out from Cobb, Walsh had asked them if he should switch up Engine 59's crews, so he and Scotty would be on opposite tours. One would work the day and the other, the night. It wasn't ideal because together they all made a strong team, but if their relationship degraded too much, it would destroy the crew anyway.

Aidan had left it up to Scotty, since he was the one struggling with the situation. Aidan may have thrown some punches, but that was mostly self-defense and temper. He loved Scotty and he'd do whatever he could to heal the rift between them.

Maybe it was the fact news Lydia and Aidan were over had spread through the family, but Scott seemed to get a little less angry with him every day. Not that they were buddies, but they could be in the same room. And it had helped when Scotty told Cobb he didn't want anybody but Aidan at his back when the shit hit the fan.

So things were awkward and the probationary status of their friendship would last awhile, but at least Aidan wasn't going to lose everybody he loved. Only Lydia.

"Let's go have a beer," Danny said when the tour

was over and they were all heading out. "You two and me."

Aidan glanced at Scotty, whose face looked as if it was carved from stone. "I could use a beer. I, uh…shit."

"We can go to that new sports bar over by the park. We just can't tell Tommy."

"Oh boy," Scotty said. "More secrets."

Aidan didn't rise to the bait. He knew there would be a lot of digs coming his way, since that's how Scotty tended to work through things. He just waited to see if the invitation would be accepted or not.

"Maybe," Scott finally said. "I've gotta do a couple of things and I might meet you there. If not, then I'll catch you tomorrow."

Aidan almost wished he'd said no outright. Every minute between getting in his truck and meeting Walsh at the new bar and getting a beer seemed to take an hour. He felt like this was a pivotal moment— if Scott showed, they might be okay again in the near future, but if he didn't, it might be a long time before he had his best friend back.

When Scotty finally walked up to the table and seemed to be waiting for an invitation to join them, Aiden breathed a sigh of relief and used his foot to shove the empty chair away from the table. "Have a seat."

"This sucks, you know. I can't even get a beer in my own family's bar because Lydia's still not speaking to me."

"I'm out until Lydia goes back to New Hampshire, at least," Aidan said. "Even after, it'll depend on Ashley. And Tommy, too, I guess."

"I'm just here because of you two morons," Danny said. "Lydia likes me again, since Ashley and I are back together."

"I think we know for a fact Lydia has questionable taste in men," Scotty said, giving him a pointed look before taking a swig of his beer. "She tends to date assholes."

"What the fuck's your problem now, Kincaid?" And why the hell had he come if he was just going to pick a fight? "You didn't want me hooking up with Lydia. I'm not. Either let it go or we can step outside and have a discussion about it right now."

Danny slammed his beer bottle down on the table in a rare show of temper, and Aidan hoped being forced to open up to his wife wasn't going to have the lieutenant opening up on all of them now, too. "If that's code for going outside and trying to beat the crap out of each other, we're going to have a problem."

"That's up to Scotty."

"That was a cheap shot. I'm not going to apologize because I have a right to be pissed, but that was uncalled-for, I guess."

Aidan had a drink, and then shook his head. "I deserve some cheap shots, but only for so long. What I did might be wrong, but I'm not going to be your whipping boy forever for it."

"I guess we'll see how it goes, then," Scotty said.

"It should go fine," Walsh said. "You're pissed because Hunt was sleeping with your sister. Hunt's pissed your sister doesn't want to sleep with him anymore, which means he's no longer sleeping with your sister. It seems like the problem resolved itself."

"I'm not pissed. For chrissake, I…" Aidan stopped talking, but when he lifted the bottle to his lips, he didn't drink because he was afraid the liquid couldn't get past the lump in his throat and he'd choke on it.

"Holy shit." Scott set his beer on the table with a thump and leaned back in his chair. "You're in love with Lydia."

Aidan flipped him the bird. It was all he was capable of at the moment.

"You love my sister. You asshole."

"Way to be sensitive, Kincaid," Danny muttered.

"What the hell am I supposed to do now?" he demanded, throwing up his hands. "When I thought he was just bangin' my sister, I could be totally pissed off. But if he really loves her and his fucking heart's broken, then…he's my best friend, so what the hell am I supposed to do with that?"

"You could hug him," Danny suggested.

Aidan glared at him, but the knot in his throat and his chest was loosening and he gave a hoarse chuckle. "No hugging."

"If you cry, Hunt, I'll hug you right here in front of God and everybody, so suck it up."

Aidan was surprised when that got a laugh out of him. He'd thought it would be a lot longer before he was able to laugh at anything. "I'll do my best not to cry into my beer."

They were all quiet for a few minutes, listening to the music and staring at their drinks, until Scott gave him a serious look. "Am I right?"

After so much lying, it was hard but still a relief to look his friend in the eye and admit it. "Yes, I love Lydia."

"Like *real* love?"

"Like the marriage, babies, dog, minivan, white picket fence, matching rocking chairs and thinks she's gorgeous in ratty sweats kind of love."

"Shit."

Aidan nodded. "That pretty much sums up my life at the moment."

"But she doesn't love you?" Danny asked.

"She doesn't love firefighters."

"What does that mean?" Scotty asked. "Her entire family's firefighters, for chrissake."

"It means if I worked at Home Depot or turned wrenches or anything else for a living, she probably would have moved in with me by now."

"Todd was an asshole," Walsh said.

"It goes a little deeper than her ex-husband, I think, though he's a huge part of it."

"She always had a hard time with Dad," Scotty said. "Even though she's the middle child, she kind of took over the mom role when Mom died, and I think being the woman of a firefighting household before she was even a grown woman was tough on her. It made some of the day-to-day issues experienced wives deal with seem larger than life, I imagine."

"It's tough even when they *are* grown women," Walsh said. "I'm sure Ashley and I being separated helped shore up Lydia's beliefs about being married to firefighters, too, especially since that's why she came back in the first place."

"Speaking of that," Aidan said, running his finger down the condensation on his bottle, "has she said when she's going back?"

"Ashley hasn't said anything to me about it."

Scotty shrugged. "Again, she's not speaking to me. Thus illustrating one of the many reasons you don't want your best friend sleeping with your sister. Everything's fun and games until the breakup, and now you're an asshole, I'm an asshole and my sister has a broken heart."

Walsh nodded, then lifted his beer as if in a toast. "Yeah, but at least your sister's broken heart will heal."

After a few seconds, Aidan couldn't hold back the laughter anymore and Scotty laughed with him. It was a start, he thought. He'd be thankful for these glimpses their friendship would survive and use them to ride out the rough times, when Scotty was still throwing him attitude. They'd be okay, though.

But he knew the weeks wouldn't feel any less long and lonely because, at the end of the day, he didn't have Lydia anymore.

THEY THREW LYDIA'S pity-slash-farewell party at Ashley's house because Danny had pulled a night tour and she had enough room for them all to sleep if they had too much to drink.

It was a good thing, Lydia thought, since they'd all jumped that hurdle at least an hour before. Some more than others. She was sipping her vodka-and-raspberry seltzer because the last thing she needed on top of unbearable sadness and heartbreak was a hangover.

"We should go put a bag of flaming dog shit on his deck," Courtney said. She obviously had no fear of hangovers because she was drinking laps around Lydia, with Ashley and Becca somewhere in the middle. "Do people still do that?"

"A *big* bag of flaming dog shit," Becca said. "One of those paper leaf bags that's like four feet tall. And we can go sneak around people's backyards and steal their dog shit until it's totally full. Then we'll put it on his deck and set it on fire."

"Courtney, you can't do that," Ashley argued, pointing a finger in her general direction and leaning close. "Only you can prevent dog shit fires."

"He's a firefighter," Lydia said. "He'd just put it out, anyway. And we'd get arrested."

Courtney made a shocked face. "They'd never know it was us."

"I hate to break it to you, but Ashley and I were born and raised in this neighborhood, so us dragging around a giant paper bag and stealing people's

dog shit from their backyards is not going to go un-
noticed."

"That's not fun at all." Becca sighed. "What are
we going to do, then?"

"I'm going to go home," Lydia said. She'd probably
go after the weekend, to give Ashley a few more days
to acclimate, but then her time in Boston would be
over. "I'm going to curl up with my roommate's cat
and a big bucket of ice cream and watch movies that
make me cry. And then I'm going to find another job
and get on with my life."

"No." Courtney shook her head. "We can still
make this work. You know everybody, so if somebody asks why we're in their backyard, you can just
tell them you're cleaning up the dog poo for them.
Like community service."

"You're shut off, Court," Ashley told her. "And
whatever you do, don't *ever* drink without one of
us with you because I think you'd make some really
bad decisions."

"I think Lydia going back to New Hampshire is a
bad decision," she shot back.

"So do I," Ashley said. When Lydia gave her a
questioning look, she shrugged. "You asked me why I
helped you and Aidan get away for the weekend when
I'd been worried about your relationship blowing up
in your face. I'd figured out you two might actually
be good together and if I helped you guys get away,
you'd fall in love and stay here and marry him and
work at the bar with me."

"That was never the plan, Ash." But, judging by the ache that intensified in her chest, her heart had decided somewhere along the way that it was a damn good plan.

Her sister shrugged. "Sometimes plans change."

"And sometimes plans get canceled," Courtney mumbled. "Even great plans that would have been doing your dog-owning neighbors a *huge* favor. It was going to be a valuable community service."

"We're not setting anything on fire," Lydia said. "We're going to leave Aidan alone, which is what I should have done from the first day I came back to Boston."

Maybe if she'd left him alone, the way she told herself to do that first night at the bar, she wouldn't be facing the rest of her life with a huge hole in it she wasn't sure anybody else could ever fill. Before Aidan, she hadn't known she was missing anything. But now it would never be the same because she missed him so much she could barely breathe.

"Maybe you should ask him to move in with you," Becca suggested. "He can make you cookies."

"Why would he make me cookies?"

"Because I like cookies."

Lydia nodded. "Of course."

The other three women immediately launched into a lively debate on what the best kind of cookie was. She didn't really care, so she drained her glass and debated on having another drink.

Asking Aidan to move in with her had crossed

her mind, but she'd never been able to muster the nerve to ask him how he'd feel about moving to New Hampshire. To her, that didn't mean transferring to a firehouse in Concord. It meant giving it up and she couldn't ask him to do that. Not since the day she'd seen how very much the job meant to him.

Maybe he'd do it, too. He might be willing to walk away from Boston Fire for her, but at what cost? He couldn't change the man he was and, if he did, was he still the man she loved?

She'd been asking herself that for days and never got an answer but a headache to go with her heart-ache.

With a sigh, Lydia decided against another drink. What she really wanted was ice cream and she knew for a fact there was a half gallon of Rocky Road in the freezer, but she probably shouldn't go get it. If she did, she'd have to share and, when it came to ice cream, she didn't play well with others. Plus, if there was any chance of her friends getting sick as part of their revelry, she thought she'd do her sister a favor and leave the chocolate ice cream out of it.

"You okay?" Ashley asked, and she realized they were all staring at her.

"Uh, yeah? Do I not look okay?"

"Becca just said she likes walnuts in her peanut butter cookies and you didn't say anything. That's not like you."

"Nobody wants walnuts in their peanut butter cookies," she said, because it was easier than explaining to three drunk women why ranking cookie types wasn't high on her list of things to do tonight. "Actually, there shouldn't be nuts in *any* cookies."

"You don't like nuts?" Courtney asked and, of course, all three of them broke out in a case of the giggles.

She managed a smile, but she couldn't giggle with Aidan so front and center in her thoughts. Not a second went by that she didn't think about and miss him. She ached for him, day and night, and there was a little voice in the back of her mind constantly questioning if going back to Concord was the right choice.

Kincaid's Pub was in her blood. No matter where she found a job, it wouldn't be the same. She had a feeling that Ashley and Danny would be starting a family soon, and she didn't see how it would even be possible for her to miss any of her niece's or nephew's lives, to say nothing of Ashley needing to cut back on her hours. She'd missed Courtney and Becca and would miss them even more when she left. And she wanted things to be good between her and Scotty again, but that wouldn't happen with physical distance between them.

Most of all, every time she tried to picture the rest of her life without Aidan, it was depressing as hell. Somehow he'd gone from the sexy guy she wanted to scratch some itches with to the man who made her laugh and held her hand and who looked at her like she was the only woman who'd ever made him smile like that.

But Aidan was a package deal. With him came a lifetime of being a firefighter's wife. She'd raise children who were proud of their dad, but afraid for him every time he went to work. He came with a brotherhood and a code of conduct and expectations.

To get the guy, she had to take the whole set. Aidan Hunt not sold separately. It was a risk she wasn't sure her heart could afford.

NINETEEN

THE KNOCK ON Aidan's door the following evening
jacked his heart rate up like a shot of adrenaline to
the chest, and he practically jogged to the door. Anybody else he could think of besides Lydia would have
sent him a text first.

But when he opened the door, he saw the wrong
Kincaid standing in the hall. Tommy had never been
to his place before and Aidan felt panic rising in his
throat. Fear for Lydia, followed immediately by fear
for Scotty. "What happened?"

Tommy frowned at him. "What happened? I
knocked on your door and you answered it with no
pants on, that's what happened. Who the hell does
that?"

"Shit." He stepped back into his living room,
knowing he wouldn't get a lecture if there was bad
news waiting to be delivered. "Sorry. Come on in
and I'll grab some sweats. It scared me when I saw
you because you've never been here, so I thought you
had bad news."

"I've never been to your place because most of the time you've always been at my place or at the bar."

"Good point." Aidan grabbed a pair of sweatpants out of the clean clothes basket and pulled them on. "You want a drink or something?"

"Nope." He sat down at the kitchen table and gestured for Aidan to sit across from him.

Uh-oh. He was about to get a stern talking-to from Tommy, which wasn't usually an enjoyable situation. Before sitting down, he grabbed a soda from the fridge just in case he was there awhile.

"What's going on with you and Lydia?" Tommy asked once he was seated.

Aidan clenched his jaw, breathing in deeply through his nose. If ever a conversation required him to think before he spoke, it was this one. "Last I heard, she was going back to Concord."

Tommy nodded. "Tomorrow."

If he knew that, Aidan didn't see the point in asking him the question, but he didn't say so. "That's pretty much what's going on with me and Lydia."

"You just going to let her go? That's it?"

"She doesn't want to be married to another firefighter, Tommy. I can't change that."

"Okay. You're right about that, because you can't change her." He nodded. "She's so much like her mother, it drives me crazy sometimes. Most of the time, actually. Let's talk about you, then. How do you feel about my daughter?"

"I love Lydia, sir. Absolutely and completely."

"Did you tell her that?"

"I, uh…"

"So, no. You haven't told her you love her."

Aidan picked at the label of his soda bottle with his thumbnail. "Why make it harder? I'm pretty sure she's in love with me, but she doesn't think she can be happy with me. Don't you think me telling her I love her will just make it worse for her?"

"So what? She's leaving you. How about what's worse for *you*?"

"I probably deserve it. If I was capable of being who she wants me to be, I could keep her. So that's on me."

"And who does she want you to be?"

Aidan hesitated for a few seconds. This had to be painful for Tommy because even though a lot of the blame could be placed on her ex-husband, Tommy had to know being his daughter played a substantial role in how she felt about it. "She wants me to be somebody who's not a firefighter."

Tommy nodded slowly, considering his words. "And that's not something you're capable of?"

The words threw him for a loop. How could Tommy Kincaid, of all people, suggest it was that easy? "I…don't know"

"Have you thought about it?"

"Maybe. A little. But when I was eleven, you told me that being born to take charge in emergencies and to save lives is a special thing and not everybody's got it. If I throw it away, how do I live with that?"

Tommy gave him a long, hard look. "I've been around the block a few times, son, and the real question is how will you live with letting Lydia go? If you really love her and you let her go for the job, you're going to start hating what you do. You'll get bitter and you'll start resenting it. Maybe you'll start having some hard liquor shots between those beers or, God forbid, getting hooked on something worse to get through the days."

"You're the worst Ghost of Christmas Future ever," Aidan mumbled.

"The bottom line is that to take care of others, you gotta take care of you first." Tommy breathed in deeply through his nose, his lips pressed together for a few seconds. "You know what I live with, son? I get to live the rest of my life knowing the only reason my wife didn't divorce me is because she found out she was dying."

Aidan didn't know what to say. Tommy never talked about his wife. He knew that was true, though, because Scotty had told him about it.

"And now I got two daughters struggling with loving firefighters and you know whose fault that is? Mine. If I'd raised them better and found a better balance or whatever, maybe it wouldn't be so hard for them."

Tommy stood, pointing a finger at Aidan. "I'm telling you right now, son, you do what *you* need to do. If being a firefighter means that much to you, then leave her alone and let her go back to New Hampshire. Make it as clean a cut as possible. But if Lydia's what you want, you need to make a decision and be okay with it. You don't owe anybody anything."

Aidan stood and extended his hand. "Thanks for the talk. And for not telling me to leave her alone just because I'm no good for her."

Tommy took his hand and, instead of shaking it, pulled him in for a quick hug. "You'll never hear me tell you you're no good. I love you, son, and whatever decision you make isn't going to change that. I'm proud of you."

Tears clogged Aidan's throat, so he only nodded and lifted a hand as Tommy walked out of his apartment. He slowly sank back onto the kitchen chair, and then he pulled out his phone.

Definitely not a text message, he thought. He tapped on Scotty's name and listened to the phone ring.

"What happened?"

Aidan frowned, and then realized it had been a very long time since he'd heard Scotty's voice on the phone. They communicated almost entirely by text, with the occasional email. "Nothing's wrong. I was just wondering if you're busy."

"Not really."

"I could use some company. Your dad stopped by."

"He did? That's surprising."

Aidan agreed. "Yeah. And he said some stuff."

"That's *not* surprising."

"I could use an ear. Somebody to talk to you, you know? And for me, that person is you, but I should tell you up front it's about Lydia."

"I can be there in twenty minutes. You got beer?"

"Yeah." A sharp sense of relief made him almost breathless for a few seconds. "I appreciate it."

Once he'd ended the call, Aidan set the phone down and cradled his head in his hands. He had twenty minutes to try to sort out his feelings so he could verbalize them to Scotty.

One thing didn't need to be sorted, though, because it was very clear in his mind. He was in love with Lydia Kincaid and he didn't have a lot of time to figure out what to do about that.

AFTER SHOVING THE last of her toiletries into her bag, Lydia zipped it up and looped the strap over her shoulder.

She was out of excuses to be here. She'd even cleaned the room and washed the sheets, remaking the bed so it would be ready for Ashley's next guest. There was literally no reason she shouldn't get in her car and start driving north right now.

No reason at all, except for the fact she didn't want to go.

Standing in the hallway, she stopped, wondering if she was going to hate herself for the rest of her life if she forced herself to leave Boston today. If she left Aidan. She regretted the distance between them already and she hadn't even left the city yet.

She heard a knock on the door and then the low murmur of Ashley's voice, followed by a man's voice. It was heartbreakingly familiar and Lydia headed for the stairs.

"Lydia!" Ashley almost ran into her on the staircase. "I thought you were still packing. Aidan's here. I'll be in my room doing stuff for a few minutes. Until you're done, I guess."

Done with what, though? Saying goodbye? Lydia wasn't sure she could do that. It was one thing to walk away from him when she'd been riding high on temper. But now, when missing him was a constant, painful companion, she wasn't sure she could find the strength.

She nodded at her sister, but she couldn't respond because she was totally focused on the man standing in the living room. Aidan looked like hell, which was about how she felt. "Hey."

"You have your bag packed."

"I'm leaving in a few minutes," she said, surprised she could get the words out without having a total breakdown.

"I don't want you to go." He cleared his throat. "I don't want you to leave me, Lydia, because I'm in love with you."

Her breath caught in her chest and she found herself incapable of making words. He loved her, and he wanted to be with her. All she had to do was accept that love and he could be hers. "I don't want to leave you, either. I've been trying to force myself to go but it's obviously not working because I'm still here."

He clenched his jaw for a few seconds and then relaxed. "If you stay with me, I'll hand in my papers tomorrow."

She blinked, sure she'd heard him wrong. "What do you mean?"

"If you can't bring yourself to be a firefighter's wife again, then I'll be something else. Anything else. I don't care."

"You can't do that. You can't just quit being who you are, Aidan."

He took a deep breath, as if thinking about what she'd said. "Being a firefighter isn't who I am. It's what I do. And yes, I *can* do something else. And I will, because the thing I want to be more than anything else is your husband. That's who I am inside. A man who loves you more than anything else. Everything else is just how I earn a paycheck or my zip code."

She was having a hard time believing what she was hearing, but hope was beating like a drum in her chest. "What will you do, if you're not a firefighter?"

"If we're lucky, we'll win the lottery, buy a private island in the Caribbean and do nothing but have sex on the beach every day." When she cocked an eyebrow at him, he grinned. "Hey, it could happen. In the meantime, I'm looking into installing fire suppression systems and a few other jobs in the industry. Saving people from fires by preventing the fires in the first place still counts. And if you really want to get away from here and go back to New Hampshire, I'll be right there with you. Maybe we can buy some cows."

Even as his joke made her chuckle, tears made his face blur in front of her and she tried to blink them away. "You love being a firefighter."

Aidan cupped her face in his hands and looked her in the eye. "I love you more."

It felt as if some knot deep inside of her loosened and she could breathe again. "I love you, too."

"You are the most important thing in the whole world to me. I choose you, Lydia. It will never matter what the choice is. It won't matter who or what or why, I will *always* choose you."

Tears shimmered in her eyes, and she put her hands up to grasp his wrists. "I believe you."

"Good. Because it's the truth."

"But don't hand in your papers," she said in a soft voice.

He looked confused, and he dropped his hands from her face to hold both of her hands. "But you said you love me, too. I want us to have a life *together*, Lydia."

"I do, too. And being a firefighter is more than your job. It *is* a part of who you are, and I love who you are. All of you. You were right, before. You're not my ex-husband and you're not my dad. I believe in you, and when you look at me, I know you love me."

He squeezed her fingers. "Promise me, if you ever feel like the job is coming between us, you'll talk to me about it and we'll decide our future together. Me and you."

"I promise." She smiled up at him. "It feels right, you and my brother being together. Having each other's backs. And Danny, too. And Ashley and I will be together at the bar. We'll have a good life together."

"So you'll marry me?"

She threw her arms around his neck and kissed

him. "Yes. I'll marry you. God, yes. Today. Tomorrow. As soon as we can."

"No!" They both looked up at the top of the stairs, where Ashley was eavesdropping with tearstained cheeks. "You're having a wedding and I need time to plan it."

"Can you wait?" Lydia asked Aidan, tipping her face back to smile at him.

"I'm not stupid enough to argue with two Kincaid women, and I like the idea of you in a wedding gown. And that garter thing. You're going to move in with me right now, though, right?"

"I'm already packed. We're not getting cows, though."

He kissed her again. "How about a cat? Oscar was kind of cool, you know."

"Maybe. What should we do to celebrate? I feel like we should do something."

He slid his hand under her hair and kissed her until her toes curled in her sneakers. "How about we go to this little place called Kincaid's Pub and I let you buy me a drink?"

* * * * *

To find out about other books by Shannon Stacey or to be alerted to new releases, sign up for her monthly newsletter here or at http://bit.ly/shannonstaceynewsletter.

Read on for a sneak preview of
CONTROLLED BURN,
the next book in New York Times *bestselling author*
Shannon Stacey's
BOSTON FIRE SERIES

ONE

"FIVE BUCKS SAYS she requested Ladder 37 when she called 911."

Rick Gullotti glared at Gavin Boudreau, then shook his head. "That's bullshit."

They were back at the station after a run and, as the lieutenant of Boston Fire's Ladder 37, he had to stay in the bay with the guys and take care of the gear. Even if they were being idiots. In the bay next to him, the guys from Engine 59 were doing the same. Stowing the gear, checking tanks and supplies. The ladder truck and the pumper engine that shared the three-story brick firehouse always rolled together, and the guys of L-37 and E-59 operated well as a team.

A team whose members loved to give each other shit, Rick thought as Scotty Kincaid yelled from the other side of the bay. "That's the fourth time that woman's needed the fire department in six months, Gullotti. Must be rough when all your emergencies happen while you're still in your lace nightgown."

"Maybe it's you she's after," Gullotti called back.

"It wasn't me she hugged with so much…gratitude."

Yeah, that had been awkward. He didn't mind being offered cookies or invited to stay for lunch, but the hugging he usually managed to avoid. Thankfully he hadn't taken his bunker coat off, so the feel of a curvy woman in satin and lace hadn't gotten through, but he was going to have to be more careful in the future.

"She was definitely grateful." Chris Erikkson—who was one of the older guys in the house, but avoided promotions due to an extreme aversion to paperwork—paused in the act of wiping down L-37's bumper to smirk at him.

Rick's phone vibrated in his pocket, and he pulled it out, anticipating a summons from upstairs. It wasn't going to take long for the story to circulate, and he knew they'd have to come up with a way to gently discourage the woman's attempt to date via frivolous emergency calls. Not only was it a waste of time and money but, if it escalated, she could accidentally burn down her house.

But the text was from Karen Shea. She was a nurse he'd dated for a while before she met a guy who had the potential to be the one she wanted to spend the rest of her life with.

They just brought Joe into the ER. Stable, but he took a fall and Marie got upset.

Shit. He'd rented the third floor of Joe and Marie Broussard's house for years, and the elderly couple had become more than just landlords. They were like family, and worry settled in the pit of his stomach.

We're wrapping up after a run. I can sneak over for a few mins.

I'll tell them. Marie's having tea and Joe's griping about having to wait for scans.

They were okay, then. And he knew Karen would keep an eye on them until he got there.

"Tell me you didn't give her your number," Erikkson said, nodding at the phone in Rick's hand.

"Who?"

"The grateful lady in the lace nightgown."

"Hell, no. It's Joe and Marie. They're in the ER with Karen."

"Damn. Is it serious?"

"Joe fell and she got upset, I guess. Nothing critical, but I need to tell Cobb I'm heading out and get over there. If a call comes in, bring my gear and I'll meet you there."

"Will do." Chris snorted. "And we'll leave you some of this grunt work to do, too. Trust me."

The emergency room wasn't busy, so he asked if Karen was free instead of asking for the Broussards. He wanted more information before he saw the older couple. About five minutes later, Karen came into the waiting room and smiled at him.

He gave her a quick hug because they'd stayed friends, but a flash of light caught his eye. There was a diamond ring on her left hand, and he took hold of her fingers to give it a look.

"That was fast," he said.

She was practically beaming. "Yeah, but when it's right, it's right. And we have a little incentive to make it legal."

It took a few seconds for her words to sink in, and he realized she was pregnant. Genuine happiness for her came first, but on the heels of that was a pang of regret. He really liked Karen and he wished they'd had whatever chemistry it was she shared with the lucky guy she was going to marry.

But how many times had he heard himself referred to as *not the marrying kind*? More times than he could count, even if he wasn't totally sure what that meant.

"Congratulations," he said, making sure she could see his sincerity on his face. "He's a good guy."

"He is." It looked like she was going to get all misty-eyed, but then she put her nurse face back on. "Okay. I probably shouldn't have called you. Marie's calmed down and it's looking like Joe's going to be punted out as soon as the scans are done. But her blood pressure was up and she looked a little dizzy when they brought them in."

"Always call me," he said. "Where did he fall?"

"At the bottom of the stairs. He was trying to measure to see about putting in a stair lift so Marie can get upstairs to her craft room and he says his sock slid on the hardwood tread because she didn't get all the Murphy's Oil Soap wiped up."

Rick sighed and rubbed the back of his neck. "The house is too much for them. And Marie won't let me hire a cleaning service for them no matter how hard I push."

"I hate to tell you this, but Joe's doctor was here making rounds, so the ER doc pulled him in. They want to talk about elder care options."

"It's probably time to start having those discussions, I guess. If he sets up a time, I can be with them and keep them honest, I guess. They're still in denial when it comes to their limitations."

Karen hesitated, then exhaled. "The other nurses and I call you because we know you, but Joe and Marie haven't updated their legal information. Dr. Bartlett already left a message at the last known contact for their son."

"They called Davey?" Rick shook his head. "That douche bag probably won't even return the call."

"I just thought you should know before you see them."

"Do they know? About the call, I mean?"

"I don't think the doctor's been in to follow up with them yet, so probably not."

He should tell them himself, before the doctor did, so Joe and Marie wouldn't be taken off guard. Their son was a painful subject and they were already having a shitty day. "We should probably make sure Joe isn't making a break for it."

Recognizing the change of subject for what it was, Karen led him through the security doors and down the hall to a curtained-off room.

Marie stood when she saw him and held out her arms. Rick hugged her, some of his worry eased by the steadiness in her slim, tall figure. Even at seventy-eight, Marie was strong. Neither of them was as strong as they used to be, though, and it was becoming a problem.

"They shouldn't have called you," Joe grumbled from the bed. Rick let go of Marie to put his hand on the man's shoulder. Taller and four years older than his wife, but not quite as thin, Joe had once been rugged as hell. Age and a stroke had taken a toll, though, and Joe was having trouble reconciling with the fact he wasn't fifty anymore.

"If a call comes in, I'll have to go, but we'd just finished a run. Pretty lady in a lace negligee thought she smelled smoke."

"Same one as last time?" Joe asked, leaning back against the stack of pillows.

"Yup."

"You said she was pretty," Marie said. "Maybe you should ask her on a date. She obviously likes you."

"Jesus, Marie." Joe scowled at his wife. "You can't encourage that or half the women in the city will be setting their tablecloths on fire."

Rick laughed and sat on the exam stool, leaving the visitor's chair for Marie. Hoping it would be a few more minutes before the doctor came back, he listened to the familiar banter between the two people who'd come into his life as landlords and become like family. And he tried to figure out how to tell them the hospital had reached out to their son because Joe and Marie knew as well as Rick did that Davey probably wouldn't reach back.

JESSICA BROUSSARD PARKED her rental car at the curb and flexed her fingers, which practically ached from her death grip on the steering wheel. Driving in Boston was certainly no joke.

Having learned through previous experience that navigation systems weren't infallible, she squinted to make out the brass numbers tacked to the front of the tall blue house. Then she looked at the address she'd punched into the GPS and took a deep breath.

This was it. Her grandparents' home.

The flight from San Diego to Boston had given her plenty of time to obsess about all the ways this trip made no sense. Whenever her father was unavailable, Jessica checked his voice mail in order to keep Broussard Financial Services running, but she hadn't known what to do about the call from the Boston doctor. Reaching out to her father had resulted in a brusque demand for her to deal with the problem before she even got a chance to tell him it was personal.

But she couldn't deal with it. The doctor wouldn't speak to her about Joe and Marie Broussard, the grandparents she'd never met, because she wasn't on the form. And, when she was tossing and turning at two in the morning, she wondered if it was because they didn't know she even existed. The plan formed—seemingly brilliant as many insomnia-born plans were—to deal with her father's problem and to meet the people David Broussard had barely spoken of, and never kindly.

A curtain in the house twitched, and Jessica realized she'd been staring. It was time to get out of the car, or drive back to the airport and force her father to call the doctor.

She climbed out of the car, bracing herself for the blast of cold air, and walked toward the front door as a pickup drove past and then turned into the driveway. Jessica paused with one foot on the bottom step, but the man who got out of the truck definitely wasn't one of her grandparents.

"Can I help you?" he asked, walked toward her.

"I'm looking for Joe and Marie Broussard."

He nodded. "I'm Rick Gullotti. I rent the apartment upstairs. They expecting you?"

No, they most definitely were not. That two-in-the-morning plan had also included not giving the Broussards the opportunity to tell her not to come. "No, they're not. But I'm…their granddaughter. Jessica."

The man froze in the act of extending his hand to shake hers, and his eyebrows rose. He had great eyebrows, which was ridiculous because when had she ever noticed a man's eyebrows before?

"I wasn't aware they have a granddaughter," he

finally said, and she could tell he was trying to be careful with his words.

"To be honest, I don't know if they're aware of it, either."

"Okay." He dropped his hand. "Do you mind if I ask why you're here? Is your visit related to the doctor calling Davey?"

Davey? Not once in her entire life had Jessica heard her father referred to as anything but David.

She took her time answering, assessing her options. On the one hand, it would be easy to dismiss him as a tenant who should feel free to mind his own business. But on the other, he knew her grandparents well enough to call their son Davey and she didn't know them at all. When it came to moving them into a better living situation and getting the house on the market, he could be her strongest ally.

"The doctor refused to talk to me and my father is unavailable. If Joe and… If my grandparents add me to their paperwork, I can help them navigate their options."

After a long moment—which he spent staring at her as if trying to read her mind—he nodded. "I'll introduce you."

When Jessica stepped down to let him go in front of her, she realized how tall he was. She wasn't sure she had an actual type, other than a preference for men taller than she was, but circumstances had led to her last few relationships being with younger men. Judging by the hint of gray peppering his short, dark hair and scruff of a beard, Rick Gullotti definitely wasn't younger. His blue eyes were framed by laugh lines, and she got the feeling he laughed a lot.

Worn jeans hugged his bottom half, and a T-shirt did the same for the top. He'd thrown a hoodie on over it, but it wasn't zipped—which meant he *had* to be crazy—so his body was well displayed. *Very* well.

"How can it be this cold already?" she asked, trying to divert her attention away from the view before she said something stupid, like asking him just how many hours per day he worked out to look that amazing.

Rick shrugged. "It's that time of year. It's going to be warmer the next few days—maybe back up to fifty—and then there's snow in the forecast. Welcome to Boston in December."

"Snow." She'd gone on a ski trip once, during her college days. There had been a fireplace and alcohol and as little snow as possible.

"I hope you brought boots."

"I won't be here that long."

He gave her a hard look she couldn't quite decipher and then opened the front door without knocking. She followed him in, trying to block out her father's voice in her head.

Crass. Alcoholic. Bad tempers. When she was eleven, she'd had to do a genealogy project in school. *They're just not our kind of people, Jessica, and you're upsetting me. I don't want to hear about this nonsense again.* That was the last time she asked about her grandparents. Her project was entirely fictional and earned her an A.

"Rick, is that you?" she heard a woman call from the back of the house, and Jessica's stomach twisted into a knot. "Did you get the… Oh. You have company."

Jessica looked at her grandmother, emotions tangling together in her mind. Marie was tall and slim, with short white hair and blue eyes. And Jessica knew, many years from now, she would look like this woman.

"Where's Joe?" Rick asked, and Jessica was thankful he seemed to want them together because it bought her a few more seconds to gather herself.

"He's in the kitchen. Come on back."

When Marie turned and walked away, Jessica looked up at Rick. He nodded his head in that direction, so she followed. Other than a general sense of tidiness and a light citrus scent, she barely noticed her surroundings. Her focus was on her grandmother in front of her and an awareness that Rick Gullotti was behind her.

Her grandfather was sitting at the kitchen table, working on some kind of puzzle book with reading glasses perched low on his nose. When he looked up, he frowned and then took the glasses off to stare at her.

"I found Jessica outside," Rick said. "She says she's your granddaughter."

Marie gasped, and Jessica felt a pang of concern

when she put her hand to her chest. "What? She can't be."

"If her hair was short, she'd look just like you did years ago, Marie."

"I can't believe Davey wouldn't tell us he had a baby."

"Davey hasn't told us anything in almost forty years."

"I'm thirty-four," Jessica said, as if that explained everything, and then she immediately felt like an idiot. "I'm sorry. I should have called first."

"Did Davey send you because that damn doctor called him?"

"I came because of the call, yes." She couldn't bring herself to admit yet that her father had no idea she was here or why.

Silence filled the kitchen, and she became aware that the Broussards had a real clock hanging in their kitchen—the kind with a second hand that marked the awkward seconds with a *tick tick tick*.

Jessica was torn. The logical analyst voice in her head—the part of her that had earned her a cushy corner office in her father's investment business— wanted her to set up a time to speak with them about the doctor's call and then check into the hotel room she'd reserved. But her inner eleven-year-old wanted to hug her nonfictional grandmother.

"It's a long flight," Rick said, stepping out from behind her so she could see him. "You hungry?"

His quiet words breaking the silence also seemed

to break the tension, and Marie gave her a shaky smile. "Have a seat and tell us all about yourself. Rick, are you going to stay for a while?"

"I'll stay for a little bit," Rick said, and though his voice was even enough, the look he gave Jessica made it clear he wasn't just a tenant in this house and he wasn't sure what he thought of her yet. "I want to hear *all* about Jessica."

Don't miss CONTROLLED BURN
by Shannon Stacey,
Available December 2015 wherever
Carina Press books are sold.
www.CarinaPress.com

AUTHOR'S NOTE

It was announced toward the end of 2014 that the Boston Fire Department would be doing a year-long test run of the 24-hour shifts worked by many of the larger fire departments in the country, rather than morning and night tours. This announcement came too late in the writing of *Heat Exchange* to reflect that change. The processes and organizational structures of large city fire departments are incredibly complex, and I took minor creative liberties in order to maintain readability.

To first responders everywhere, thank you.

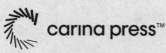

 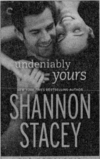 
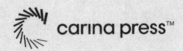

New York Times Bestselling Author

BRENDA JACKSON

The Grangers

**She's all he's ever wanted.
He's everything she'll ever need.**

Business mogul Dalton Granger is passionate and gorgeous, but private investigator Jules Bradford won't give him the time of day. She knows all about the youngest Granger— the charming bad boy.

But Dalton is more complicated than that, and he's determined to show Jules that behind the bravado is an honest heart, a devoted son and brother…and a man whose own life is in peril.

Jules is the only person who can protect Dalton, and they embark on a mission to save his family and legacy. But when their late nights in the office become early mornings in the bedroom, Jules and Dalton realize they have more at stake than they ever imagined.

Available now, wherever books are sold!

From *New York Times* bestselling author

LAUREN DANE

What won't he do for a second chance?

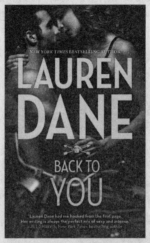

Rock star Vaughan Hurley puts everything on the line to prove to his ex-wife Kelly that he's a changed man, and the only man she needs. And there's only one way to do it…

Pick up your copy today!

Be sure to connect with us at:

Harlequin.com/Newsletters
Facebook.com/HarlequinBooks
Twitter.com/HQNBooks

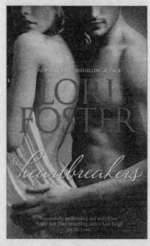